Homeward BOUND

JOURNEYMAN SERIES ONE

Heather,
Enjoy the ride!

GOLDEN CZERMAK

Homeward BOUND
JOURNEYMAN SERIES ONE
by
Golden Czermak

Cover Model: Caylan Hughes
Cover Photography and Design: FuriousFotog
Editor: Kellie Montgomery
Formatting: Cassy Roop of Pink Ink Designs

WARNING: This book is for mature readers only. Not for children. It contains adult themes, violence, coarse language, sexual situations, nudity, and paranormal themes.

Acknowledgements

Eric, I could not have done any of this without you. From the tireless nagging about words and plot lines, to the countless days and nights spent away from you cultivating not only this story but the Furious brand in general- your patience knows absolutely no bounds. For that, and especially your love over the past 18 years, I am forever grateful.

FuriousFans, what can I say? There are *way* too many of you to name individually here, but I am frankly blessed, humbled, and amazed by all the support you have shown. It truly does mean the world to me and never would I have imagined being able to do any of this without it. The fact that there are, literally, millions of you around the world blows my mind each and every day. Here's to new adventures, especially now with Gage Crosse, and of course more as the future becomes the present.

Last but certainly not least, Caylan Hughes. I think your sheer presence and personality are enough to explain to those that know you, but in case anyone reading does not: You. Are. Gage. Back in November 2014, I never would have imagined when that bulky (haha yes, I went there) red-haired model showed up in that massive white truck, that such a great friendship would be kindled both in front of the camera and in real life as well. We've only just started my man, with Gage and with all the rest. Thank you for your friendship, your inspiration, your love, and more.

Homeward
BOUND

CHAPTER
one

ONE NIGHT IN HOUSTON

THE NIGHT WIND WAS BITING as it gnawed through the drizzle that cloaked the rusty factory in gray. Lifeless leaves clung to withered trees while their skeletal branches tapped against the peeled metal and worn stone, rattled by the tormenting breeze. The place had a look of being long abandoned, but shadowed figures moving between the cracked panes of glass betrayed the dead air.

At a distant side entrance, a beat up truck crept off the county road onto the middle-of-nowhere property with its lights off. Mud squelched under its aged tires while lightning cleaved the sky, illuminating "Danger" and "No Trespassing" signs tucked in amidst the overgrowth lining the narrow driveway. Three indistinct figures were sitting inside the 79 GMC quad cab as it slid off into the cover of dense brush. Its doors swung open as the vehicle came to a slow roll, then stopped shortly after.

Joey Mosely was first out. He darted from the rear seat toward the back of the truck, light puffs of his steamy breath trailing behind like a train. The young man was in a wrinkled white tee, tight over his muscular chest, along with a pair of weathered jeans and a hand-me-down Member's Only jacket. Extending an arm, he pulled himself up into the truck bed, crouching in front of a large weatherproof box positioned underneath the rear window. Two additional boxes were on either side; all were tightly shut.

Fingers like chopsticks felt around in his jacket pockets, touching the all too familiar softness and crunch of wadded paper. A frown met the first ball of gum wrappers he pulled out, the disappointment growing with the candy ones that came next, and yet more so with the countless sticky notes that somehow fit inside too, all useless since the ink had bled out long ago. Flinging them aside, he dove back in and thankfully after a few seconds found the hard metal he was looking for, removing it before inserting the oddly notched cylinder into a round keyhole at the top of the lid.

Ancient glyphs of different shapes and sizes were painted along the outside. As the key turned and the tumblers moved, the symbols glowed with faint energy and the cool metal surface became warm to the touch. The lid slowly rose by itself with a whisper, like voices carried from long ago and a force blew through the opening into Joey's chin-length hair, causing it to whip up briefly then flop back down to block his view.

Sweeping away the stray black strands, he reached inside where a plethora of arcane weapons, items, and technological devices waited – tucked haphazardly amongst rich fabrics embroidered with even more charms and symbols. The contents seemed to glimmer eagerly with each flash from the passing storm, waiting to be picked up and used.

Adrienne Elkins slipped herself out of shotgun position. The denim jacket she wore with her solid black top and jeans fit her late twenties figure quite well. She surveyed the area for any signs that their approach was noticed. The forest was dingy except for the now faint pricks of lightning and white light of the waning crescent moon that streamed down through the treetops. Thankfully, nothing indicated they were in any immediate danger; even the crickets chirped in chorus uninterrupted.

Grabbing her *Cougars* baseball cap from the glove box, she tucked up her long brunette hair and then reached back into the door's side pocket.

Out came a pair of plain daggers, the first one placed in a small ankle holster while the other found a home securely on her belt. Adjacent to it a larger one already dangled, its silver blade etched with three circular Solomon sigils and the Elder Futhark runes Thurisaz and Uruz along the handle. She took a long, deep breath of crisp air before she returned her attention to the surroundings. The night was brooding, different than usual.

It was then that a beast of a man lumbered out of the driver's seat, his heavy black boots sinking into the soggy soil. Dressed in a tight gray tee and a denim jacket with the sleeves ripped off, his muscular yet intricately inked arms stretched as he swaggered toward the front of the truck in a pair of absurdly snug jeans. Glancing at his baby, a gloved hand ran fondly down the brown and white hood; she still had plenty of go left in her, the old girl. Halting to take in the gloom around them, he rapped his husky fingers on a thigh-mounted custom MK23.

"Gage," Adrienne said softly, not wanting to jar him out of any deep thought. "Joey's got some new gear for us in back. He..." She stopped, noticing his right hand tapping on the gun. "Seriously? You brought it with you to a clearing... again?"

Without a word, he turned and winked a green eye at her.

She rolled her hazel ones in return.

Lifting his hand off of the holster, he ran it slowly through his thick mop of black hair. There was just enough wetness for it to fall perfectly into place when he was done and he looked over toward her, head cocked. "I always thought that cap had a fitting description of you written across the front, darlin'," he said in a deep accented voice, a finger pointed squarely at his forehead.

"Untrue," she shot back without any hesitation. "You know I like my men older, more experienced. I don't think you know much about that, right? Experience? Perhaps with some, you'd manage to hit something with that weapon of yours."

He glanced over, seeing a little more sass in her step. "I can hit plenty of things with my weapon, gorgeous. Especially if they're moving at the speed you do," he said casually.

There was silence as she shook her head, the slightest hint of a smirk escaping from beneath the brim of her cap.

He moseyed to the tailgate as Joey greeted them, holding three sets of what looked like head bands.

"So my man, what do you have prepped for us tonight?" Gage asked. Leaning forward, he rested those large arms on the edge of the truck like a big kid eagerly awaiting toys.

"Mostly the same old cutty, stabby, keep-the-biters at bay fare," Joey responded, casting a lingering stare at Gage while he rubbed on his dark beard, much thicker than his own. His arms looked truly massive pressed up against the tailgate. Shaking his head, he coughed before struggling to continue. "But I… uh… thought we could give these new guys a whirl."

He raised the gadgets to show them off in more detail. They were circular headbands, each outfitted with a battery pack, small microphone and several rows of light emitting diodes. "I've been working on these for the past few weeks: voice operated UV lights. Perfect for any tight spots we may encounter in there."

"How do they work?" asked Adrienne, shifting herself over to the back of the truck next to Gage for a better view.

Joey handed them each a unit then flipped a switch on his battery. There was a brief pop and a hum which lingered for a few seconds before fading.

"Well, as you know," he said, "we always seem to get caught in some kind of close combat situation when fighting these guys. Hell, when we're fighting pretty much anybody. With these, we should be able to loosen their grip if we get pinned and things get particularly… necky."

"Some of us like necking," muttered Gage, throwing a glance over towards Adrienne, "and being pinned. Isn't that what you told me the other day, Ady?"

Her middle finger shot up. "Yup, I recall mentioning just that."

Joey laughed then squatted, looking down at the truck bed.

"If you two kids are done," he said, pulling his hair into a loose bun and placing the device on his head. "Now let's say you do get caught in a tight spot, all you'll have to do is say these magic words and you should be set: 'light 'em up!'"

The unit beeped and in an instant the floor was bathed in an otherworldly blue light, the air buzzing gently.

"Oh, this is good!" Adrienne said, reaching in to pat his shoulder. "Nice one J!" Yet again Joey didn't fail to impress with his tech prowess. He was always the hard worker, even more so since the loss of his dad about this time last year. She started to ponder: had it already been a year since that fateful night? The blue began to fade away at the edges of her vision and it grew dark as sights and sounds, horrible in memory, threatened to rush in.

Then came the screams... *Noooo!*

She snapped back and her gaze now twinkled in the moonlight. She brushed away what could have been an overflowing tear, wondering if anyone had noticed, and smiled.

"Thanks!" he beamed. "Deactivate." The lights on his unit flickered, then faded and the area became bleak once again.

"Good work, my man," said Gage, his words unexpected. Adrienne and Joey exchanged puzzled looks, waiting for a smart ass chaser to the compliment. It never came. Instead, Gage thumped a fist on the tailgate. "Now let's finish up and get to business."

They had come to rural Houston that night to complete a clearing of a local vampire coven, which was a focus-grouped way of saying 'exterminate the damn place and everyone inside of it'. The Order of Journeymen, despite years of gradual dissolution and dwindling numbers, still prided itself on committee-approved correctness, often with a panache for the superfluous and verbose.

This particular coven was small, estimated at no more than six vampires, yet they managed to raise a host of questions being at the epicenter of seventeen unexplained deaths and three disappearances across the counties in the area. The attacks were getting more brash and the collateral damage drifted ever further into the public eye. The latest kidnapping was no exception, with County Sheriff Mike Blake missing for over a week.

Lucky for the team, the heightened awareness of a missing elected official along with an ample amount of local press investigations made things easier for them. With a little detective work and lots of greased palms, they were led to this derelict plant.

Joey removed a series of small grenade-like items from the box, passing a few carefully to Adrienne before clipping the rest to his belt. A couple of knives were also pulled out and he tossed Gage some ammo clips, painted blue, along with a few vials of holy water. Although most of the traditional folklore about supernatural creatures was false, some of the elements were tried and true.

Joey hopped over the tailgate and pressed a small button underneath the rear bumper. For a brief moment, the truck seemed to shimmer from within before returning to normal. He reached back into the bed and pulled a baseball bat off a side mount, a sharp blade slotted into the barrel.

"Hope *Bolo* gets lucky tonight," said Gage.

Joey looked at him, slapping the handle to his palm and returned a thumbs up.

Gage turned his attention to the magazines, ejecting a spent gray one from his gun and slapping in one of the new blues, tucking away the spares in his holster pockets. He checked his phone for the time and noticed the battery had drained quite a bit before switching it into vibrate mode. That's when he noticed Adrienne pacing in his peripheral vision.

"What're you thinking?" he asked, approaching her from behind. A large, calming hand touched her on the back.

She had just adjusted her belt for what had to be the hundredth time, then looked down the same path he had earlier. She placed her hands on her hips. "I'm not sure," she said gently. "Something seems off. Not necessarily the situation..." she paused at that notion, letting out a scant chuckle: *killing vampires had become the norm*, "but the why".

"If it makes you feel better, I agree," he said, folding his arms while also looking down into the dark. "It's been what, a couple months at least since we've heard of any blood-sucking in the area? In fact, the same amount of time since we've heard of *any* supernatural shit going down. It's been all quiet, then outta nowhere we have this beastly feast right in our backyard." He shuffled, looking uncomfortable even for the mighty Gage Crosse. His knuckles cracked as he went on. "Hell, I thought we had driven them all out west toward Pine Springs…"

Joey stepped up beside the two of them and Gage took in the faces that were with him, looking to one, then the other. Who would've thought he would be with anyone, especially a team, for over a year? Certainly not the self-expressed loner himself.

It hadn't been all rainbows, roses, and unicorns by any means (well, there was that one unicorn about eight months back). The nights were still as long and as harsh as they'd ever been, though he supposed notably less than the pre-company days. They had all been through much together and he was certainly glad to have them by his side. He gazed at Adrienne for a moment longer.

Especially her.

"But," he snapped, "we can dwell on all that afterwards." He strode to the back of the truck one last time. A serrated steel machete lined with combat sigils caught his attention. Yanking the blade out of the box, he closed it up tight and tossed Joey the key.

"You both ready?"

They nodded and looked to him for direction.

"Alright then! Let's do this!" he said, taking point as they walked together into the dark.

CHAPTER
two

THE VAMPIRE COVEN

AFTER A SHORT HIKE, the trio arrived outside the crusty building, more ominous up close than it was from afar, searching for the nearest way in. Much to Gage's disappointment there wasn't a gaping hole they could simply waltz through, but Adrienne soon spotted a door off to the right in a smoker's area, coated in brown vines and rust.

Joey knelt in front of the entrance while the others covered him. He reached into a side pocket in his jeans and pulled out several lock picking tools, nimbly working to refine his breaking-and-entering skills. "This is so much easier with a video game controller," he said in frustration as the door didn't yield right away.

A rustle came from the bushes; Gage honed in on the sound, but it turned out to be just the wind.

"*Voila!*" Joey said proudly after a few more moments. "Master lock picking skill achieved."

Gage pushed the corroded door open slowly to minimize the sound of moaning metal and ushered them inside once there was a gap large enough. One after the other they entered the darkened room.

A few windows lined the crumbling walls, damp and sweating with black mold, while rows of benches and tables ran down the center. Refrigerators and microwaves on the far side rested against flaking safety posters and corporate notices that had long gone unread. In the corner stood two vending machines, one full of expired snacks and the other stuffed with cobwebs and spider spawn.

"This is definitely the right place," whispered Adrienne as she pointed to the open fridge doors. Inside were trays of blood and assorted body parts, marinating at room temperature on the powerless shelves. If anyone had been hungry, they definitely weren't now as a bitter stench of vinegar and death wafted into their noses and stung their throats.

Joey made his way toward a hallway to the left of the entrance, rounding the corner straight into a massive spider web that completely covered his face. Its maker dangled right at the corner of his eye and quickly he shoved it into the wall, smearing bug guts across the factory's posted injury record. From the looks of that weathered document, this place hadn't won any awards for a safe work environment. Ever.

That's when the distant patter of footsteps echoed from the silence ahead.

Without words the team split: Adrienne holding back in the break room while Joey slid into a supply closet midway down the hall. Gage, in typical fashion, stayed put with arms patiently folded across his chest.

A man, outwardly in his early forties, walked around the corner. He was tall but thin and dressed in plain, everyday clothes that were dirtied from a distinct lack of washing. Groaning, he tried to light a cigarette with a stubborn lighter that was only delivering sparks. He took a few more steps down the hall before noticing Gage blocking the way ahead.

His breathing labored as their eyes met. Those long arms fell to the side, protruding out as yellowed fingernails inched their way into sharp claws. His eyes narrowed as the cigarette fell from his mouth, now agape as if to scream. But no sound came. Instead, his teeth became razor-like and deadly.

The two stood facing each other like a standoff in the Wild West.

"Well, you gonna make a move?" Gage whispered impatiently. "Time's wasting and we ain't all undead."

The vampire charged down the hall, surging off the ground onto the walls. As he rushed by, the supply closet the door opened and Joey stepped out, *Bolo* in hand.

The vamp's charge was met with a power jab to the gut. Winded, he stumbled before engaging with Gage in a furor of fists and talons.

Gage knocked the creature into the left wall, then to be fair sent him into the right, dislodging flecks of paint and debris that threatened to cause a sneeze. But there was no time to lose focus. The beatings continued, ending with a heavy boot to the chest that sent the biter flying back down the corridor on his back.

Sliding to a stop, his large brown eyes locked in on a passing streak of silver.

"Night night!" said Joey as he swung the bladed bat down like an axe. With a single strike, the vamp's head was hewn.

Gage finally let loose a sneeze. "Man, it's fucking dusty in here!"

Adrienne came chuckling from the break room and walked past the two of them to the end of the hall. She turned to say something sarcastic at them, but cold, dead hands yanked her around the corner before she could get a word out.

Gage and Joey bolted down the passageway and rounded the corner. They met with the sight of …

… Adrienne standing over the hunched body of a female vampire, middle aged with curly blonde hair. She was wiping blood off her silver dagger with her shirt, the vamp's neck cut clean from side to side. The wound shimmered with a faint yellow light.

They both gave her a startled look.

"I guess you're good then, no need for a dashing rescue from two handsome men?" asked Joey with half a smile on his lips.

"Good for now, studs," she said, pointing at the center sigil on the blade before twirling it in her fingers and sliding it back onto her belt. "Trusty number fourteen."

"No need for the extended warranty, Solomon guarantees product effectiveness will last three thousand years or more after one's death," said Gage as he kicked the vamp's limp legs. He gestured toward the next set of doors. "Badass ladies first."

Pushing through, she led them into the main factory area. It was a jumbled mess of machinery from ages past, cracked and entangled with vines which were likely the only thing still holding everything together. Mills and lathes sat beside things so degraded and unrecognizable that their original purpose was long lost to history.

The ceiling above stood broken, pillars of cascading moonlight peppering the floor while dust motes danced in the coolness. Despite an abundance of flakes, the air in here was fresher and less rimmed with rot.

To the left stood another set of double doors, a faded sign split in two overhead saying 'Reception'. Straight on were the supervisory offices and conference rooms and to the right was the factory proper, complete with boilers, furnaces, and danger.

"Well, this definitely checks the mark for a warm and welcoming post-apocalyptic vibe," said Joey. "Remind me to get a postcard before we leave."

"We should look in the offices first," said Adrienne, pointing to the shadowed hallway ahead of them. "See if any are holed up inside before hitting the main area."

Gage nodded.

After few steps, their plans changed as a brawny female vampire strode in from the black and stood in the center of the entryway. Her fangs were bared, ready for attack. She was a big beast of a woman, probably extremely slow and ungainly and-

She came at them with a quickness they had never seen before. In an instant she was upon them. Adrienne and Joey barely had time to dart out of the way as she rushed by, a near invisible streak.

"What the hell!" exclaimed Adrienne, hitting the unwelcoming dirt. "This one's been drinking some top shelf red. Everyone watch out!"

She rushed by again and Gage swung his machete, slicing through nothing but air. He scowled as a claw grazed his back and tore into his jacket.

A follow up punch sent him to one knee, then another scrape came across. Grimacing from the sharp heat now radiating across his back, his blade clanged on the ground.

Adrienne looked up and saw another vampire running toward them from the factory floor, shifting deftly around and over the equipment. His features were as sharp as the teeth he bore.

She stepped in front of Joey as the vamp leapt high and grabbed hold of her shirt, sending them both careening into a stack of wooden pallets. Several splintered under their weight and the rest scattered across the floor as the duo clamored for the upper hand. The monster made his way on top first, straddling her. As she was immobilized, he wasted no time moving in for the kill.

Joey drew one of his knives and ran toward them, thrusting it deep into the vamp's back.

He recoiled in agony, knocking Joey away.

The attacker loosened his grip on Adrienne's arms and she used the opportunity to strike. Her fist connected with his jaw, sending several teeth flying. Shuffling to her feet, she flipped the blood sucker onto his injured back and in the same swift motion released a dagger from her belt. It pierced his undead skin, pinning his hand to the wooden boards.

Meanwhile Gage unleashed another flurry, whipping the air to no avail. A flash surged by, bumping his shoulder hard.

Frustrated, he tried again.

"Will... you..."

And again

"Stay... still..."

and-

Thunk!

The edge bit into something solid and a thin cloud of red floated by.

"Gotcha at last, Helga," said Gage through his gritted teeth, twisting the blade in place.

She squirmed as it continued to hack and saw its way through the rest of her.

Gage flicked the machete at the end of his volley, sending her head soaring from her body like some sick, deflated balloon.

The other dagger came off Adrienne's ankle like a bolt, piercing her attacker's remaining hand. The vamp was now secured to the pallet, contorting his back and legs in all manner of unnatural shapes, underscored with even more abnormal sounds. She took out her final blade and thrust it deep into his heart. A golden glow pulsed from the wound and a loud shrill escaped before the sounds of gurgling took over.

The three of them took a moment to catch their breath, but if this mission was telling them anything, such time was fleeting. How true that was.

In the ever-dark ahead of them a new shape emerged: smaller, younger, and more agile. He stepped forward, extending claws so far out they looked like kitchen knives attached to his fingertips. With a single unwavering swipe, he cut through nearby pipes as if they were putty.

"The fuck kind of freak show is this?" asked Gage.

These were not normal biters; so far from them.

"You have got to be joking!" exclaimed Joey, fishing one of the grenades off his belt. It hummed through the air, landing close to the monster's feet before exploding in a fountain of dazzling purple.

The vamp screeched as his skin peeled from the radiation and the corrosive light blinded him.

Joey took the chance and grabbed *Bolo* off the floor, dashing forward to cleave.

The vamp stopped and sniffed the air. He knew something was headed his way fast. Sure enough, as Joey swung he seized the bat by its handle, flinging both it and its owner down the length of the hall.

Joey tumbled into a dingy restroom, crashing between the single sink and a lidless, sludge filled toilet. It smelled atrocious. The area was very small, with little space to swing and absolutely no places to hide. Even if he wanted to fight he was weaponless, the arsenal he was carrying scattered down the passageway.

Hunching like a big cat, the vamp ran at him, scraping the floor with those massive talons and leaving deep lines in the concrete.

"Light..." said Joey.

The vampire jumped, landing atop his next meal, sending the air straight out of Joey's lungs. He couldn't get a deep enough breath to say anything more.

The vamp reared those sickles back to strike but suddenly began to convulse, digging feverishly at his own chest. Unable to retract the claws in time, it began cutting into its skin while something undulated beneath the surface as if alive. From the writhing, bulge a shower of maroon gave birth to the tip of a machete blade.

Gage withdrew the sharp end and with a powerful lunge, jabbing it into the vampire's neck. Grabbing hold of the creature's head, he started to pull while pressing down on the machete for leverage. The veins in the vamp's temples threatened to explode from the pressure. Bones began to shatter like tinder and before long the beast's body crumpled to the ground. His head followed a few moments later with a soft *thud*.

Joey breathed hard as he filled his lungs, looking up to Gage towering above him – godlike with fists clenched in the faint light that spilled in from the doorway. It highlighted every striated detail as he looked down and extended a bloody hand to Joey, pulling him up onto wobbling feet.

"Ya okay, big man?" asked Gage, pulling him closer for stability.

Joey placed a hand on Gage's large chest, feeling a little heat swell in his cheeks. A bit more 'added balance' was apparently needed so he moved in a touch closer. "Definitely am now."

Gage raised the corner of his mouth, turning to see Adrienne approaching. His smile widened as she arrived.

"Are you both alright?" she asked through her huffs.

They nodded, Gage taking a moment longer.

"Good to hear," she said, noting all of their cuts and bruises. She rubbed her shoulder to calm the fiery pain before adjusting her gloves. "Glad you guys look as good as I feel. I don't know what the hell these things are on, but thank God that should be most of them if our count was right."

"Yeah, these fuckers are much more powerful than ones we've dealt with before." Gage looked around cautiously. "There should be one more in here somewhere and they'll likely have answers. We gotta find 'em."

"Well," said Joey. "I can assure you of one thing." He pointed behind as he reluctantly stepped back away from Gage. "This bathroom right here, is clear."

Adrienne handed him his fallen gear. "Let's go."

They proceeded in step down the deserted hallway, checking out each decayed office. They were empty save the undusted furnishings and paperwork, caked with years' old layers of filth and squalor.

Then a lone cry pierced the silence.

"What was that?" asked Joey.

"It sounded like a child," answered Adrienne. "It's coming from the conference area." She extended her dagger to indicate the way.

"You know, wouldn't it be nice to fight something in the warm, midday sun one of these days?" Joey grumbled as they set off into the gloom.

"Keep on dreamin'," said Gage. "In fact, I'm laying out tomorrow and getting a tan." He extended his arms ahead, inspecting each one in turn. "Could almost pass myself off as a ghost."

"Hate to disappoint you but it's going to rain, Casper," Adrienne whispered.

Gage replied with something indecipherable under his breath just as the cries grew louder. They continued the further down they went, peaking outside a set of three doors. The main conference room was ahead, two smaller ones at either side. All were shut and locked from the outside, but thin, rectangular panes allowed a look inside.

They each took one and looked in.

Joey slowly glanced through the murky glass. It was a standard conference room on the other side with a long mahogany table and cracked leather chairs around the outside. Bland and commonly corporate, nothing else was of interest.

In Adrienne's, the furniture had been removed and body parts were stacked in the middle of the room, a veritable vampiric buffet. She gagged a bit at the sight of the carnage; this part never got any easier. As she looked on, she was extremely thankful that she couldn't smell it.

Gage looked in his room. Most of the windows were blocked by several large conference tables that had been upended and hurled against the far wall. The accompanying chairs were haphazardly strewn about, yet a definite circular space was left clear in the middle. There, dead center, knelt a little girl dressed in pink. She was turned away from them, long blonde hair curled halfway down the back of the frayed dress.

The cries continued.

Joey got to work picking the lock and the door soon creaked open. The trio entered slowly and approached the girl with weapons in hand. She hadn't budged despite the obvious sounds they were making.

The cries were now much louder now, too.

"I don't like this at all," said Joey. "Creepy supernatural children are the worst." He and Adrienne inched around to the front, Gage hanging back with his gun drawn and pointed squarely at the back of her head.

"Careful Ady," said Gage as she stepped forward.

The girl didn't move, despite tears streaming through the dirty fingers covering her tiny face.

"What's your name?" asked Adrienne, scanning for bite wounds. She couldn't see anything and there was no reply, so she asked again.

The sobbing faded and the girl's arms sank to her sides. "Why do you want to know?" she asked through dark and narrow lips. Her eyes were closed, still wet from the tears falling moments earlier and her skin had a porcelain glow.

"Because we want to-"

"Help?" she sneered, turning to the side. "Helping me… it's far too late for that."

As her hair fell away, Adrienne noticed two distinct puncture marks on her neck. "So, you've already fed?" she asked.

There was no reply.

Gage was already growing tired of this exchange, shifting from one leg to the other and back again. To keep from having an aneurism, he sent his eyes to drift around the room: what a dump this place truly was. However, something caught his eye. In the corner he spotted a long length of rope amongst some fallen tiles and signaled to Joey.

Adrienne was unfazed and continued her line of questioning. "What is your name? Have you already fed?"

"Nancy," she snapped. "But I don't see why that's important. My last name is Hardy too, in case you wanted to ask me that particularly stupid question." She paused and took in a deep breath. "Mortals. Oh and yes, I have fed."

"On what?"

There was a long stretch of silence before she leaned toward Adrienne.

"Those missing persons," she whispered, flinging her bloodshot eyes wide open. "All of them." She lunged forward, grabbing Adrienne by the throat. Her timid mouth smirked as it split into two fleshy petals, each lined with rows of fangs. Adrienne was transfixed in horror.

Finally, Gage thought, nodding to Joey. Like a whip, he threw a lash of holy water across her back, tossing the empty vial aside. She seized up as he reached around to empty more down her throat. She coughed as it sizzled its way into her stomach.

Joey rushed in to bind her hands, avoiding her deadly bite. Before long the guys had secured her from above. While she stood with arms overhead, choking smoke continued to belch amidst her attempts to scream, which changed from childlike to monstrous with unsettling ease. However, as Gage approached all fell silent when he pressed the barrel of his gun to her forehead.

"You done flapping those jaws?" he asked, not really looking for a reply. "You're on my time now princess, so let's chat." He holstered the pistol, grabbing a nearby chair. Flipping it upright, he fell into the old leather and stared at the apparent eight-year-old ahead of him.

"So lil' miss Nancy," he said. "You've done a pretty good job here with this coven of yours. Those seventeen deaths make a lot more sense now, your squad of roided up vamps tearing up the streets."

She shifted her arms, straining against the ropes before staring into him, sniffing the air. "You're so… intense," she said, sniffing the air as if to pick up on a whiff of his manliness. "Here I am, at a disadvantage. A studly, tattooed man stands in front of me and knows my name, but sadly hasn't even told me his before tying me up for a little bit of bloody fun. How rude."

He cringed hearing those words come out of her, although she was probably far older than she looked. "Gage," he said, scowling.

"Interesting," she noted, eyeing him from head to toe. "You wouldn't happen to be THE Gage Crosse now, would you?"

"The one and only."

She giggled, managing to make it sound malicious. "Well, Gage, your reputation precedes you. In all my years I've never sensed someone as… wild as you. It certainly doesn't strike me as a quality the Journeymen would seek out for their ranks, at least the order of old. But then again, that may explain why they are now in such rapid decline."

"This ain't about me sister," he said, pointing to her bound hands, "or the Journeymen."

"Oh but it is," she countered, realizing they had no idea what was going on. She giggled again. "You and your fellows are so in the dark about what is happening right now in the world."

"That's why I have you here. Enlighten me."

"Now, where would the fun be if I did that?"

"Fun?" he asked. "Well, let's see. It seems this dumb J-man has you by the balls." He raised an eyebrow. "If you actually had any. You're the one all tied up, princess."

"For now," she replied, her mouth stretching into a wide smile.

Gage rose from his seat, pulling another vial from his pocket. He unstoppered it and dripped some holy water on her wrist, sending a burning trail along her forearm all the way down to her elbow. She winced when he did it again on the other arm.

"See? Now there's the fun! So, do you have anything to tell us?" he asked, slumping back in the seat.

"Color me disappointed, Gage. I was expecting better. Where's that champion of champions who slayed over a hundred vampires during the raid to rescue that gutter trash?" she said spitefully, nodding toward Joey and Adrienne. "Oh, I've heard the stories. Now, here you stand, alongside this bitch vampire-slayer and her pet nerd. All three of you apparently impotent in extracting information from a mere child." Her childish giggle frolicked in the silence. "It'll be fun sucking the marrow from your pathetic bones."

Gage had reached his limit. He kicked away his chair and cocked his gun, shoving it right in her face. "Darlin', I'd like to see you try."

There at last was a hint of the legendary Mr. Crosse. She leaned in closely, seeing the fire in his eyes and his finger calmly resting by the trigger. "Ok. I'll bite," she whispered. "The demons are on the move, the Noctis planning something huge. All monsters are mobilizing in response."

Gage grew a shade paler when he heard mention of the Noctis, those bastards. That ever growing band of demons had taken away his life, his everything, three years ago. This life on the road for revenge was all that he knew now because of them.

"Mobilizing?" he asked, not sure that he wanted to hear the answer. "For what?"

She sat still for a moment before continuing, "To fight against them… or to join them. A war is coming unlike any we have seen before."

"And the vamps?" Gage asked, looking down the bridge of his nose at her smug face. "What are you blood suckers planning on doing?"

"Well, us vampires aren't into being the play things of demons. The werewolves though, I hear they love to wear collars."

Gage looked to his teammates, who had already cast their tense eyes his way. "We need to talk," he said, walking over to a corner for privacy. Adrienne and Joey were two steps behind.

"You heard what Princess Plaque said," he whispered. "We apparently got some serious issues coming over the horizon. If the Noctis are actually moving, then something big is about to go down."

"That's assuming she is telling us the truth," noted Adrienne. "What reason do we have to trust anything she says?"

"Good point. I don't trust her as far as I could throw her… which could be pretty far so never mind that," he said. "But the fact is, she has these mega-vamps under her control and it makes me think there is definitely more here than just a regular clearing. We need to-"

A loud *snap* cut through the silence.

They spun to see a segment of rope careen through the air and a pink streak bolting for the exit. Gage drew his gun and fired several shots. One after another the glowing rounds hit with indigo shockwaves, but he had missed. The bitch was fast.

"Dammit!" he hissed, jerking his head as Adrienne and Joey gave pursuit.

The two reentered the main facility on the hunt. Nancy was so small, easily obscured by the equipment and impossible to spot on ground level. Adrienne took to a nearby ladder and climbed, careful not to lose footing on the greasy metal. She scanned the area keenly, spotting their target as she bolted between two grinders.

"Over there!" she shouted, pointing toward the front of the building.

Joey raced in that direction.

Adrienne started to dismount and noticed Nancy wasn't going to exit through any of the main doors. Instead, she hung left and took a concealed set of stairs, presumably down to a lower level.

Both pursuers now sprinted toward their target but stopped cold when they heard her scream. Such a horrific scream, brimming with pain. As quickly as it began it was silenced, a distinct growl rose in its place, low and terrible.

They both knew what was coming.

Sweat formed across Adrienne's forehead, stinging her eyes as she drew the silver dagger. "No, it can't be," she beseeched.

Joey shuddered. He hadn't heard this sound since that horrific day. Misty eyes appraised the room, floating down to the ground beneath them. A tear rolled off his cheek to the floor. He hurled his eyes toward Adrienne, whose gaze was already waiting.

That's when the seventh one showed up, breaching beneath them in a blast of concrete and splintered boards.

Joey fell to the chamber below and hit the bottom with an ankle first, then his head. *Bolo* fell from his grip, rolling a few feet away. All became blackness.

Adrienne was flung like a rag doll over forty feet into nearby machinery.

She tumbled and struck metal but fate had kept her conscious. The runed dagger waited nearby. Wincing, her labored breaths churned dust into the air as she crept its way.

That's when the creature came into view. A monstrosity much taller than a human stood before her. Pale like milk, skin stretched sickeningly thin over its skeletal body and a pair of membranous wings were folded on its back, fingers moving like spiders at the joints. Golden eyes with dark circles stared pitiless into her from the shadows while drool poured from its fangs. This was a primal vampire. Rare, deadly, and uncontrollable.

Why in hell would the coven have a primal?

She crawled closer to the dagger; it was a necessity if she wanted any hope of survival. The ones she still had would have no effect against this powerful of a thing.

It began to inch toward her. Tattered were its beige clothes and on its left side, a tag caught a gleam off a shaft of moonlight. A gold star was upon it, inscribed with 'County Sheriff' and the name Mike Blake off to the side. He wasn't going to be arresting anyone soon.

She stretched for the blade. It was still too far away. She slithered further across the floor and he took another step. Then another. Before long, he was running full speed toward her, claws scraping against rusty mills. Mangled metal convulsed in his wake.

The dagger still lay out of reach. Fucking hell! Closing her eyes, she waited and withheld a scream and he leaped into the air, claws ready to tear her apart.

A whirl of silver propelled across the room, striking Mike. He collapsed into a boiler and both fell to the floor with a thunderous noise. Pulling himself up, a large machete stuck out from his side. Shrieks let loose when he yanked out the smoking blade, tossing it aside. Blood so dark it could be mistaken for oil spewed onto the floor. His eyes narrowed when he saw the attacker, ire rising with each flap of spread wings as he barreled towards Gage.

He braced himself for impact and they crashed through the door frame back into the conference room.

Mike grabbed Gage's left shoulder and started to sink his talons into the ink, but something went wrong. The pentacle tattoo smoked and his ashen skin bubbled as if acid were on it and a rancid stench rose to fill the air.

Gage continued to pound Mike's face and body.

Howling, Mike wrenched his injured arm back then powered Gage into the wall, free arm upon his chest and wings tightly clamped on his wrists. Bones cracked as his jaw unhinged, rows upon rows of fangs hung from the grotesquely wide maw. As he roared, shreds of flesh and dress flung themselves over Gage's body.

A clawed hand rocketed toward his face. Gage knocked back hard, jostling Mike enough for a miss except for a single hook that carved deep into the flesh above his left eye. The sting was insufferable. His vision became a crimson blur.

Mike lashed out, throttling Gage's neck. The beast slammed him several more times against the wall, causing it to crack and rubble to fall from above. His grip tightened and Gage grimaced from the pain.

Darkness encroached. Blood drenched teeth filled what little view remained. It was inevitable, Gage was going to die.

But not today.

"Light 'em up!" her angelic voice cut through the darkness.

The room became bright like a blue fire that burned from all sides. Mike's putrid flesh seared and his grip waned. No longer was Gage contained, Mike scratching at his own face in misery.

Gage reached down and drew the gun. In one swift motion he raised the barrel and pressed it hard against sizzling forehead.

"Ya marked my face," Gage said, placing a finger on the trigger. "Lemme return the favor." He pulled it back and in a cobalt flash Mike was ended, collapsing to the ground in a headless mass. A moment later black blood rained down on the convulsing heap.

Adrienne stood behind, tending her side while Joey was propped against what remained of the door frame…or maybe it was the wall, it was hard to discern.

Gage let out a long sigh. "Good timing," he said.

"That was an awful line, Gage. Just awful," she replied. "Deactivate."

All their units turned off in unison.

They bent over and each grabbed Joey by an arm and staggered from the remains of the room. As they exited, her hand touched Gage's arm and they both felt themselves stir. Gage glanced in her direction. Funny, he never really noticed over the last year how beautiful and graceful her features were. Until now, like some switch had been flipped.

Another monster had awakened and this one made it very difficult to walk.

"Something wrong Gage?" asked Adrienne, catching him limping along.

"No, nothing," he deflected, voice slightly shaking. He thumped his thigh. "Just the ol' leg. Must've hit it hard in there."

The trio soon emerged from the darkness they had entered, looking worse for wear but alive. They ascended the hill and tossed their gear into the back seat of the truck, gently helping Joey inside.

Adrienne climbed back into shotgun and removed her cap, her head sinking back into the seat. Finally, a breather.

Gage trudged over and got in the driver's side. He paused, closing his eyes for a moment. Opening them again, he glanced to his phone and oddly the battery was nearly drained. Without a second thought, he plugged it in then grabbed hold of the rear view mirror to study the gash above his eye. It was deep, likely to leave a scar.

"Dammit," he said, lightly touching around it with his finger. "Fucking vamps."

The keys jangled as he cranked the ignition, reversing the truck back along the driveway and onto the main road. This particular job was completed, though it had raised further questions about what the vamps were doing across the state. Not to mention the Noctis, who'd obviously started enough of a scare to mobilize sharpened teeth and God knows what else across the nation. But all these great questions could be addressed a little later that morning.

Now was time for the morphine of music, which blared through the truck speakers and filled the cab. Joey sat alone in the rear seats, turning bat in hand. Adrienne nursed the back of her head while staring out into the passing fields. The monochromatic blur was hypnotizing. Gage looked to her, then back at Joey. He raised the corner of his mouth, catching one more glimpse of his newly earned scar before pressing down hard on the gas. The engine roared in reply, rocketing them down the empty road as the wind rushed in through the open windows.

The biting air had lost its teeth and the simplicity of motion was exhilarating.

CHAPTER
three

REST STOP

THE LONE TRUCK CREPT its way down empty, potholed streets and the sounds of classic rock rode the otherwise silent breeze. Ahead, the cold light of Montgomery's Gas and Convenience spilled out through the sprinkling rain into the long night, a beacon of color amidst a perpetual sea of gray.

Joey propped himself up in between the front seats and reached out to the radio, turning the volume all the way down. "Hey, they're open! We need to stop."

Gage took a look at the fuel level; there was still plenty of go left and he really wanted to get back to base. Exhaustion was setting in and the sweet call of his downy pillow made it that much more difficult to keep his eyes open. "The gas is good man, ain't no need." He reached back for the radio.

"But I'm hungry and need to pee," Joey persisted, bouncing slightly as he slunk back into his seat.

Gage looked back at him. "Seriously, what are you, five? You couldn't have taken lil' J for a walk while we were in the woods?"

He grumbled something more under his breath and begrudgingly flicked on the turn signal. Joey was glad he couldn't make out what was said.

The cab jostled as Gage hurriedly drove over the chasm masquerading as a drainage dip. It could have easily knocked out the wheel alignment of any other vehicle, but the GMC was already so far gone that the jolt might have even fixed it. Thankfully the early hours also ensured there were plenty of parking spaces to choose from, so naturally Gage settled in diagonally across several at the front of the store.

"You okay to walk?" asked Adrienne, looking to the back seat. Joey had taken quite a fall earlier.

He nodded as he started to change shirts. "Oh yes. One can always find strength when on a quest for donuts."

She shook her head. "But these are boxed convenience store donuts, J. You know, basically cardboard. They're nothing like the ones from Humphries." It was hard not to let her mind drift on a cloud of sugary splendor. It had been some time since they last ate.

Joey looked as if she had slapped him clean across the face. "Um… So?" He shifted in the seat to take a more studious posture. "Granted all donuts are not created equal, and you have the cake versus yeast debate, and I'm not saying that I wouldn't love the warm, fresh taste of Gage right now."

His eyes shot open. *What the fuck Joey!*

Adrienne blinked and mulled over what she thought she just heard. Her head cocked to one side, to the point it looked broken, and she gave Joey her 'Oh my God you didn't' face.

"What did you say?" she asked.

"Greengage plums," interrupted Gage nonchalantly. "It's one of their best flavors. What's it those fancy reviews say? 'So complex in taste and texture'. Isn't that right Joey?"

By now Joey was redder than the blood stained shirt he was still entangled in. "Yeah… Yeah it is," he stuttered, finally getting the soiled shirt off and a clean one on. "I'll be back in a few. Either of you need anything?" he asked, desperately trying to shift the focus off of himself.

"Nah, I'm good man," Gage replied.

Adrienne was holding back a massive laugh, taking great pleasure in watching Joey squirm awkwardly. "Teriyaki beef jerky would be great. Oh, and snag me some gum please. I doubt they have greengage plum flavor, but if so, make that priority number one."

Joey narrowed his eyes, but avoided looking directly at her while darting out of the back seat. He couldn't get into the store fast enough, nearly colliding with the slow-opening automatic doors. If they didn't know better, it was almost like he hadn't been injured at all.

Both shook their heads as their bottled up laughter finally let loose.

"You know there hasn't been a plum flavor on the Humphries menu in nearly six months," stated Adrienne, confirming the count on her fingertips.

"Oh trust me, I know," said Gage with a chuckle. He turned his attention to his cell phone, the corner of his lips turning down. "That's weird."

"What is it?"

He showed her the screen, pointing to the upper right corner. It had charged a whopping five percent since they left the coven. "Huh, I guess something is wrong with it. Should've done more than that in a half hour, right?"

"Here, let's see," she said, taking his hand and gingerly sliding out the phone. She risked a lingering touch. His skin contradicted his gruff exterior and was invitingly soft, save the fresh scuffs across his knuckles.

He peeked over her way and she pretended to be none the wiser, pulling on the charger. Smiling at him, she inserted it into her phone and all seemed to be well. It chirped and the charge icon popped in as usual.

"We'll see how it goes with mine. You've always had bad luck with things…" She paused, realizing what she said wasn't necessarily in the best taste, given his history. "…especially with tech," she added.

"You ain't kidding," he said as relief fell across her face.

"Sorry for saying that," she said after a brief pause.

"What, about the bad luck? No worries, gorgeous. We've all had our fair share of it. It's a nasty world out there." He looked out his window at the stars beyond the store canopy. "Full of teeth, claws, tentacles, and hell, a thousand other hurtful ways of taking anything ya value away." He looked her way again, now fighting his own thoughts. He definitely cared about this little team of his. They'd become close, like family, over the last year. They kicked ass together and he would stack them up against any of the finest Journeymen still out there. Yet something was dangerously itching for him to want more, to be more, with her. "Surprised it hasn't gotten worse than it already has," he continued. "Guess that's a testament to the job we manage to do."

"Yup," she said, her voice a little unsure. "Even so, it's hard to care about things in this line of work, isn't it?"

Her words betrayed her mind. It was incredibly easy to care for things, like the rugged man beside her. She had been developing more robust feelings, those waters rising during the lull in supernatural activity in recent months. The team was able to get to know each other more personally, day in and day out without the imminent threat of being eaten or worse, hanging overhead. Those emotional floodgates were now exceedingly close to breaching. She looked from his beard down across his right arm, well-lit under the fluorescent lights. It was covered from shoulder to wrist in roses, intricately detailed in black and white shading.

"I've never asked you what your ink actually meant, have I?" she asked.

"No, but you've certainly burned a hole in me staring so many times."

She bumped his arm. "Whatever, you ass. Like you've never stared at me before."

"Only that hat you wear all the time, cougar queen."

Her eyes had to be the strongest part of her body, always getting a workout around him. From the rolling of course, not the gawking. At least that is what she had convinced herself of. "So, going back to this tattoo of yours."

"The roses," he said softly. "They were Momma's favorite flowers. Back during the days I traveled alone, I would close my eyes thinking on the past and I swear I could smell their sweet scent- as if I were standing right there on the front porch of the house we lived in. Silly as it sounds, those nights felt a little less cold because of that. I got this tattoo after a while, as a reminder that Mom is always with me and that I would never have to close my eyes again."

Something was certainly awakening between the two of them. Gage had never seemed vulnerable before, yet here he sat opening up. Adrienne didn't know if that was for the better or worse. Regardless, she continued.

"That's amazing, Gage. My mom nearly killed me when she found out I had a tattoo, even after explaining it had something to do with her."

Gage quickly perked up. She had ink? How was this so? If he hadn't noticed before, that meant it was hidden, very well hidden.

"I had no idea ya had tattoos, Ady," he said, not so casually searching her visible skin.

She raised a finger. "Tattoo. Just one."

"You'll have to show me sometime you rebel, since I showed you mine," he said, leaving his mouth open with a hint of those perpetually white teeth. "Oh and don't get Momma wrong. The sentiment is great but if she saw me today, all inked up like a thug, I probably wouldn't be her favorite son anymore."

"You have a brother?"

"Nope, only child. I'm her favorite and only," he stated matter-of-factly.

A little laugh escaped her smile.

"I'm sure she would still care about you, Gage," Adrienne said faintly as she found a prominent vein which rose above the detailed ink work. With a finger, she traced the ridge across the bloom on his imposing shoulder.

That felt unexpectedly good. He labored to hold his eyes open, but his feelings were amplified with them closed. The artificial glow slipped away, wrapping him in a momentary blanket of nothing but her touch.

The vein road-mapped into his bicep, which she rode without hesitation, detouring along the way to other floral sights across his arm. This was simply incredible, a nurse's wet dream that was quickly becoming her own. She was soon back on the main highway, riding down into the dense cluster of petals on his forearm.

They laughed again when she reached his wrist, lifting her finger before both fell into a pit of silent stares. Thoughts began to mount as their heartbeats started to climb.

Should I try to kiss him? No. That wouldn't be right. But if I did, maybe it would feel right...

Why have I never noticed how gorgeous she is? That hair, my God... Those lips... Fuck my life.

Adrienne, would this really work? He's like a brother to you. But just look at him.

Gage, do you really want to go through with this? You know the life that we live. Love leads to one thing. Pain.

"What is taking him so long?" asked Gage, breaking the hushed exchange that threatened to spill over into action. There was always something he could be impatient about.

She pointed ahead into the store. "That right there. I don't think he'll ever grow up."

They both watched Joey make beelines up and down the aisles from one delicious junk food delicacy to the next. During his mad dash, he rounded a corner too quickly and knocked over an end cap display, sending assorted flavors of chips flying across the floor.

That sent the portly shop keep trundling over, flamboyantly waving his arms in a fit while Joey haphazardly threw a few items back on the display.

Gage chuckled. "That's what makes him special."

Joey filled up his bags then reached into his pocket, tossing some cash on the counter. "Keep the change!" he shouted, bounding out of the store and back into the vehicle.

"Good God!" said Adrienne. "Got yourself a bit of a boost?"

"What?" asked Joey, tossing her a bag of beef jerky. He had already demolished a pack of chips, starting in on some cookies. An empty energy drink can made its way into in the plastic bag tied around his wrist. Thankfully for him, a tinny *clang* indicated there were more full ones inside.

"I swear that guy's wife is a beard," said Joey, a cookie hanging from his mouth as he rifled through the bag for something to wash it down with.

Adrienne nearly choked, since she agreed.

"You fuckers set?" Gage cut in; bed was calling his name. "Let's roll, and gimme a damn cookie for waiting on your ass."

Adrienne nabbed a chocolate chip one for him and took a fleeting look down at her cell phone as they set off. The indicator showed that it had already increased fifteen percent. Something was certainly wrong with Gage's phone, which had since died.

CHAPTER
four

A MEETING AT MONTGOMERY'S

THE PORTLY EUGENE MONTGOMERY was counting the money left on the store counter, snorting under his breath when the front doors dinged.

Better not be that little prick again, he thought, having only just cleaned up about half of the mess left by the whirlwind that was Joey Mosley. *Sexy as he is, that boy is a menace.*

That's when a pungent odor stabbed at his piggish nostrils.

"First you trash my store, boy, and now you try to smoke in here? Take those damn matches and your cigarettes outside," he snapped, looking up with a snarl.

It wasn't Joey.

There, instead of the young man, two uniformed police officers stood in front of him, imposing like statues.

"Oh! My apologies officers," he said with a tinge of surprise and a frown. The coins in his hand fell through his stubby fingers, dancing noisily on the glass. "I didn't mean… Crap… I thought you were someone else."

They said nothing as the shorter officer removed his cap, placing it over the clattery change. His buzzed hair, stocky build and gruff expression weren't putting Eugene at ease one bit. If the guy hadn't been wearing a police uniform, he could just as easily have been there to rob the store.

Eugene peered over to the other man. He stood at least six inches taller and was far ganglier. His expressionless face and cold focus added to the unease that pervaded the room.

"So, can I help you two fine gentle…" his voice trailed off as the doors chimed yet again. Eugene shuffled over and craned his neck to see who was coming in. Sweat had begun beading on his brow and he took a large, salty gulp when he saw who had stepped inside.

A middle aged man with sharp features had waltzed in, his scuffed boots crunching over the array of candy bars and chip bags still strewn on the floor. Dressed in torn skinny jeans, his white wife beater had yellowed from months of accumulated stains. On one wrist he wore a luxury watch, dulled by fictitious gold and on the other a pair of handcuffs dangled loose and free. As he sauntered closer, his steely eyes gazed down a beak-like nose, never leaving the rotund man behind the counter.

Eugene wrenched his eyes away, noticing a large red smear on the man's chest as he settled in between the two policemen. A smell like natural gas followed.

"Good… evening…" Eugene stammered. "Can I help *any* of you?"

The prisoner spoke. "Are you the purveyor of this fine establishment?" he asked in a raspy voice. As he gestured with his arms, the handcuffs reflected the overhead lamps, sending their light dancing uncomfortably across Eugene's face.

"Yes, I am."

"Then indeed it is your lucky day," he said coldly. The prisoner continued, pointing a finger toward Eugene. Something told the shop keep that this wasn't the kind of luck one wished for. "I have a couple of questions that need answering and you… well, you are the man for the job."

He waved his pointing hand and the policemen fell back a few steps.

Shorty broke away and walked toward the door. After a quick look around, he found the switch for the "OPEN" sign and flipped it. The letters faded as he returned to the other officer's side.

Eugene felt a rumble in the pit of his stomach and his heart began to pound in his chest. He couldn't focus on any one thing, desperately needing some comfort in this extremely uncomfortable situation. Maybe if he could move his hands beneath the counter and press the silent alarm or maybe if he could snag his shotgun to pepper these assholes, he would feel better and safer. All was for naught when the effort was stopped before it even began.

"Ah ah ah," said the prisoner as both cops reached for their weapons. "I know what you're thinking. We've no time for company just yet. You and I still have to chat."

The sweat stung as Eugene tried to watch the detainee through squinted eyes, still catching brief flashes of light from off the cuffs.

The man leaned forward. "So my good man, have you had any visitors tonight?" Good lord his breath was terrible, as if strips of meat were trapped between his teeth since the days his shirt was pure white.

"No," said Eugene amidst a cough that brought up a little bit of sick with it.

The prisoner's look screamed *liar*.

"No… one of any importance," Eugene corrected, coughing once more.

"Hmmm," pondered the convict. "Is that so? I'll be the judge of that."

Just my luck, Eugene thought. *What kind of gangland crap has that son of a bitch brought on me?*

"So this 'nobody important.' Who was he?" The man picked up a quarter and started to tap the glass with it.

"Some kid" he told him, "maybe in his early twenties. I didn't catch a name."

"A shame," he replied, pausing to look at the coin in detail. He placed it back on the countertop before picking up another, shiner one. "Paid by cash did he? Well, it's a good thing he wasn't all that important."

Eugene fell silent, as if he stopped breathing.

"So, was he with anyone else?" the man pressed, continuing to knock the countertop with his fresh coin.

"Nobody in the store," Eugene replied. The tapping grew faster and he wiped his forehead with a sleeve; was the heating unit on? The air was notably hotter and patchy sweat stains had formed under his arms and across his lower back.

"There was someone out in the vehicle, well two actually: a man and a woman. I couldn't see either of them very well." The non-stop tapping was getting to him, now beating against the inside of his skull. "Stop it!" he exclaimed before dialing his voice way down, "please?"

The prisoner flicked the change toward Eugene, striking him on the chin. "So there were three total," he said, looking over his shoulder. With a head jerk the cops promptly stepped up to each side. "The vehicle they were in, was it a truck?"

"Yes," he answered curtly. Maybe a shift in tone would get these men to leave. "Are we close to being done; I was quite busy beforehand…"

Ignoring him, the questioning continued. "So do you know where were they going? Where they live?"

"What the? How am I supposed to know that? I have no goddamn idea!" *Who are you guys? What do you want? Just get out!*

The con frowned. "Listen-"

"Look! You listen!" Eugene shouted. "I told you! I! Don't! Fucking! Know!"

"No *you* listen here you bloated meat sack, things are about to get really messy for you."

"Go to hell!" he snapped, sending a glob of spit onto the man's face.

Wiping the phlegm that caressed his cheek, the prisoner blinked. His gray eyes were suddenly black with a flowing ring of deep crimson.

"Been there already and hated it, as you're about to find out." He swung his arm, the handcuffs crashing into the countertop and shattering the glass.

The officers rushed in and grabbed Eugene, holding him firm as he attempted to get free. They were so much stronger than he was. Unnaturally so. They yanked him hard across the demolished counter, scraping his body over the hundreds of razor edges inside and like a limp doll they hurled him onto the floor before going to scoop him back up.

The prisoner surveyed the splintered glass like he was shopping for jewelry, looking for the largest and most beautiful one he could find. There it was. Reaching in, he removed a long, knife-like shard and turned to face Eugene, who was still struggling with his little bit of might.

"Please…" he quivered, shaking uncontrollably on his cracked legs as fear overtook him. "I'll do anything. Just let me-"

His eyes met those empty, red rimmed pupils as a thin line of prickly heat glided over his neck. Warmth flowed from of the gash and over his chest, oozing down his body like a broken egg. He had no choice but to continue looking at the unforsaken gaze drilling into him, gasping for breath before his round body toppled.

The man removed his boots as Eugene expired, a faint whisper of breath skating across the shiny pool. He stepped into the brackish liquid, still pleasantly warm, and used one of his bare feet to shove the body out of the way.

"*Spiritum meum, victor erit,*" he uttered in an abyssal tone that shook the walls. "*In malign positus, loquar!*"

The store lights flickered and showered the room with sparks as the blood snaked under his clothes all the way up his body. Rushing from his collar, the tendrils wormed their way around his lips as he continued to speak in a long lost, guttural language.

"Onoskelis, it is I," he said demonically.

A few minutes later a voice boomed, coming from all directions. It was fathomless, forceful, and feminine. "What news do you bring, Stolas?"

"Tonight we have confirmed that the Hardy coven was, at last, decimated."

"Excellent work," she said. "You and your company will be rewarded. That little bitch learned what a mistake it was to turn against us, as will they all in time. Now, we must focus our attention to the north and the wendigos-"

"Your grace," he interrupted. "The coven was decimated, but not by us."

It grew eerily quiet.

The buzz of the freezers took over, echoing in Stolas' ears as he remained outwardly calm. However, the shadow inside strove to maintain composure.

His host's skin became itchy and it was impossible to remedy.

"Onoskelis?" he said nervously. The long pause remained for nearly a minute more. Cautiously, he carried on with the report. "Based on the use of Solomon weaponry, scientifics, and other trace evidence at the scene, we believe the attack was carried out by a small team of Journeymen. Specifically-"

"Gage... Crosse," her voice resonated, toppling boxes from the shelves. Gage had managed to find a way to be at the epicenter of nearly every major supernatural event over the last couple of years. He was certainly a man on a mission after the death of his parents and that made him extremely dangerous, especially to demonkind. She could respect that, but also knew that if he was involved then there was a definite threat to their immediate plans.

"Yes," Stolas confessed meekly. "We have reason to believe he is based somewhere in the Houston area with this team of his. We are working to find out where that is but it is heavily warded, as is his transportation."

"Is there reason to suspect he knows anything of our plans?"

"Well, not in detail. There were also no prisoners taken but, there is no way for us to know what Hardy told him before her demise."

"Hmmm," she replied. "We cannot afford to have that behemoth poking around. You are to keep your distance and remain where we are at our strongest: in the shadows. Our plans are making considerable headway and any suspicion about or attention on us shall be kept to an absolute minimum. Is that clear?"

"It is, your Grace."

"That brings me to the manner of your contact with me, Stolas."

He swallowed hard, noticing the shorter cop had stepped forward a few paces, fitting gloves over his hands.

"How did you come about finding enough blood to use this spell?"

"The... shopkeeper," he disclosed.

"The shopkeeper," she repeated. "Who happens to own the store that infamous demon slaying menace had just... fucking... visited?"

A hand latched onto his arm, spinning him around. Shorty had him, brandishing a small iron blade resembling a railroad spike. Demonic seals were engraved down its entire length.

A few feet away, the spindly cop murmured with his head bowed and Stolas realized what was happening too late. He attempted to step out of the pool of now stale blood, but his feet were frozen, the liquid around them crystallizing into icy clamps. He was trapped like a rat in a cage.

A coughing fit followed as the taller cop's whispers picked up pace. Umbral mist laced with red belched from Stolas' mouth with each uncontrollable hack.

I need to get out of this sack of skin! he thought while closing his eyes as he tried to eject from the host. There was no guarantee that there was anyone nearby to repossess in time, but that was a risk he was willing to take and it was certainly better than the permanent fate he knew was coming.

The shadowy form of a night raven spawned briefly, ready to take flight, but suddenly glitched back into the body that now anchored him.

"You have made some mistakes in the past, my not-so-wise feathered friend," Onoskelis chastised. "Perhaps those herbs you've been so fond of have clouded your judgment. But knowing *that* particular Journeyman is so close to us and our plans, we must be far… far more careful. We can afford no more mistakes like this and we cannot afford your grand levels of stupidity any longer. *Vale, Stolas!*"

The store rumbled once more and she was gone.

Before he could get another word out, the iron spike made its way into his chest. Shorty smirked as he turned the blade and Stolas convulsed; sooty vapor wafted out of every pore yet was heavy and sank to the floor. Holding onto the weapon, Shorty pushed Stolas backwards.

Hell did not await him, nor Heaven. The unmitigated dark of the abyss swallowed his corrupt demonic soul before he hit the floor, utterly and unquestionably dead.

The gangly cop then walked over to the counter, grabbed a shard of glass, and placed it into Eugene's hands. He turned back to his partner. "I'll prepare in here," he said peacefully.

Shorty nodded, exiting the store. He walked to the police car parked under the filling station awning and settled calmly into the seat, lifting the radio. Pressing the button, he spoke with authority, "This is Officer Sullivan. We have a coroner's case at Montgomery's Gas and Convenience."

CHAPTER
five

THE FIRST TIME

YOU KNOW THE TIME OF the morning where if sleep evaded you, none of the options laid out on the proverbial table for rest were going to pan out? As luck would have it, that's exactly the time Adrienne found herself in. The sun was still well below the horizon and she couldn't sleep if she wanted to.

I bet Joey is still awake too, she thought as she walked down the hall, poorly trying to justify her own insomnia. *That was a lot of sugar, caffeine, and whatever else shoved into those slender cans he was knocking back like a crack whore turning tricks.*

On the other hand, Gage was probably sawing enough logs to add a third story to the Lodge. That goddamn grizzly tease, innocently snoozing up there while she was down here, wide awake with him fully on her mind.

She stumbled her way into the kitchen, her vision blurred by fatigue and the annoying flickering above the sink. A certain man was tasked with fixing that light and he had obviously made it a top priority. Squinting between its random flashes, she looked out the tiny window.

The GMC was parked caddy-cornered to a gold '80 Z28, its classic American lines making Gage's baby look downright clunky in comparison, kind of like its owner.

Beyond the vehicles pitting themselves against each other, the trees swayed with a trance-inducing dance and just past the grassy expanse a section of the metallic ring that surrounded the property shone in the moonlight. The rain had also started to pick up; still a drizzle, it would likely be a steady downpour within the next hour.

Parched, she sluggishly opened the cabinet where the drinking glasses should be, only to find there were none inside. A glance down at the sink showed her where they had gone: swimming in a cesspool of dirty dishes while a large air bubble belched at her with a pop.

Sigh.

As she started cleaning and cursing under her breath, a huge mass entered the room and loomed behind her. Stepping up, it grabbed hold of her shoulder and she twirled, flicking off the dagger that was still on her belt. She quickly raised it high and let the tip sink in, releasing a small trickle of blood.

Fuck, it was Gage – no third floor construction project was going on tonight.

He wiped the stream of red off with a single swipe from his thumb and then rubbed his beard with the other hand, all while letting out a beastly yawn. He stood there, shirtless as usual, in another pair of tight, low riding jeans that looked nearly identical to his countless other pairs.

This pair seemed to have the magical ability to get tighter the more he moved, showing off all the goods both front and back. She idled on his barely contained behind before reality threw her back.

"Really?" she snapped.

"What?" he replied, reaching into the sink to pick up one of the used glasses. "It's just *moi*, gorgeous."

She pushed him hard, knocking the glass back into the dishwater, sending some of it splashing across her already grimy tank top.

"Oh I don't know," she said with a another Gage-induced eye roll. "Maybe the fact that we *just* cleared that coven full of…" She paused as her mind wandered between the circus of vampiric freaks they fought and the primal that nearly killed her. "Sorry, I just haven't had a chance to chill out yet or get rest like *some people*. I mean shit, I can't even get a glass of water for my parched soul without having to navigate my way through a level of hell left behind by you and Joey." She waved her hands frenetically over the pile of dirty dishes before crossing them in an attempt to look imposing. Her head was cocked to one side.

Gage wasn't taking the bait; in fact he had some of his own.

"My bad, my bad," he said, raising his arms in surrender. "After all this time I thought you could handle the stress of monstrous beasts." He calmly turned his fingers downward.

"Most beasts I can," she said. "Yourself included."

He shifted a bit closer to her, turning her away from the sink and pressing her against the central island. He leaned in toward her ear.

"I doubt that," he whispered. "Certain monsters were made to make people scream."

"Oh yeah, I bet you make all the ladies scream with this," she said while darting her hand out to grab the front of his jeans. There was much more there than she realized; than she wanted. Her eyes shot up to his as he raised an eyebrow in agreement.

"Not just the ladies darlin'," he corrected. "*People* scream. Better watch yourself. Don't get lost and become… prey."

It was suddenly very warm. She found herself looking straight into his eyes, unable to pull away, eagerly wet underneath her jeans.

"I don't get lost easily," was all she could manage to say.

"We'll see."

At that moment, Joey walked by the archway separating the kitchen and dining room. He was carrying a couple of empty bags to the storeroom for supplies. As he passed, he stopped about halfway and saw two silhouettes; Adrienne pinned with Gage looming over her. His hulking back and shoulders were easily twice her width, arms triple the thickness. Joey spent some time studying them, transfixed by Gage's shape for what seemed like forever. He realized he should leave before he was seen, but as soon as he started again, the floorboards turned him in.

In the low light Gage looked up and he zoned in, eyes drifting from Joey's disheveled hair down the open flannel shirt laid over a lightly furred chest, past the bulging jeans all the way to his muddy boots and right back up again.

Oh how he loved to make people scream. He tossed Joey a wink, which sent him on his way.

ADRIENNE LAID BACK IN her comfy bed wondering what had happened earlier.·

She had heard a little creak and soon after, Gage had pulled himself away from her and went back upstairs. She took a moment alone at the kitchen table to finish off a glass of water before somehow ending up back in her room. The journey back up here was a blur as he would not leave her mind, filling it with an endless cycle of thoughts and possibilities.

The rain beat against the roof, the normally restful sound causing a calamity in her soul. Part of her was outside, dancing by herself joyously in the rain. Another was tucked up underneath a tree locked in a passionate kiss, while yet another was here in her room gazing out at all the dancing and kissing going on. She focused in on that piece, searching for an answer.

As she looked upon herself from the outside, she had the most difficult time understanding what feelings she could read on own her face. Was she content to be up here alone? Was she sad? Did she long for the time under the tree with another, or for a solo number in the rain?

Why was this so damn difficult?

Speak to me Adrienne!

There was no reply.

Frustrated, she got out of bed and propped herself up against the window sill. The steady beat of rain drew her attention back out the window where she found herself again, dancing solo. As she watched, she felt pretty satisfied. That is, until a figure walked up to her and a hand grabbed hers, bringing her close. It was Gage, soaking wet from the rain as well. Together they held each other in the deluge, perfectly still with no other motivation to move. Immediately all felt right.

That was all she needed to know.

She crept down the hall as to not wake Joey up, though the heavy roar of the storm would have muffled any noise she would make passing by his door. Before she knew it, she had arrived outside Gage's room. The door was cracked open and there was a small amount of lamplight coming from inside.

She pushed the door open and peeked inside. She was nervous that she was even in his room, especially so when she saw the sight of what sat on the edge of the bed. Gage was there with arms rested on his thighs, looking down in deep thought.

This is a mistake, she thought, inching back out of the room. While she retreated he happened to look up; little did she know he had been wrestling with the same things.

"Hey there," he said softly. "Whatcha up to?"

"Oh, um. Just checking to see if you were alright. You left in a bit of a hurry downstairs."

"I'm good," he said, leaning back onto the bed. His body looked amazing in the soft light, every single cut and line calling out for attention, especially those tempting v-lines that receded into his jeans. "How about you, darlin'?"

"Me? I'm okay," she replied, wanting to touch him everywhere.

"Ya sure?"

"Yup."

He slowly laid himself all the way down on his back. "Well, I think the door frame can hold itself up. Come on in," he said while patting the open space to his left.

Part of Adrienne still contemplated leaving, but her desires pushed her forward. She closed the door behind her and moved across the sparsely decorated room, bachelor-like in its level of simple and clean. The lines of the furniture were straight like the picture frames on the wall, each holding vintage images of construction workers on beams high above New York City. After a few strides, she sat down gently beside him as he laid there perfectly still.

He looked up at her beautiful brunette hair and skin, dewy like the morning, while she looked down at his ruggedness, so hard and captivating. The veins she had traced earlier in the truck were apparently only the tip of a very large iceberg; they criss-crossed everywhere on his body. As she pondered another road trip along them, she saw a large lump forming in the front of his jeans, growing with each passing second.

He raised a hand to run her hair through his fingers. It was luxuriously soft and when he withdrew, the smell of tea tree and mint trailed behind.

"Did you get lost on your way here?" he asked her.

Adrienne thought she would be ready for this. Part of her wanted to bolt out the door right then but as she continued to look down, she saw that the bump had grown a significant way down his pant leg. She knew that he went commando from his all too frequent plumber impressions and this must have been the reason why. But no way was it that large. Was it? How did it even fit in there? She had to know, primal instincts hastily taking over.

"I must have taken a wrong turn," she replied, resting a hand on his left leg. No sooner than she touched him, a wet spot formed at the end of the bulge.

Good lord.

"Well, I did warn you about what would happen," he said with a pulse that made the spot grow a little more. "I'm about to show you a lot of things, darlin'. You best be ready."

She wasn't.

His stare, rooted and green, commanded her to stay put. A sudden heat formed at the back of her neck as he stood up in front of her and unbuttoned his jeans, motioning for her to do the rest as he placed his hands down into his back pockets.

The zipper began its way down, a forest of veins and thick lines plunging into the confines. She had seen these jeans so frequently over the last year, never once imagining she would be getting inside them. Yet here she was.

He was still pulsing as the zipper fell, the spot in his jeans growing larger.

Once the jeans had been unfurled, she grabbed each side just above the front belt loops and pulled down. They didn't move. She tried again and slowly but surely they lowered, fighting her along the way.

A few seconds later they were stuck again.

She reached around, grabbing his tucked hands. He resisted a bit, forcing her to lean dangerously close to his still caged monster. With her head mere inches from him, he finally moved his hands with hers over his ass, and the jeans were free to move again.

They had slipped down far enough for her first glimpse of the beast: the base was so wide with thick veins roping down the shaft. Her heart leapt while she backed her head up and continued to drag the jeans downward, his large balls swinging free along with the rest of him. There was certainly no shortage of Gage anywhere.

All of this was so surreal and in a world where garden gnomes were alive, that was saying something. She wanted to touch it so badly, just to see if it was real, but that wasn't going to happen right now.

As she reached out her hand, he firmly grabbed hold and lifted her up to his face, pressing her hard against his body. Each one of his striations was hard as marble, his skin soft to the touch. It was difficult to describe the feelings coursing through her at that moment, but dizzy with excitement was probably the most accurate.

Gage didn't wear cologne, yet had a natural musk that she had caught faint whiffs of before. Now that she was so close to the source and not in a life or death battle, she simply wanted to be drenched in it. Needing more of the intoxicating scent, she tucked herself in closer to his neck and drew a long breath.

That's when he leaned in, pulling her back by the hair to bite her lower lip, transitioning into a kiss. His lips and beard were supple and the trace of peppermint on his breath mingled with her own. It was a kiss that seemed to last a century, setting her legs to tremble while she shivered uncontrollably.

Seeing the effect he was having on her was like a drug and he powered on.

He took time to undress her, placing her back onto the edge of the bed while slowly pulling off her top. He savored the moment, running over her velvet skin with the tips of his thick fingers. Her bra soon joined the shirt on the floor and he caressed each of her breasts in his hands. As he looked at them in the golden lamplight, he spread his fingers and went in to tease a nipple between his teeth. And so the other would not be jealous, he followed suit and did the same to it.

She let out a low sigh that forced him to stand up. He squeezed his sizable self in between those voluptuous mounds for a couple of slow strokes. Responding like a faucet, he knew that he needed to slow down before he cascaded over the point of no return.

There was no way she was going to get out of screaming.

He pushed her back onto the bed and she bounced a couple of times. Bending over, he grabbed hold of her jeans and they came down along with her panties. As they fell he saw her tattoo on the front of her hip; a small heart was laid on a bed of olive branches in the shape of the infinity symbol. No wonder he'd never noticed it before tonight.

Her jeans continued to rolling off her slender hips as Gage took the chance to sample her, his beard tickling between her legs as he enjoyed playing with his long tongue. She tasted good, so good the beast wanted some of its own.

Adrienne watched as he stepped over to the nightstand, bouncing in all the right places, coupled with that perfect amount of swagger. He pulled the top drawer and opened a wrapper, setting the torn packet off to the side. She caught glimpse of an 'XL' emblazoned across the front of it and swallowed hard as he kicked a hip out, flexing his glorious buttocks in a way that defied gravity.

She still shivered with excitement and perhaps now a hint of fear.

Sheathed, he walked back in front of her, his thigh tattoo catching the light as he grabbed hold of her legs, setting them around his neck. He flexed and countless lines danced across his muscular quads..

Don't look down, she told herself as the quivering subsided. Of course that meant she instantly took a peek at what was coming. The condom strained against the entire length of his rod, every ridge looking as if it was going to burst.

Holy shit! she thought as his broad head rested right against her door and she was about to let him in. When he starting swirling it around, the shivers kickstarted again.

At last he entered, pushing his power tool into the welcoming warmth. It was a tight fit and she writhed in silent, agonizing joy after only a couple of inches. Double digits still remained. This was going to be an incredibly long... *oh my God!*

Her firm hold sent waves of pleasure down his shaft. He looked over her naked body as he throbbed in reply, wondering why they had waited so long for this. The feelings were beyond incredible and she was even more so.

But she wasn't going to control him. Each time it looked as though comfort was setting in, he taunted her by sliding in a fraction deeper, her wetness making it easier the longer they went. He definitely loved being in charge of the situation, but noticed that he was now over halfway in. Nobody had ever lasted to the end of a battle with this beast before yielding a scream.

Unbeknownst to him, Adrienne had been screaming since the first moment they became one. As he continued to press on, the exhilaration of the night became too hard to contain and she overflowed onto the covers.

It was time.

Her flow allowed Gage to push himself deeper and as he plowed all the way in, he grabbed her and rolled completely over. Now on top, she screamed as he went balls deep, pulling back before charging in once more.

And again.

Oh Gage!

And again.

Ahhhhhhh!

Her eyes couldn't focus as the world became a blur.

He flipped her back over and furiously drilled her, grinding away until the pressure built so much he couldn't hold back. Waves of euphoria overcame them both as he surged, unleashing a carnal bellow before pulling out and collapsing in a massive, meaty heap at her side.

Her vision slowly returned to normal as he laid there utterly spent.

Soreness began to take over the lower half of her body as she looked over to Gage, now facing her way with an emerald fire in those eyes. Sweat had beaded across his back and forehead and he breathed heavily.

"Was that a scream I heard from *you?*" she asked, tapping his nose lightly with a finger.

His brow furrowed. "I dunno what ya speak of," he said.

"Of course not," she said back, looking at the ceiling.

Gage loomed into view, pressing his chest against hers while his hair had molded into the textbook definition of bed head. "I don't scream," he said with a underlying growl. "Now take that back or there may be some punishment."

"Well," she said. "Fortunately someone has me immobilized."

He leaned in for another welcomed kiss.

CHAPTER
SIX

THE LODGE

THE BIRDS CHIRPED THEIR melodious morning vocals despite it being another dreary and overcast day. Per Adrienne's weather prediction, the sun worked to burn its way through the thick mist and cloak of gray drizzle that did not want to leave.

The Lodge, as it was know by the team, sat quietly on its grassy mat nestled amongst the trees. It was a plain but spacious two-story wood cabin, inviting at first glance if not overly rustic. A separate garage, which also doubled as a workshop, was a leisurely stroll from the main house. It was dubbed Joey's Supernatty Funhouse by Gage, even though he was frequently in there using the makeshift gym set up in the front.

From there and other spots around the property, glints of metal could be seen snaking in and out of the ground like a shiny thread. The power of iron being ancient and fundamental, Joey's father Arthur created the continuous barrier from thousands of molten railway ties before they moved in to use the land as their base of operations. The setup was sufficient enough, when coupled with masking and renewal sigils, to keep the place off of the map while physically repelling most supernatural beings.

Along both sides of the dirt path between the two buildings were less arcane stacks of lumber to fuel the cabin's wood burning stove and fireplaces. Gage could often be seen out there chopping after his workouts, getting in his cardio while keeping the place well stocked.

Overall the place was simple, but it was home.

Upstairs in the Lodge, Joey had awakened earlier and sat alone beside his bed with the lights off, the room cast in a monotone shade not far off from the ink shading along his left forearm. He could have sworn he heard muffled screams from down the hall overnight, wishing it was his imagination but suspecting it wasn't after what he had seen in the kitchen.

Gear of all shapes and sizes found itself scattered all over the comforter and floor, while gadgets at various stages of completion adorned multiple rows of shelves lining all four walls. Resting peacefully in the corner of the room, a set of radios sat atop a small desk, their displays dark from inactivity. Beneath their tiny peg feet, a collection of scribbled notes offered some cushioning for the already scratched, antique surface.

Joey's room, similar to the JSF, was a "chaotic mess of ordered purpose," meaning that from the outside it looked as if a hurricane tore through on a nightly basis, but he knew exactly where each and every item was, or at least where it *should* be in those cases when Gage came in for an unsanctioned raid.

Joey cleared an area in the center of the bed, his nerdy if not somewhat twisted sense of humor evident in the zombified arm print clawing its way around the edges of the blanket.

He lifted his phone from its charging dock on the nightstand and slung himself on his back, head landing squarely in the center of the fake blood splatter that was printed on the pillowcase. Teasing some of his long, dark hairs between the fingers of his right hand, he clicked on the photo gallery with the other and navigated to a special folder that he had dedicated to Gage. One at a time, he began to flip back through the pictures.

He paused briefly on a selfie that caught his eye; this was one he had been sent after Gage had finished a wood chopping session back in June – God what a tease. Covered in sweat with his trademark eyebrow lift, sunlight glistened off the moisture pouring from Gage's tight body. The unique angle of the shot instantly made Joey think of the view one would have should they be... engaged in nightly cardio, so it was easy to imagine the tree canopy that was in the shot dissolving away to become a ceiling. Perhaps a bedroom ceiling. If he had to admit it: his bedroom's ceiling.

He stirred a little before carrying on, stopping at a photo of Gage and himself after their last vampire clearing several months back. Joey's full sleeve hadn't been finished yet, so the black inks that were peeking out of his bloodied shirt stopped just above the elbow. The both of them stood next to each other, arms around each other's shoulders, cheesing hard. A quick swipe showed a nearly identical shot, but Gage had playfully stuck out his tongue.

Smiling loosely, a chuckle worked its way out as he brought a piece of hair down to his mouth and nervously chewed on it. He wondered if he was reading too deeply into things between the two of them.

Could there ever be anything but friendship here, Joey?

Gage always seemed to up the level of flirting between the two of them when he needed something- be it some tech to tinker with or a task that needed to be done.

Would this amount to anything other than an emotionless fling? Do you want it to?

Joey didn't mind however, since he enjoyed feeling wanted and needed during those times. After all it was Gage, and his friendship meant a lot to him.

Should something happen, would your friendship be irreparably changed?

He continued to ignore the voice nagging in the back of his mind, shutting his eyes and sending himself into a world of what could possibly be. The drab melted away and the room was now full of warmth. Gage came in and settled beside him on the bed, wrapping those burly arms all the way around him. It felt like it was going to be good, forever.

Joey... stop ignoring me. Do you love him?

He finally took notice of his own questions, pondering on the last one for a while. Gage was someone who managed to hold his attention, oftentimes for way too long a stretch. For some reason, he would keep him high on a pedestal, whether it be his personality, the way he made him feel, the unknown of whether or not he felt the same way, or maybe because he showed a dominant side Joey found intriguing. Whatever it was, Gage was the one making him think 'wow, this guy talking to me... and we are friends... and I like it.'

But sadly, forever wasn't going to start today. Joey's eyes cracked open and the stodgy gray of the ceiling welcomed him back to reality.

Bummed, Joey sighed as he looked around the empty room. Gage hadn't come in, wasn't there, nor was he holding him. Perhaps if his brown hair was longer and more tousled things could be different, but he wasn't that girl.

His mind was far from the chaotic mess of ordered purpose he knew how to handle. It had become plain chaos in there and the trips he was making down Feelings Avenue would most likely remain one way. Gage wasn't coming toward him in the opposite direction and his life was certainly going to keep on trucking whether or not Joey was in the other lane.

So with that, Joey tried to evict him from his thoughts, or at least keep things focused on the platonic. But shit, before long he was once again thinking about his ripped body, chiseled jaw, and gruff but characteristic manscaping. That's when he found himself reaching to unbutton jeans in order to ease some of the growing tightness. If the statues of Perseus and Poseidon tattooed on his forearm could close their eyes, they surely would right about now.

Gage had walked out of his room and was stepping down the hall when he paused in front of Joey's cracked bedroom door. He was about to knock and check on him, when through the thin gap he noticed him lying down on the bed. Retracting his hand from the distressed door frame, he watched for a moment as Joey made his way into the front of his jeans and his head slowly slid back into the soft pillow. His left pec flexed, striations cutting across the musical score and red flowers that adorned it.

Gage debated watching the entire thing as his eyes followed the few petals drifting down from his shoulder to elbow, but his stomach heeded the call of breakfast and took back over.

Knock! Knock! Knock!

Joey's hands shot back up toward his chest, the jolt nearly sending his phone into his face.

"Morning, bossman," said Gage without the slightest indication he had noticed what was going on mere moments before.

"Oh! Um… hey! Hey there G," Joey stuttered awkwardly as he casually stretched, then buttoned up his pants.

"Are ya getting *up to* anything?" asked Gage.

"Nothing. Just um… chilling a little."

"Ya can't *beat* that first thing in the morning," Gage said with an amused smirk.

Joey caught on to Gage's not-so-subtle wordplay, replying, "Yeah, it's such a stress reliever. So what's the deal? You seem more chipper this morning than usual. Did you have a good night?"

"Oh yes," he responded, "I had a great night. After the downright exhausting fun of the last few days, it was nice to finally unwind. Plus, I have nothing official on the calendar today, so it's a win all around."

Yeah, I bet you had such a great night unwinding with her, didn't you? Joey thought callously.

"That's just plain awesome," Joey said, careful not to let his thoughts slip. "I think I'll take the opportunity to play around in the Funhouse today and see what kind of coolness I can devise for our future missions."

"Hell yes," said Gage with a massive Cheshire smile. He took a quick glance out the window and noticed the sun hadn't peeked out from behind the cloud cover. "Oh and since I can't tan today thanks to the weather, figured I would get more wood chopping in at the lean-to after breakfast. Speaking of, Ady's already downstairs whipping us up bacon and eggs. Ya hungry?"

Joey's stomach rumbled at the mere mention of food, but the thought of Gage chopping wood wouldn't leave. "More wood?" he asked, knowing full well there was more than plenty of it stockpiled. He looked down, catching a glimpse of the photo that was still pulled up. Quickly he closed it, hoping

Gage hadn't seen anything.

Of course he already had. "Well, it's decent cardio as you know and also great practice for sport fucking," the big guy replied with a wink.

"What?!" said a bewildered Joey. He looked up to where Gage was just standing, only to find him already gone.

How the hell could that moose of a man move so fast?

Just then, one of Joey's radios began chirping, followed by another, then another. Soon they were all sounding off, the instrument panels flared up like slot machines as Joey rushed over to see what was going on. He quickly scanned over it all, not knowing where to focus until the flickering amber light on the smallest radio drew his attention. His heart was in his throat as he flipped over the comm switch and listened.

"Oh damn!"

CHAPTER
seven

AN UNEXPECTED CALL

Shortly after, Joey bounded downstairs, rounding the corner into the kitchen. The smell of bacon greeted him along with the pleasing warmth from the wood burning stove. His pleasant mood was short lived when he noticed a similar sight to the night before. This time there were no silhouettes.

Gage clearly stood behind Adrienne with his hand on her hip. He gently rubbed it before leaning in to give her a peck on the cheek. Nabbing a glass of water, he headed over to the breakfast table and sat down.

"Ah there's my man!" Gage said, smiling large.

Joey nodded, giving a half-assed grin in return before walking over to the cabinets himself.

"Excuse me," he said to Adrienne as he reached over for a large tumbler.

"Morning there J," she said happily. Her mood was quite elevated as well.

"Morning," he replied lightly, filling his glass to the brim with pulpy orange juice. He popped the container back in the fridge and kicked the door closed with his foot.

He took a seat across from Gage, visibly excited. Guzzling down most of the juice, he then thrust his elbows on the table, hands gesturing at a hundred miles per hour, narrowly missing the glass with each pass.

"Guys! Get this! The channels are lit up about the Noctis. Like all of them... even Gold!" he shouted energetically.

Adrienne nearly dropped her spatula. Setting it down, she turned to face Joey. "Really? That hasn't happened in a little while. Never too soon though, if you ask me."

He nodded. "Yeah, last time it happened was the Incursion of 2010 and before that way back during World War II with the occult stuff the Nazis were dabbling in. Dark times, the both of them."

Gage appeared at a loss. "The... Incursion? My bad. I guess I've been so wrapped up in dealing with these damn red eyes since getting introduced to this world I forgot to attend my supernatural history lessons."

Joey's face lit up like a beacon. "Well-" he began.

Adrienne jumped in before he got anymore out, picking up her utensils. "The Incursion was a huge deal for the Journeymen five years ago. You know that the Order is far from perfect these days, a lot of that due to major losses in numbers. A lot happened gradually but most occurred during the Incursion. It all started when there was some internal strife amongst the powers that be on the Council-"

"When isn't there?" Joey horned in.

"And one of them," she continued, "feeling as though his voice was being suppressed, went rogue. He was a powerful archmage, a human named George Thurston. He had some pretty wild ideas on humankind and how we fit in the hierarchy of things."

"Yeah," said Joey, crossing his arms. "Right on top with the any supernatural at the bottom of his grimy boot. Didn't do much for the relations between them all. The wiz then had the bright idea he should steal away with the Grimoire of Shadows from the deepest recesses of the vaults. The shit stored in there you just don't mess with; they're locked away for a host of reasons, none of them good."

Adrienne loaded their plates with hot bacon from the pan. "He used the book and coupled it with his own magic in an attempt to gain more power for himself, enough to try and punish the Journeymen for what they'd supposedly done to him and bring his vision of an enslaved supernatural world to fruition. However, his plans backfired when he found a complicated spell that could open a doorway to ultimate power and used it."

"Which was his dumbass move number two," Joey interjected. "Those dusty grimoire spells are incredibly powerful and even their names are meant to scare you away from casting them. It takes genius level talent to do that and an even greater mind to understand what it is those spells are actually doing. Most, if not all, of the incantations and recipes were sprinkled with unequal dashes of riddles and consequence. Of course that time was no different, Georgie taking what the spell was at face value. Again, his dumbass move numero dos. A little humility over hubris would have gone a long way."

Adrienne continued, her voice dipping into sadness. "Yup. After the doorway was opened, it quickly became evident to Thurston that it was a massive mistake. We really don't know what it was, but it called itself Andhakara, a name or creature that nobody has found referenced in any of the lore books. It was dark, gruesome, and pitiless, some accounts saying it was so appalling that looking upon it could drive you insane. Now I don't know if that's just exaggerated writing from one of the chroniclers, but we all knew that it desperately wanted to be here, in our world. That's when shit hit the fan. Thurston was killed almost immediately trying to placate it and thankfully the Order knew he had the book, so mustered a quick response to the situation. Only a small part of the being managed to manifest itself here before it was stopped using everything the Journeymen had brought to bear upon it. Sadly though, not before there were a lot of casualties and an even longer list of lasting impacts. You'll notice if you ever see the present day Council: humans are outnumbered on it these days."

Joey shot a sideways look toward her while she heaped scrambled eggs onto their plates. *Thanks for your input,* he thought with a hue of rancor. *I'm the knowledge base, bitch.* He got up from the table and went to the fridge for some more juice.

"The icing on the cake?" he said as the liquid poured into his glass. "Andhakara was never actually destroyed. It was only banished back to where it came from, taking the book along with it. So, it's still out there, along with its brethren. We can thank Thurston for yet another opportunity for an apocalypse, as if we didn't have enough options already waiting." He looked over to Gage as he sat back down in his seat. "So you can see big guy, Gold channel being active again means the Order is concerned about the Noctis in a big away. Something is definitely happening with these demons up in the North, along with other movements in Eastern Europe and Australia. Not to mention the mobilizing of monsters in response even here in Houston. Whatever is happening, it's global and it's scary."

Adrienne came by to set their plates down, returning to grab hers and another cup of coffee before joining them.

"I thought they were big trouble," Gage said as he started eating. "But damn, this is bad news."

Joey nodded. "What I was able to gather from what I heard upstairs is that they – the Noctis – are positioning themselves for something massive based on the scale and distribution of their activity. They haven't made any offensive moves yet, appearing to be on hold. Nobody seems sure what they are waiting for, but I would not be surprised if the Order called an Assembly within the next few weeks, my guess would be around Halloween, to address the situation."

Gage crammed more food into his mouth, freezing at the mention of a meeting. "Say what?" he murmured. "I guess I missed that class too. We have mandatory meetings?"

Adrienne let loose a titter, as did Joey. He slapped the tabletop before taking another drink. "Dude, you have definitely been kicking ass off the grid since day one."

"Um, yeah," he said nonchalantly. "That's what we do as Journeymen out here in the field; aka the real world. I thought this was more of an 'individually owned and operated' type of thing anyway, doing things my own way, how I like it, to help people."

"Yeah that's sort of how it works, most of the time," Adrienne replied, lifting a bit of crispy bacon and teasing it between her teeth. "But it's like a franchise and we sort of have to keep within the lanes of the brand. Mandatory meetings are rare though and normally only happen when a big deal like this is going on."

Gage snatched the bacon from her fingers and ate it, rolling his eyes mockingly. "Well shit. Where's the fun in that?"

Joey chuckled. "No fun at all but I'm sure they'd make an exception for you, after all the action you've seen… and caused first hand."

Gage was unamused as he scraped up the last bit of food off his plate. He glanced over to their plates and noticed they had barely begun eating. Slow pokes.

"Yeah," affirmed Adrienne. "Maybe you could just conference call in."

Joey laughed and actually slapped his knee. "Special exemption granted to the world record holder for the number of ass kickings delivered over the three years since his unofficial induction."

"You two can fuck off," Gage said with a fat finger pointed toward each of them. Yanking his phone from his pocket, he tapped the corner on the table. "Calling in would be just peachy, if only this piece of shit would stay charged. It's deader than a double tapped zombie… again."

"Ugh, no idea what's causing it?" Adrienne asked, shifting from humor to concern. She was still puzzled by the issue, but maybe it was just a simple hardware issue.

"Other than it being a POS?" he responded. "Nope. I changed out the battery with a spare. No effect. Rebooted. No effect. I'm thinking after I flog on some logs I'll pop into town and get another one. That way, I can be sure keep tabs on you two bastards and also conference in when the suits call their manda-"

Suddenly, the sounds of *Don't Fear the Reaper* blared from the mobile phone, cutting through through the conversation and suppressing all the sounds in the room.

Slowly, Gage turned the screen and watched as it continued to ring.

What the hell?

There was no telephone number displayed as the screen flashed briefly, followed by several rolling glitches. His thumb hovered over the jittery answer button, but the phone died right as he brought it down.

Everyone sat quietly.

"I thought you said your phone was dead?" asked Joey.

"It was," said Gage to his reflection on the shiny screen.

"Well, something's definitely up. Want me to take a look at it today?"

He pressed the power button a few times to no avail. "Yeah... sure thing J. Work your magic on it because it's dead again. Would be nice to know what the hell is going-"

As if he were being mocked, the phone sprang to life again at full power. The screen jumped around but this time Gage was quick to answer it.

"Hello? Who is this?" he asked sternly, lifting the speaker to his ear.

Patiently he waited for a reply, but only the static spoke, accompanied by heavy riffs of bass.

"Hello!" he repeated again.

The interference continued as the undertones became more profound.

"Gage?" Adrienne asked while reaching out an arm. "What do you hear?"

He pulled his arm back, raising his index finger before placing it into his open ear, listening intensely.

The base continued to rumble over the static, yet patterns seemed to be forming. Were they words? He continued to listen, closing his eyes in an attempt to block out all other stimuli.

A few moments later distorted words arose out of the noise, interlaced with bursts of static.

"Gage... you must..."

The voice was sharp and deep; the words hurried yet commanding.

"Who is this?" he demanded.

"Gage you must... go... Gage you must go!"

"Wait... where do I have to go?"

Joey looked over to Adrienne and mouthed, "EVP?"

"Seems like it," she whispered. "But there's no way a ghost could be here at the Lodge."

"This is really weird," Joey muttered as they returned their attention to

Gage, who was still shut off from the world in concentration.

"Where do I need to go?" he repeated.

The crackle and fizz of static filled his ear until one word boomed out from its depths.

"HOME!"

His eyes sprang open as he let out a short gasp.

The words repeated over and over, getting louder with each successive mention.

He pulled the deafening phone away from his ear as Joey and Adrienne exchanged fast glances, her arm now clenched around Gage's forearm. He was visibly disturbed.

The words sank back into the ocean of static before the phone went dead once more.

"You okay big man?" asked Joey, noticing the intensity of Adrienne's concern.

"Yeah," he said, breathing deeply. "I'm alright." He set the phone on the tabletop and pushed it away, sniffling. "Fuck."

"What?" asked Adrienne.

"It told me to go home."

"Back to Denver?" she asked.

"Yeah," he replied. "Haven't been there in over three years since… that day."

Something didn't feel right about any of this.

"Why on earth would you have to go there now, because that voice told you to?"

He didn't know what to say.

"It could be a trap," said Joey. "It almost screams one to me."

Gage was still trying to figure all this out for himself. Why home? Why now? It made no sense.

Joey elaborated, "We have no idea what that was; for all we know the Noctis could have found a way to hack into your phone and are trying to lure you into a death zone. You do have a reputation of being a demon slayer after all. One of the best."

"If not the best," said Adrienne in agreement. "I mean, why would you get such a mysterious call to go home now? After all this time? It seems incredibly smoky to me, especially since the activity on the radios just flared up."

"Smoky. Haha. I like that," Joey said with a chuckle. "But seriously, look at it this way too. If this is an actual supernatural event and not a technological one, whatever did it had to be incredibly powerful in order to get past the defenses here. Hell, I'm not sure how that's even possible now that I've said it. Now I don't know about you, but I wouldn't want to be toying with anything that could do that. We have a lot of crazy stuff happening right now with these monster alliances and movements. It's just dangerous out there man, especially without a plan."

"So yes," Adrienne said. "We agree it's a trap."

"You could be right, darlin'," Gage said, but something gnawed at his gut, pulling him toward the road. "But, what if it's something else?"

She closed her eyes, folded her arms on the tabletop, and collapsed her head between them. "Like what?!" she asked, shooting back up in amazement that Gage would still consider going.

"I dunno. All I know is something's telling me I need to go to Denver."

Her hands flew through the air, slamming back on the table. "Exactly! 'Something'! You've no idea what it is, Gage. So you're just going to take off? Just like that and go home? With all this shit about to happen here."

Oh boy, thought Joey. *Lover's quarrel in three... two...*

"Geez, I ain't going to be moving there Adrienne!" he shouted. "I'm just looking into this."

"By yourself," she countered. "You don't even know where to start looking. Or how long this will take."

"Oh for the love of all that's holy. Home. The fucking voice said 'go home' so I'll start there."

She shook her head.

"What if this could help with the Noctis?"

"What if it *is* the Noctis!? I swear Gage, you can be so fucking reckless!"

"Excuse me?"

She crossed her arms and shot him a silent glance.

Well this is awkward, thought Joey as he stared into his empty glass, wishing he had more orange juice.

"Fine," she said. "If you're going, then I'm going to go with you. Two sets of eyes are better than one."

"Oh no, no," he said. "First you said this was too dangerous and now you want in? Can't have both, sweetheart. Plus, I work best traveling alone."

Damn those words cut deep. Even to Joey they stung a little bit. "Hey now!" he said.

Gage let out a loud groan and slammed a fist on the table, shaking the plates. One danced its way off the edge and onto the floor, shattering into several pieces.

"I guess the past year of working with us has held you back then?" asked Adrienne coldly, with a stare that could freeze her cup of coffee should she glance at it. "The mighty Gage Crosse being forced to drag a team around with him."

Ady don't drag me into this, thought Joey as he bent over to pick up the pieces of plate.

The chill of her words fell on Gage's broad shoulders and he pinched them together. "That isn't what I meant Ady…"

"Sure sounded like it to me."

"This is different."

"How so?"

"It's-"

Ugh, enough of this! "Look you two," Joey cut in. "Just shut up and go else we will be here all week! It's obvious you both like each other. Shit, it's so drippingly obvious that it's pooling on the floor and I'm gonna slip on it. You both should look at this as a means to get to know each other better. After all, that's what road trips are best for."

A look of embarrassment fell across Adrienne's face while Gage sat unfazed, his arms now crossed tightly over his chest.

"Plus," Joey continued as he walked over to the trash can and placed the broken pieces of plate inside, "it'll give me a chance to get caught up here;

listen in on this new demon chatter and talk to some old buddies of mine to see if there's anything we can do to either stem the redeye's activities or to help the Order prepare for what's to come."

Gage lowered his head and ended up blowing a raspberry. "Fine," he said snidely in Adrienne's direction. "Guess we have some packing to do. So much for an event-free day."

With that, the team ate the rest of their breakfast until the scraping of silverware on plates became the dominant sound in the room. Soon after, the kitchen emptied out in record time.

CHAPTER *eight*

MAN'S BEST FRIEND

THE STREETS OF WHITTINGHAM had grown gloomy in the wee hours of the morning; the sun still sleeping, yet to burn away the ample fog that had rolled in off the green hills.

Through the mist, the sounds of quick footfalls rose as two figures raced down Eaves Green toward its intersection with Ashley Lane. A small farm was nearby, bleakly taunting with opportunities and places to hide, but a solid stone wall blocked their way. Rows of tall evergreen hedges grew right up against them, all working together to keep the riffraff out.

"Dammit," spat one of the men as a cockerel crowed, the eastern horizon growing brighter. Time was wasting and he quickly glanced across his shoulder to check if anything was on their heels. Nothing living was there, but a gray shroud masked everything including their pursuers; there was a moment to figure something out, but it would not last long.

He snapped his head forward, searching high and low for any break in the irregular cobblestone, or perhaps a thinned out part of the hedge that could be pushed through. If so, they could then hole up somewhere on the property- in the barn, under equipment, anywhere but the open road- until it was safe to slip away. He knew that continuing to run, especially with the coming dawn, would guarantee their capture.

The man grew a bit frantic when he couldn't find a way in. Stress was on his face though he was fairly fit, displaying no real signs of fatigue beyond the nervous panting building from his chest.

Dressed in a dirty but tailored black suit and dingy cream shirt, the lack of entry gave him little choice but to resume dashing along the road, all the while looking as his fancy shoes pattered lightly against the asphalt. Unfortunately, nothing but solid rock continued to greet his efforts.

No, he thought, adamant about not going back to 2 Eaves Green. The two story detached house right sat off the road and was so typically British on the outside, but it was the inside that terrified him so. The torture that he endured there was… memorable to say the least, forgetful the most. It was the closest thing to experiencing actual Hell on Earth, right there between the home's beige stone walls.

As he ran, he gripped the strap of a fashionable canvas shoulder bag tightly as it bounced around his right shoulder with each lengthy stride. He had managed to steal it away when they fled.

If anyone were looking out their windows at that moment, they'd likely think it quite an odd ensemble for a man to be wearing out in rural England while jogging in the middle of the night. Yet when one is kidnapped, a change of clothes isn't normally an option that is offered.

The man's wardrobe paled in peculiarity to the person he was traveling with and should those same people still be watching from the safety of their homes, peeking coyly through their window shades, they'd likely think themselves drunk or dreaming.

"Would ye stop fretting, Henry!" came a low and assertive growl from behind, the words spoken with a defined West Country accent, "yer making things difficult. That there's a farm we're passing, not a castle, so there's bound to be a drive nearby. Methinks there's one just east, up on Ashley."

The gravely voice didn't come from a man, but a large bipedal wolf that rushed past toward the crossroads ahead. Around his neck was a chain collar with tremendous links, the swinging end molten and issuing sparks as he went by. When he arrived at the intersection, he dropped to the pavement onto all fours and sniffed at both the air and ground.

"Way ahead is clear," the wolfman stated, raising a long arm eastward as he rose back up on his hind legs. There was a wound on his left one, causing him to stagger a little when weight was placed on it. "We need to head up that direction."

"My apologies, Geirolf," Henry responded with much needed relief as he strode up to him, patting his furry shoulder. However, as his canine partner turned to face him, there was no comfort to be found in the face staring back.

Henry gulped before asking a question, knowing full well what the answer would be. "Is it them?"

Geirolf's face indicated that indeed, their time was up. He snarled as his arms flared out to the side; claws flicked out like switchblades brandished for an attack.

Quickly Henry turned about, just in time to see six monstrous shapes at the fringe of the mist. The shadowy forms looked for all intents human but stood twice as tall, with twisted animal-like shapes attached to their silhouetted bodies. Yet out of the curtain of fog ordinary men emerged, their irises ablaze with red set against scleras darker than the night.

"The demonic bastards," Geirolf muttered between his gritted teeth. "They've already discovered our absence."

That was too fast, Henry thought. *How did they see through the charm so quickly?*

The six men, different sizes yet all considerably huge, charged at them with great speed. There was no time to think, only act.

"*Regna terrae, cantata Deo, psallite Cernunnos*," Henry began, extending an arm out to help him focus before continuing the passage, "*Regna terrae, cantata Dea psallite Aradia. caeli Deus, Deus terrae…*"

As he continued to speak the incantation, all six suddenly decelerated as if their energy were being drained away. However, the power of the words was weak, spread across them all when it was only meant for one. This was not going to hold them for long.

Geirolf knew that Henry would only be able to slow them for a little while and could not stop speaking the invocation. With no other options, he took a breath and thrust a hairy hand into Henry's bag. The protective enchantments on the bag seared his supernatural form and the smell of burning hair filled his nostrils, but he rejected the urge to scream, pushing it deep down inside. A short time later, he found what he was looking for, pulling out three palm-sized stones between his singed claws, still smoldering. They were flat like coins, each marked with a pentacle on one side and lines of invocation on the other.

With haste, he brought them all to his snout and breathed over them. The symbols awakened, sparking between the etched lines as he targeted the three closest demons, now kneeling on the ground, and flung the stones their way.

They twirled and whistled through the air, landing at the knees of each possessed man. The sparkling trails shot off to form stars before encircling them, each in their own individual traps.

"Goodbye, ye filth," the werewolf said calmly but with antipathy. "*Exorcizamus.*"

The glowing pentacles leapt to life on the command, closing upon their hostages like massive bear traps. The human receptacles were unharmed by the gnashing teeth, but the smoking darkness that poured out of their orifices broiled under the onslaught of lightning. The vapors sank to the road and then beneath it, sizzling as the earth drew them back down to Hell.

The remaining possessed men were still upright, but with fewer numbers the invocation had doubled in strength and their movement slowed as if they were running through molasses.

Henry knew that soon he would need to choose only one to complete the exorcism. He looked to Geirolf, who had reached down into his wounded leg and removed a set of iron braces. Inserting the bloody metal into his mouth and over his teeth, he licked off the blood and nodded to signal that he was ready.

Henry selected the burliest of the group on which to pour all his focus.

The others, now freed from the effects of the spell, immediately sped up and leapt into the air.

"... *Benedictus Dea, Matri gloria!*" Henry stated, finally completing the ritual.

A force thrust the massive man to the street and he writhed as an antlered form was ejected. Dark and terrible, it ascended no less than twelve feet above them, lunging toward Henry on hoofed feet, trying to possess him by force. With its shadowy talons mere inches from his face, a breeze whooshed all around them, catching the smoke and gently dissolving it away.

Henry choked as his fears were allayed; he was less than two seconds away from emptying the entire contents of his bladder down the front of his suit pants.

However, there was little time to compose a complete thought as the others had engaged Geirolf in battle. Their attack met with his sharp claws and powerful teeth crushed bone, fists flew, and serrated silver slashed its way through fresh dog meat. The back and forth continued for several minutes until Geirolf, wounded heavily by the argent blades, took hold of one of the men and clamped down on his neck.

The body shook uncontrollably as the host died and a gigantic black mass in the shape of a chimera was cast out by the iron surrounding his teeth. It had the traditional lines of a wolf, but spread out huge bird-like wings and whipped its serpent like tail. After roaring so loudly that anyone within a mile would have been woken, it dashed off toward the north for reinforcements.

"Blast!" Henry snapped as the shadow melded back into the mist. He reached into the bag and pulled out a banishment stone, shouting *Daemon Ejicio!*"

The stone pulsed and red swirls of light spiraled out toward the man, held a good way off his feet by one of Geirolf's considerable arms. He continued to stab at the hairy limb with his blade, even as the lights struck him and wrapped around tightly like ropes. The wolfman then released him, allowing the spell to continue carrying its prisoner off to the west and out of sight.

"Are you alright?" asked Henry, concerned by the amount of blood pooling beneath the pads of Geirolf's feet.

Grabbing the silver knife sticking out of his arm, Geirolf jerked it out and threw it to the ground. The pain was indomitable and he couldn't hide a grimace. "I'll be fine," he lied, "but we should get going while we can."

"I agree," came a strangely welcoming female voice from behind, "oh but wait, on second thought, I think not. Your luck and your time have run out."

The two saw a tall woman standing in the middle of the street, dressed in black leather pants and a short but matching jacket covering a dark maroon shirt. She glared callously at them with her demonic eyes, thick blonde hair floating down her neck to her shoulders. She remained silent with an arm raised as if about to give a signal.

A small army of goblin-like creatures appeared out of the fields to the south. It dawned upon Henry with the rising sun that there had truly been no means of escape this day.

A large ogre, hideous and bloated, approached from the west. "I take back," it said, words barely formed over its grunts.

"No," the woman forbade, "the overseers at Number 2 failed in their simple obligations, unable to keep this unimpressive man and his... pet from escaping." She looked back at the outlying hills; there in the distance a little over a mile away was a massive construction operation. "When you want something done right these days," she said faintly, "you have to do it yourself. I'll take them."

Geirolf and Henry were bound in warded chains, crisscrossed around their hands and feet, and set in the center of the goblin ranks as the mysterious woman confidently led them onto the site. It was desolate and dirty, all remnants of what had been there long erased by the vehicles and machinery parked haphazardly around the property.

Her feet crunched along on the brittle mud, which transformed quicker than a blink into tufts of dead grass that pushed up between the spaces in scattered debris, like stubble on a scabby chin. She had walked through a hole in the force field that encased the entire site, which also had an illusion spell over it to conceal what was beyond.

The prisoners were quickly ushered in as the goblins filed away into the fields, the ogre bringing up the rear and following all too closely for Geirolf; its stench was foul enough at a distance, but it was downright unbearable when the closeness of its breath teased his ruddy hair.

Once the four were inside, a group of hooded figures robed in black and gold rushed in and began chanting a guttural mantra. The hole began to shrink in response and within moments was closed firmly.

Henry raised his head, having kept it down since departing the farm. There were huge piles of rubble strewn around numerous derelict buildings, all aged from years of neglect and decay.

There was a large structure to their right; two stories of mottled brick that had once been a sanitarium, having declined and since closed after allegations of abuse and fraud putrefied its reputation throughout the community. It was primarily an institution for the mentally unstable, although a hospital ward had been in place for more traditional medicines and treatments.

Sweeping sets of broken windows set in off white frames wrapped around all sides, while a set of four dank columns lined the chunky, cracked steps up to the entrance. There was no door to the building, only an opening where one should have been.

That would not be their destination, the woman veering sharply to the left toward an old church on the grounds. Built of heavy stone, it was brown and weather-beaten, the once colorful panes of arched glass reduced to thin, jagged edges. A craggy steeple rose up through the dead shrubbery, its godforsaken presence towering over the rest of the area.

As they approached, a distant scream cut through the eerie silence from across the courtyard, catching in Geirolf's ears. He looked over to see if anything could be made out. There was no one or thing to be seen, yet the wretched sounds continued to come from behind the facade of a deserted shack that stood all by itself on the far end of the property.

Poor soul, he thought without much more time to dwell on matters. Before long they had reached the bottom of the church steps, which rose up to a pair of doors, firmly shut.

"My God," said Henry, bringing a hand over his mouth.

Aghast, he realized the lights at the base of the stairs – which he thought were adorned with cast metal heads – were capped with real ones, impaled right through the bottom. They cast a sickening orange glow on the walls and a wash of red spread out on the ground beneath them.

He wondered if they had been tortured prisoners, demonic soldiers that had failed their master's bidding, or mere innocent souls from the town nearby. Knowing what he knew about these foul creatures, the last option was the most appealing. Desperately, he wanted to look away from the macabre sight, but could not bring himself to do so. He wanted to be far away from there, in the security of a safe house, but there was no means of escape.

Summoning what strength he had left in him, he managed to tear his watery glance away and bow his head. With few to no options left, he cupped his hands and began to pray silently; his words sending itches down to the woman's bones.

"I don't think any of your gods will hear you here, Mr. Abington," she interrupted. "Especially the one you're trying to speak to."

Defiantly, he continued and with a smirk she waved a hand, the doors creaking open by themselves.

The ogre grunted, pushing them forward and into the pew-less nave, still dark with the remnants of the night. The faint smell of incense still clung to the walls and the inside was oddly devoid of other demons. There was an air of peace about the place, which in turn made it more eerie.

Ahead of them was a simple stone altar, heavy and rectangular, covered in rich black satin. It sat underneath a marvelously detailed apse and in the days the building was alive it must have been a sight to behold.

"Grolg, bring them," she commanded, snapping then pointing to the altar as she made her way behind it.

The lumbering beast hit them both in the shoulder, driving them along with arduous *thumps* until they were about ten feet away. There, he forced them each down to their knees, Geirolf struggling to keep himself conscious from the pain now coursing in his body.

Through labored breaths, the wolf cleared his throat to address her. "Who are ye?" he asked between the hard gasps and wheezes.

"*Elasa impamis om-*"

"In the common tongue, ye stupid bitch!" he bellowed, resulting in a cocky laugh out of her pompous face.

"Quite the mouth on you… Geirolf is it?" she asked, tapping a finger on her chin while scrutinizing him. "If I recall, that means 'wolf spear' in Nordic. My, my, what an unfitting characterization for such a pathetic beast, unless of course it was referring to your sharp tongue."

"Cut to the chase, she-demon," he retorted, spitting up blood. "Are ye going to answer my question or not?"

"Do you really think that you are any sort of position to be asking questions, mongrel?" she snipped. "In any case, we have all the time in the world to discuss matters before getting to know each other on a first name basis." She then spoke directly to Henry, "Sadly, you're not blessed with as long a life, so won't be around for the best parts."

She dipped below the altar and removed a carafe of wine, pouring it into a plain chalice before taking a long drink. It was bitter but refreshing, something she couldn't experience when in demon form, and it quenched her thirst if only for a short time.

After another swig of wine, she swished it around her mouth and reached back underneath the coverings. Out came a large silver dagger, its triangular blade twisting down its entire length and tapering to a sharp point. She swallowed as the tip clanged on the altar.

"Now I know that I should really start with that one," she told Geirolf, pointing the knife over to Henry, "but this proverbial spear that you are named after… I'm fascinated by it and want to test it against my own metal."

Methodically, she walked around the stone slab and stood imposingly ahead of the werewolf. With no warning and a quick flick, she cut across his snout and he heaved in agony, blood gushing from the wound.

"Geirolf!" Henry shouted, receiving a hefty strike from Grolg as a reward. He dropped onto his hands, fighting for breath, knowing that Geirolf didn't have much blood left. The amount pooled on the floor was staggering and who knows how much had leaked out between here and the farm.

"Silence meat bucket!" she yelled. "It's not your turn… yet." She grabbed hold of Geirolf's muzzle, squeezing it where she had just cut it before pushing it off to the side. "So tell me fluffy, what do you Journeymen have to do with this activity along the Devil's Highway? What exactly are you all looking for?"

There was silence.

Enraged, she slapped him hard across the face, sending more blood to the floor.

"I do not know," Geirolf replied softly, determined not to let her break him, though inside he was hanging by a thread.

"Oh come now, traitor, surely the higher ups told you something? If not there, then what about the reconnaissance happening in Michigan? The buzz in New York? Why in Lucifer's name is your Order messing around in things they do not understand?"

He returned to silence and she raised the knife to cut him again.

"Stop it!" Henry shouted. "Just stop! He wouldn't know! He's not even part of the Order, so how the hell would he know anything?!"

"Yet he chose to help you," she responded coldly to his request for mercy, thrusting the dagger into the wolf's shoulder, then again through his upper arm.

Geirolf winced, but remained vigilant.

"Well, my dear Henry," she said. "It seems as if you are right. The mangy mutt has absolutely no idea."

"Yes," Henry replied with relief. "That's what I've been telling-"

"So, there is no need to keep this treacherous hound around, is there? Grolg, eat! Be sinfully gluttonous!"

Geirolf looked to Henry with tears forming in his bloodshot eyes; the heaviness of the ogre's footsteps counted down his impending doom.

Before long Grolg was right behind him, placing those giant hands on his shoulders and opening his mouth.

"Goodbye old friend," Geirolf said, biting down hard on his back tooth and cracking a hidden L-pill full of silver nitrate. As he swallowed the solution, the acid burned his throat and he convulsed, Grolg dropping him to the ground. In seconds, his heart stopped beating and his brain was dead; Geirolf had passed, leaving behind the naked body of a man sprawled on stone tiles.

The woman looked to the dead prisoner, halting the ogre's second advance on him. Partly impressed by his fearlessness and massively upset she didn't have the information wanted, she turned her attention to Henry, the red of her eyes burning more intensely than ever before.

"Your turn," she said, turning the dagger in her hand while stepping over his way.

Suddenly the church shook, kicking up dust all around them, nearly knocking her off balance.

"Onoskelis, it is I," a voice resonated daemoniacally from all around.

She cursed mildly under her breath and was visibly furious at the interruption. She threw the dagger to the altar, Geirolf's warm blood splattering across the delicate coverings. Signaling to Grolg, she walked toward the vestry.

"Make sure our remaining guest is kept comfortable until I return," she ordered. "Just be sure to not kill him."

As she opened the door and stepped through, Henry's pained screams echoed through the cavernous church. Snapping her fingers, she answered the call as the doors closed behind her. "What news do you bring, Stolas?"

THE DEMON AGARES WAITED in room at the very back of the vestry, listening in on the ongoing conversation between Stolas and Onoskelis while stroking his long, wintry beard. He was dressed conservatively, ironically in something that one would likely wear when attending Mass.

His face, creased and experienced, held a deep crested frown as he took in the exchange.

"*Vale!* Stolas!" boomed her guttural voice from the other room. A second later the set of heavy doors flung open and she glided through, snapping her fingers to slam them closed again.

The church had become her own little sanctuary, away from the constant bickering and stresses over in the sanitarium. The vestry acted as another layer of peace in her otherwise chaotic world.

She took a prolonged breath, striding over to her elder attendant and with a quick blink transformed her eyes from red and black to the host's original light blue.

"That damn idiot, Stolas. I can just see him trying to escape in his final moments or pleading for leniency."

"Your Grace," said Agares, blinking with his demonic eyes. "Were you able to gain any information about the Journeymen from the prisoners?"

"Not yet," she replied, eyeing herself in a full length mirror in the corner of the room. "Grolg is tending to the human now. The werewolf literally bit the dust."

"By tending to, do you mean eat…"

"No matter," she said nonchalantly, eyes still transfixed on the reflection of her human self. Her fingers teased their way through her hair and she let out a puff of breath from her slightly open mouth.

"You know Agares, I think that I actually prefer this body to my real one," she said to his utter surprise, a hand rolling all the way up from her ankle to her inner thigh. "I think that her name was Betty, before I took up residence. Betty's legs are so smooth, far less hairy than my-"

"Onoskelis!" he cut in with a fearful tremble. "If any of the Knights were to hear you speak in this manner about such things!"

"You forget your place Agares!" she snapped back, walking over to the window. Placing a hand in the windowless arch, she watched as her winged horse, a grand symbol of stature in the old times, took a shit in the middle of the cemetery.

It had once been a graceful and pure Horse of Eden, from that very garden of the same name. After the fall, all manner of creatures that resided there either died or were stolen away, as this one was by the the demon Bael and later given to Eligos, commander of demonic forces on Earth. Its coat, once as white as freshly fallen snow, had been transformed into soot. The demon's malice further corrupted it, transforming it into the winged terror that roamed about outside.

"I've nothing to worry about, now that fool Eligos is gone and we've obliterated the last traces of his die hard followers," she said to Agares. "Wouldn't you agree that things are far better now with me in charge?"

Agares began to nod but any words hung back. Indeed Keli had managed to wrestle power away from one of the mightiest Knights of all time, but traces of her inexperience were everywhere and the coup was messy and ill-planned, nearly failing at the last moment.

On the other hand Eligos was an incredibly respected demon with a great deal of knowledge about warfare from all sides: planning, strategy, foresight and tactics being amongst his highest aptitudes. Agares believe he would have been supreme asset in the times ahead, his charisma and charm able to woo even the most devout naysayer.

But all those hopes and prospects died when he did and they were left with a she-goat claiming his steed as her prize, along with command over all demonic forces upon the Earth.

He realized his pause was on the cusp of being too long. "Indeed Onoskelis," he finally agreed, "things are vastly improved."

She grunted, taking no note of his compliment or praise. "How many times have I told you to address me as Keli? Why is this such a hard thing for everyone to do?"

"Your Grace," Agares continued, "Keli, no offense is intended but you must understand that the other Knights… they are always watching and listening with their spies. Do not underestimate them."

"Yes, yes, fine."

Agares now needed to discuss with her a topic he knew would send her over the edge. Walking casually toward the door, he paused and turned to face her. "There have been some reports, whispers on the proverbial winds so to speak, that there is someone that may be looking to supplant you. The demon Dajjal has been…"

Her eyes flashed back into demonic form. "Don't you dare speak his name in my presence again!" she shouted at the top of her lungs, a vein throbbing across her forehead. "Otherwise I will make sure you're on the quickest flight back into the fire."

Your time will come, disrespectful she-goat, Agares thought while bowing his head respectfully in turn, taking her outburst as confirmation that it was time to leave.

"Yes, of course Your Grace, my sincerest apologies," he said as the doors closed, catching one last glimpse of her before they shut loudly.

CHAPTER
nine

HOMEWARD BOUND

THE GMC BARRELED ITS way down Route 287, the hum of rubber rising above the classic rock pumping through the speakers.

Gage bobbed his head with the beat, tapping the window with his knuckle. Good thing he was a Journeyman, hell anything but a singer; his career would be over long before it ever started.

Adrienne had sat quietly the last few hours listening to the music herself, reflecting on the whirlwind that had overtaken the last couple days. She looked over as he turned up a bottle of water with one hand, letting the liquid fall effortlessly into the corner of his mouth. Not a drop was spilled while he sat with the other arm extended on the steering wheel, slightly flexing.

Thoughts whirled in her head and she had to get some of it out. "Gage," she said. "Can we talk a for second?"

"Yeah," he said, belting out the chorus line before reaching over to turn the volume down. "My singing that bad?"

"What? No," she denied. *Well maybe a little.* She exhaled slowly. "No,

Gage, I wanted to tell you that I'm sorry for the argument we had before heading out."

To her amazement he said two words she never expected. "Me too."

She examined his face, which now showed hints of being troubled. The Great Wall of Gage was going up brick by brick, but part of him wanted it down, to be far on the outside of it, or have them both tucked safely within its protection.

Leering at the passing mile marker, she just blurted it out. "Is this going to work?"

"You mean… us?"

"Yup," she replied. "Are we rushing into this without really feeling it out?"

He didn't answer right away, honestly not knowing the answer himself. He had asked himself that question a hundred times on this ride alone.

"Well, it's not like we don't know each other, Ady," he finally said.

She nodded.

"You're right. Over a year we've lived with each other, me having to tolerate your ass," she said with a laugh. "I mean we've been fighting vampires, ghouls, werewolves and things I can't even remember the names of over that time. Shouldn't that, if anything, bring people closer together instead of tearing them apart? I guess if this was a perfect world like in movies and books that's how it works. But shit, Gage, the crazy ass real one we live in is so far from perfect."

He cast a look her way before returning his eyes to the road. "The world may be imperfect darlin', but there are some perfect things in it."

She blinked in awe. Where had the real Gage gone? This man's words managed to wrap around her like a warm blanket, enveloping her very soul. Yet as great as this was, she was still stuck with a foot out in the chill of reality.

"Maybe I just feel undeserving?" she questioned.

"Of what, or who? Me?" he asked.

She didn't answer, afraid of what might be said.

"Doll, you're far from undeserving," he responded, sending over a large hand to massage her thigh, "so far from that. Look, I've found your everyday demons are easy to understand: Murder. Death. Kill. Then repeat. It's what they do and it's what makes us know what to do. Nice and easy, right? Predictable? Normal folk are a totally different animal, complete with their own inner demons that manage to complicate the simplest of things. Especially mine, Ady, and there are a lot of them."

Adrienne took her hand and placed it on top of his.

Gage continued, "I've been struggling to keep my past life and my current one, with you and with Joey, separated. Hell, I think all JMs do that to some degree as a sort of protection. But, the last two days have had my *vastly* cool and collected mind twisted in a thousand different directions. Each one of those can be traced back to one thing." He pointed a thick finger her way, "You."

She blushed, but really connected with what he was saying. She had been doing the exact same thing these last couple days.

"But I'm willing to try this if you are," he said without any hesitation. "Our past lives are who we are just as much as the ones we're living right now. There ain't no sense in keeping part of us locked away in a box since it all makes us who we are, right?"

Damn, Gage had become a psychologist; a sure sign the world was ending soon. But, she found herself again agreeing with him.

He smirked as the original Gage came back. "I mean, it could all suck... through no fault of my own of course."

She pinched him hard.

"Ow!" he shouted. "Damn, this girl has a bite on her! Told ya that ya liked that sort of thing." He shook his head mockingly and tapped her thigh with a fist. "Vamp hunters, I tell ya. Bunch of pain freaks."

"Thanks a lot," she said sarcastically, "but you've made a compelling case, Mister Crosse. I'm willing to give it a shot. I definitely can't say there won't be a few hiccups along the way."

"No doubt and definitely a ditto here. But we live in a world where nightmares are real." He turned his palm up and grabbed hers. "They're gonna take every chance to get in the way of what we have planned."

Glancing in the rear view mirror, he switched into the fast lane and gunned it as fast as the engine could take them. "*Non Omnis Moriar,*" he muttered. "I live by my motto: 'Not all of me shall die'... so bring it bitches."

Hand in hand, the two fell back into silence as the truck zoomed past Fort Worth. The long drive ahead of them had just gotten a little bit easier.

GAGE DROVE ON FOR the next four hours, zoned out and letting his mind wander.

Adrienne had long passed out with her mouth agape in that sexy 'I'm about to drool down my neck' sort of way and a chuckle sprung free as he took in the sight. If his phone hadn't died again he would have snapped a memento for later use.

You really like her don't you? said an unwelcome voice from deep inside, barging into his thoughts. He really didn't feel like having this conversation with himself right now, but took on the challenge of quieting himself.

"Yeah I do. There are definite feelings here," he answered. "We've sorted this out, so there's no need for any doubt."

Oh, so bringing her along on this reckless mission was the right thing to do?

"Yes it was."

But you're putting her in jeopardy by getting closer to her, especially not knowing what you're about to swagger yourself into; you're the walking definition of selfish!

"No, I'm not. She's in the life too and both of us are already in the crosshairs of God knows how many different creatures and factions. Why not take this opportunity to enjoy the time we have together?"

It's irresponsible, that's why! Totally! Love in this life is nothing for us, except for pain.

"And sometimes love is the key that is missing in our lives" he continued to battle, a headache brewing beneath his temples from all of the back and forth.

The voice needed to shut up, as weariness was settling in. Looking at the endless, dark asphalt through squinted eyes was exhausting and the call of sleep lingered over the big man.

They had made it just outside of Amarillo, Texas when Gage pulled off on Exit 76, riding the access road to the first motel off the highway. The minuscule Atomic Inn blazed in full neon glory amidst the lackluster lights of the surrounding services.

A faint drizzle began to fall on the windshield, bathing his view in a kaleidoscope of circular color and cascading drops. When the truck rolled to a stop in front of the manager's office, he yanked the key from the ignition and just sat for a moment with both eyes firmly shut. The stillness was so inviting, coupled with the slow patter of rain. He could have stayed there all night, but alas the longing for a mattress overruled.

CHAPTER *ten*

THE ATOMIC INN

ADRIENNE OPENED AN EYE as she lazily came to. She seemed to be developing a bit of a habit of waking up at odd times in different rooms with Gage. Of course, he was up and about somewhere, nowhere to be seen.

She sat up to take in the room, which by all appearances was sorely outdated. Its walls were solid wood paneling and the bright furniture sat on a heavily patterned carpet that had to be straight out of the 1970s. The covers that she rested underneath were no exception, the arresting floral pattern powerful enough to send the sanest mind straight to the asylum.

A musty odor clung to the air and the lingering smell of stale cigarettes ingrained in just damn near everything.

Gage emerged naked from the bathroom, washed his hands and set to vigorously brushing his teeth, the striations in his arms and shoulders flexing nonchalantly with each stroke. How could a man make the most mundane things in life so astonishingly sexy?

As he swaggered back and forth, he waved from below and his masculine scent pushed aside the staleness of the room. He must have showered too. Precious gems of moisture clung tightly to him as he leaned over the sink to rinse his mouth, those massive lats catching the overhead light.

"Stay right there," she said.

He didn't move.

"God damn, that back of yours. One day I'll get used to it, but today definitely is not that day."

He paused, hands on the countertop to let her take in the sights before adding a slow rolling hip pop. From there he raised his arms into a double bicep flex, every muscle embossed in that insanely thick back. Bringing his elbows closer together, she saw muscles she had never noticed before and time just went ahead and stopped. An eternity with that view would not be a bad thing at all.

Gage glanced down, already growing and leaking, desperately wanting to turn around but she was still solidly transfixed on her view. He waited a few more seconds, continuing to rise and then just made his move.

Concentrating as he turned, her eyes dropped as he came into view.

There he stood, reaching full attention and looking surreal as ever. He had never before been this generous and solid. Unquestionably the sight turned him on and a stream of expectation escaped the tip of his head, flowing down along his shaft until a dozen gratifying inches later it dripped onto the floor.

She walked up to him, playfully pulling off her shirt and panties before tossing them aside, coming to rest on her knees. Looking up from below, he towered over her, the monster cutting through the middle of those eight remarkable ridges and crowned by his expansive chest.

"You know what you're doing, darlin'?" he growled with that distinct drawl.

She answers by grasping it with both hands, each unable to close fully around him. With a few long strokes she teased out a few more streams before bringing him to her, his advancing sweetness dancing on her tongue. Her lips went on to caress his head, taking in a few inches with each loving suck. Her tongue flicked underneath each time, sending waves surging up his spine. Those massive arms reached up to grab hold of his hair and before long the mop became a tormented, seductive mess.

Arms falling to the back of her head, he guided her all around his sizeable balls. The sight of that coupled with himself being so full instantly drove him wild and a lush idea leaped into his head; something he hadn't been able to do before with anyone.

Taking one of his hands, he escorted her head up the shaft towards his throbbing head, bracing himself with the other one before bending over to meet her. With shocking ease he was able to and when there, took himself into his own mouth. There they kissed with himself raging in between, sharing in the now ceaseless flow.

Adrienne started to show her excitement on the carpet, the sheer elation of what was happening becoming too much. She pulled away and looked in his eyes. "Flip me," she said before clutching at his beard.

Gage didn't wait, the look in her eyes said that she wanted the B and nothing short of that was going to satisfy her. In an instant she was upside down, cradled in his arms, making quick work of him while he had access to all her goodness.

Her eyes had zero choice but to roll back as his beard met her skin. Though his soft hair exhilarated her hundreds of times with each touch, this was no timid beard ride; this was a rodeo. He dug in with such intensity that she nearly came. She looked down and he filled her view, the carpet passing by underneath until she felt her back against the wall. Once settled, she tried to service him a little more but only managed a single lick before he tore into her again. Each thrust of his tongue sent her closer to heaven.

She shifted herself and at last managed to grip him and went to work, countering each move he made with one of her own.

There against the wall they both battled it out, sliding across and knocking over the lamp on the nightstand, then the nightstand itself. He was pressing her so hard it was a miracle the wall hadn't dented. She gained the upper hand, his balls beginning to contract in ecstasy.

Snatching her from the jaws of victory, he threw her onto the bed and got on top before she had a chance to recover. His dick filled her mouth and his tongue worked her door. Thrust after thrust from both ends showed her who was boss and soon she found herself vanquished. Pleasure gushed into his waiting mouth while he continued to pump away, before long flipping around to splash himself across her breasts.

He collapsed beside her, himself a wrecked heap. He peered over her way and was amazed by the volume.

"Good thing I pulled it out, eh? You might have drowned."

She didn't answer nor did he push her for one; the sounds of heavy panting all they could muster.

They could clean up later.

CHAPTER
eleven

PANCAKES AT THE CRISPY BISCUIT

Light from the neon wonderland just outside the window filtered in through the cheesy curtains, pouring a pallid mix of colors across the crumpled sheets and towels.

As Adrienne stretched beneath them, she tried to yawn but her jaw twinged. It was sore, but not in an insufferable way; in fact it felt sort of euphoric. After giving it a quick rub, she settled in to try and sleep for a few more precious minutes.

However like clockwork, the bathroom door opened and heavy footsteps approached. She propped herself up and saw his hulking frame come into view, complete with an enticing smirk.

"When nature calls, you listen," Gage said, leaping into the bed and sending her flying.

Laughing, he quickly caught her and drew her in close. For a moment his smile faded away, replaced with a look of concern. Keeping one hand around her he used the other to prop up his head, staring deep into her eyes.

"You need warning labels," she said. "Big, bright ones."

"Oh? You know I can do big. Bright's not so much my thing," he said, letting go of her. He snatched one of the pillows, tucking it under his arms. "But I think this should provide enough cushion for the pushin'."

She didn't know whether or not to roll her eyes. "You sure about that?"

"Well," he replied, tossing her a condom. "There's really only one way to find out, gorgeous."

THE REAR DOOR SLAMMED after Gage threw their duffle bags in the back of the cab. His stomach grumbled while he watched Adrienne walk with bowed legs into the diner across the street. As she waddled in her black jean shorts and red halter top, he couldn't help but beam from his own handiwork.

Locking the door and setting the defenses, he made his way over to The Crispy Biscuit himself, noting the bombastic 'All You Can Keep Down' sign that clung to the front door as he entered.

Pancake special today? Jackpot!

As he walked in, it was like he stepped through a time portal and transported back in time. The place had a genuine 50s diner vibe, complete with checkered floor, ultra shiny chrome trim, and a colorful jukebox in the corner that rolled out the oldies.

Adrienne was seated at a booth by the windows facing the other services. She had already ordered their drinks by the time he strolled over, collapsing into the bench seat across from her.

"Whatcha going to get?" he asked her without touching the menu cradled between the condiments.

"I'm not too hungry actually. I just need some coffee to fully charge my ass. Maybe some snack things from the gas station over there before we leave." She pointed out the window to the service station, now bustling with activity.

Gage perked up in his seat, eyebrow rising. "Something up?" he asked.

"No, not really," she replied. "I'm just a bit… sore. Everywhere. I wonder who made that happen?"

He raised a hand meekly just as the waitress dropped off their drinks; a pot of coffee for Ady and a large glass of ice water for Gage. She was a pretty little thing, young and blonde. Her glossy white name tag read "Audrey".

"Have you decided on any food this morning?" she asked in an excessively effervescent voice.

Gage widened his eyes so much they nearly fell out. "Well first off Miss Audrey, I will take a mug for some coffee as well. Ya seem to have been drinking a lot of it this morning, am I right? It must be a-freaking-mazing."

Adrienne sank her face deep into her palms, wishing she could push herself into another dimension.

"No sir!" Audrey pressed on. "Just super duper happy to be here!"

"Well alrighty then!" he said with a large shit eating grin. "Super duper! I will take one of your pancake specials too; the one advertised on the ginormous poster in the door over there."

"Okie dokie!" She turned to Adrienne. "And for you, ma'am?"

She spread her fingers and looked through them guardedly. "Oh nothing, thanks. I'm fine with just the coffee."

Audrey cocked her head the side as if that was an unacceptable answer. "Little bit of a headache there?" she whispered.

"What? No…" Adrienne said, dropping her hands to the lacquered tabletop. The silverware bounced with an awkward jangle.

Audrey nodded profusely, scrunching up her face. "It's okay if last night's libations don't wanna get to going. I'll bring you a couple headache powders," she said, raising her hand up to cover her lips. Her voice dropped to a whisper. "I keep extras in my purse for just such occasions." After a friendly wink, her attention fluttered back to Gage. "And those pancakes will be right out!"

"Oh darlin'," he said as she took off. "Can I also get some bacon, lots of it? Big boy here."

Audrey nodded and all but skipped her way into the kitchen.

Adrienne shook her head as she disappeared behind the doors, only to look back at Gage with a start. He was staring back at her through the dark lenses of his runed sunglasses. They appeared designer, but faint sigils of sight were etched into the lenses, allowing him to see things the naked eye could not.

She felt like burying her face again but at this point it would only draw more attention their way.

"I saw nothing," he said disappointed, taking the glasses off and hanging them from his v-neck.

She busted out laughing. "Wait, you expected to see something with those... on her?"

"I swore she could be a kobold since there ain't no human that chipper. But nope. I guess she shall live another day; lucky for her."

It was still too early for this stuff. Adrienne snatched her mug off the table and filled it from the pot while shaking her head. She took a large gulp; it was a bit bland but she didn't care at this point since it still managed to awaken that dormant piece of her soul.

Audrey popped back a few minutes later with a cup for Gage and dropped off the largest stack of golden pancakes they had ever seen, along with a mess of greasy bacon spitting happily from the plate.

Gage promptly tore the buttery discs apart with his fingers, pulling them into bite size nuggets.

Nothing surprised Adrienne anymore. Topped up mug in hand, she continued to watch him be an outright heathen, shredding his way through the entire plate of pancakes. Finally, he grabbed up a fork, shoving bacon between those fluffy chunks before slathering it all with syrup.

He popped a piece of the sticky, salty sweetness into his mouth which melted away without the need for chews. "This is too good," he said with an orgasmic expression on his face.

The taste was divine; so much so he couldn't help but shovel in more.

"Call me chipmunk," he said with bloated cheeks.

"A sexy as hell chipmunk," she replied with a laugh.

"You know it," he agreed.

During the exchange, a bit of syrup escaped down into the bearded forest, a trace of shininess lingering on the surface.

"Gage, you have something…" Adrienne said, pointing to her chin.

He stared at her blankly as he ate another piece.

"Right there," she pointed at him directly.

He didn't budge, expression never changing. More food went into his mouth.

Then came the eye roll. "My God, never mind. The way you eat is so messy… kind of like sex with you."

"Exactly like it," he said, unruffled. The last of his stack was now consumed. "And you love it. Oh but these pancakes though! I think they may actually be better than sex. I might have even came a little." He peered down the front of his jeans. "In fact I did, a lot more than last night."

She leaned back and folded her arms. "Ass!"

He didn't reply or look at her right away, opting instead to stick a stray bit of bacon between his lips. With it dangling there, he stuck out his tongue before drawing both inside. "You ain't getting either of those today," he said, motioning to the waitress. "Another round, my dear!"

CHAPTER
Twelve

FAR FROM HOME

G AGE HAD POLISHED OFF four stacked plates in the diner before Adrienne suggested they get back on the road.

Hunger satisfied and belly a bit bloated, he stood at the pumps of the Buy-N-Fly topping off the truck while stretching both arms over his head. Apparently his little sex talk back in the diner hadn't sat well with Adrienne, who'd stormed off to pick up some last minute foodstuffs inside.

Twenty dollars and some change later, he took a deep breath of robust fumes rising from the gas cap and flung the handle back on the pump before strutting his way toward the convenience store doors.

Inside, Adrienne had been standing in a deceptively short line for what seemed like forty years now, an assortment of sweet and savory snacks tucked into each elbow. Gage always managed to keep the truck well supplied with water bottles so there was no need to pick up anything additional to drink; a good thing too since she was out of room on her makeshift shelf.

A squat woman stood behind the counter, her head so close to the surface that it appeared to float. Wearing a deep creased scowl, she moved at a pace that would make a sloth proud. Adrienne convinced herself that she may actually be one, her unflattering hairstyle reminiscent of a sloth she had seen in a zoo many years ago. At least there was only one person ahead of her now, but the sluggish clerk had only just begun the what-should-not-be-so-tedious job of checking the man out.

As Adrienne shifted her weight from one leg to the other in anticipation of a lengthy wait, the smell of cigarettes enveloped her, entangled with acrid wisps of sweat and BO. She repressed a cough as an unwanted gaze fell on the back of her neck amongst other, lower, parts of her body.

Three fetid workers had walked in, grimy and foul from road construction, settling in the line behind her. They had stopped a little too close for comfort.

"Mmm would you look at that," said the one closest to her in a low voice, his foggy eyes tracing a path up her legs. Weathered and ghoulish, he might as well have been drooling from his dip-filled mouth and by the looks of the dark lines that stained his chin, that had likely already happened a few times earlier in the day.

A younger man shuffled up beside him, dirty blonde and cleaner yet no less unpleasant. "Damn, you right," he snarled in a voice that did not suit his appearance in the slightest. "Fine piece right there."

A shudder began to clamber up her spine as she could make out the sounds of prolonged sniffing; thank God she couldn't see what was happening. There should be some kind of disinfectant for airborne stares from scuzzy sources, especially for situations like this. She would definitely buy a crate or two of the stuff, even though she had no idea if it would be remotely enough to dissolve the feeling of disgust that had caked itself all over her.

The last of the three hung back, heavyset in a safety vest that was two sizes too small. Smacking his gum loudly, his mouth was so overstuffed that saliva bubbled up at the corners of his lips, sputtering with each word that he belched. "Betcha that one's a great ride."

Grunts of agreement were exchanged between the men, adjusting their gnarly belts as if to try and draw her attention.

As if, she thought, so tempted to turn around to give them a piece of her mind. After thinking it over, she spun around to-

"May I help you?" the cashier cut in.

- take advantage of it being her turn and the slothful clerk being free at last.

"Ah, thanks so much," said Adrienne, squinting at the clerk's faded name tag as she dumped items on the counter with relief. "Martha, is it?" she asked as she flexed her elbows a couple of times to get the blood flowing.

The look on Martha's face remained unchanged. The scowl was obviously permanent; a next level variant of the resting bitch face.

"Well alrighty then," Adrienne said crassly. "I'll just take these things here and, um, some of those condoms too, the ones in the blue box."

She pointed to the display behind the register in an attempt to let her newfound admirers know she had an other half, without actually having to look at or talk to them.

"Well, ain't you a lucky one?" the closest man gruffed, the other two chuckling discordantly.

"Nah, I'm the lucky one," a familiar voice interrupted. It was Gage as he approached from behind, grabbing Adrienne squarely on the hips and patting her right cheek a couple times. "And the blue box ones are too small for me darlin'. We need those right there in the black box, with the XL remember?" He made sure to put much emphasis on the X and the L.

Turning around, he winked at the men before striding off. They eyeballed him in return, scoffing and whispering amongst themselves as he swaggered by.

As the clerk finally rung up her sale after the longest wait ever to spend sixteen dollars, Adrienne discovered that Gage had gone again.

Ugh, where's he at now, she thought, stepping away from the counter. It wasn't long before she saw him browsing in a nearby aisle.

"I already have stuff," she said to him, waving the bags around to grab his attention.

He was having none of it.

"I'm just double checking," he replied. "Oh! Did you get any cinnamon gum?"

She sighed, her face decidedly neutral. "No, I didn't."

"Well, we have to curb the potential for dragon breath. Nobody wants that. No, no, we must get some."

She tried really hard not to roll her eyes again as she trundled over to the assortment of gum and began looking.

Gage continued to browse, eventually finding his way outside of the food aisles. There he spotted a gray flannel shirt on one of the few clothing stands in the store, along with a matching hat. His eyes grew wide. *Wahoo! Two jackpots in one day!*

He quickly scanned the other racks; they didn't carry much worth buying, cluttered with way-too-small tee shirts and caps sporting one liners about beard rides, guns, and 'your girlfriend'.

At last Adrienne found the right gum and looked around again to see where he was. Could he not stand still for a more than a few seconds?

"A lil' help here," came a distinct voice from behind.

Adrienne spun to see him with both arms stuck straight up, the unbuttoned shirt straining across his flared back. She shook her head as she walked over, setting down the bags and grabbing hold of the loose ends.

"Stuck are we?"

He was unamused. "No shit, potato head."

"You have a way of getting clothes stuck on you, don't you?" she asked sarcastically. "Just as well you don't own many."

She attempted to pull and the shirt didn't move.

Great, this was actually going to be a struggle. As usual, Gage found ways of making life markedly 'easier'. Undaunted, she tried again and after a few heftier tugs, his back finally gave up its hold and the shirt was on, stretched only slightly. Upon a second glance, perhaps a little... or a lot more than slightly.

"You really should trademark that back," she joked. "It would go perfectly with the others."

He smiled. "I'm building up quite the collection of TMs, eh?" He grabbed each side of the shirt and did a twirl, pausing dramatically each quarter turn to accentuate his features. His abs and countless obliques looked exceptionally good with the direct lighting overhead. "Whatcha think?" he asked, head tilted with narrow and seductive eyes peeking through a tuft of hair that flowed over his forehead.

She looked him over, mulling over how utterly ridiculous he looked while also thinking it was without a doubt one of the sexiest things she had ever laid eyes on.

"Well, you model wannabe," she said. "You're looking pretty damn lumbersexual. Flannel actually looks hot on you, so if ever this Journeyman thing doesn't work out you could always dabble in some modeling; get yourself on a romance book cover or two."

"Ha! Damn right you'd want to read about me. But, I like to think of myself as more metro," he stated. "However, I really like this shirt and this hat! Makes me look like a grizzly fucker."

She laughed heartily as he put the cap on over his untamed hair. "That you are, Gage. One grizzly, hung, buff, metrosexual fucker. Jesus, you have to be one of the most confusing men I have ever met." She stopped him moving for a moment, a major task in its own right, and her hand grazed across the fine hairs on his chest. "And I wouldn't have it any other way."

They stood for a moment in the middle of the aisles looking at each other, uncaring how awkward looking the scene might appear to others.

The front doors sounded and the all-too-familiar huffs of arrested breathing soon followed, ending the romantic interlude.

A bloodied man shuffled his way into the store and fell into the main counter, splattering red everywhere. He was holding his side, from which his life oozed out of an extensive wound.

"Call 911!" he exclaimed through short breaths. "There's two huge bears or some shit out there and they're… eating people!"

Adrienne and Gage faced each other, tenacious expressions flashing across each of their faces.

"Always an adventure!" she said.

He shouted across to the perma-scowl, who was frozen with an upturned nose in front of the bleeding man. "Get that man medical attention and be quick about it!"

She didn't budge.

"Now!" he bellowed. His voice rattled her straight to the core and as if a switch had been flipped, she hustled over to the phone.

Adrienne and Gage rushed out, dropping their bags off beside the entrance before continuing on toward their truck.

The scene outside was sheer pandemonium: a sea of panicked people had arose out of nowhere like some frenzied crop. The two of them had to dodge their way through the mob, the crowd running in any and all directions. Some searched for safe haven in the convenience store or over at the diner, while more were banging hard on the locked doors of the motel, desperately seeking shelter.

Upon closer inspection, Gage noticed that although the rabble was scattered, they were generally moving to the east and away from something, as yet unseen, beyond a line of big rigs parked on the other side of the station.

As they neared their vehicle, terrifying howls blanketed the screaming crowd. The hectic action seemed to stop whilst the sound blasted its way across the frightened masses.

"That doesn't sound too good," Gage said.

"Not in the slightest," said Adrienne nervously. "Recognize it?"

"Sure don't," said Gage unfortunately.

No sooner than the roars ended and the shrieking of the crowd took over, two monstrous shapes bolted around the foremost K-Whopper. They were slightly larger than Kodiaks, with reptilian skin that glistened in the low slung light and lustrous manes of rust colored feathers that ran down the entire length of their backs. Their heads could pass for large dogs, filled to the brim with salivating canines. They were actually quite beautiful yet absolutely terrifying.

The lead creature was holding something tightly in its jaws, a body by the looks of it, but it was hard to make out with all the commotion. It bit down hard, splitting whatever it was into two pieces that fell off to each side. They continued to rush toward the station, tearing between a couple of cab overs, shredding the metal like paper and shattering glass.

About a hundred feet away, a family of four had taken refuge by the side of their silver minivan, hoping it would shield them from the hungry eyes that were searching for prey.

Adrienne watched helplessly from afar as the parents, themselves quivering in terror, tried to comfort their children's cries which were acting like a lure, drawing the attention and fury of one of the beasts.

"Move!" she shouted vehemently, placing herself at risk of being targeted by either of the monsters. "You have to get away from there!" she cried, but it was to no avail, her voice unable to carry itself over the cacophony in between.

The beast swung its tail at the van, bulldozing its way through the roof, getting stuck halfway across the ragged metal that had peeled away. As it tried to pull free, the wheels resisted like nails on a chalkboard and each powerful tug left thick skid marks imprinted on the concrete.

Likely addled from fear, the family stayed put during the onslaught instead of taking a chance to run for safer cover.

Adrienne shook her head as she stood there dumbfounded.

The creature's tail came loose with a deafening snap and the van lurched up on two of its wheels before tipping over, crushing the cowering group underneath its unforgiving weight. Her gut wrenched as the creatures didn't even bother rifling through the debris to consume them, instead stomping by as their heavy footfalls cracked the pavement. What a waste of life.

One of the beasts headed straight toward a couple of defenseless bikers over at The Crispy Biscuit, desperately trying to get their Harleys started while the other one took to beating itself against a lifted black Dually that was parked at the motel. Inside, the passengers were screaming like little musical sardines as they were tossed around mercilessly.

Adrienne and Gage finally reached the GMC and he leapt up into the bed, unlocking their magic box of goodies. He tossed her a marked long sword and pistol, grabbing his own MK23 from its holster before removing his now favorite machete and a rune stone before slamming the box closed.

"What the hell are those things!?" shouted Adrienne.

"Bunyip I think. Haven't seen one in real life though and I might have skipped over a lot of the lore, since Aussie cryptos ain't normally on this side of the world."

He donned his sunglasses. Through the lenses he saw their heads were pulsing with intense colors: yellows and reds shifting hues around the sinuses. The corners of his lips fell to a frown and he added begrudgingly, "From the looks of it they're berserked. Lucky us."

"Good lord, what are they doing here in Texas of all places?"

"I dunno but they're definitely a little far from home," he said, racking the slide. The sound was pure comfort to him. "Wouldn't surprise me one bit if the Noctis or some other faction was behind this."

"Yup, I agree. So how do we take them down?" she asked eagerly.

"Well," he started confidently while holding up the gun and machete in turn. "I assume they're gonna be like most of the things we encounter on four legs: hating bullets or the sharp end of a sword."

Adrienne abandoned all her eagerness in no time flat. "So that's it?" she said with heavy disappointment in her voice, waiting for a bit more detail, like what kind of bullets were useful or if any specific symbols and marks would put them down faster.

As expected, nothing more came from Gage on the matter.

"So… that's all we have to go on?" she muttered. "Call J."

"Yeppers!" said Gage with a playful nod as he ran toward the motel, "and phone's dead again. Ain't this fun?"

"No," she replied to herself before running after him, "it's not fun at all."

The bunyip continued to beat itself against the side of the buckling truck, trying to get at the tenderized morsels inside. It used its claws to pry off the doors as if it were some huge tin can. The passengers had since blacked out and large bloody patches stained the side windows and dashboard vinyl. If they weren't dead, they were certainly pretty close to it.

Meanwhile, the two men on motorcycles managed to flee the scene in the nick of time, missing the jaws of death coming for them by mere seconds. Instead of chasing after the racing bikes, that bunyip turned its attention to a construction vehicle parked close by and it let out a satisfying puff from its monstrous nostrils.

Standing there, appetizing and at the ready with an arsenal of tools, were the three garish men who had brashly commented about Adrienne's figure earlier. The heavyset man pushed by his colleagues and slapped a long black wrecking bar across his fatty gloved palm.

"Come on, ya sumbitch!" he yelled.

On command, the mighty beast lunged forward.

Back at the motel, Gage popped a couple of rounds straight into the creature's legs. They pierced its flesh without issue and it winced in obvious pain, retracting its body from the truck as a thin liquid flowed out from the bullet holes. Now that there was a confirmation that bullets worked against the thing, Gage focused in like a laser, his confidence pegged high.

The monster roared angrily at him as he continued forward unabashed, its tail lashing against the weathered doors, bashing splintered dents into the wood.

"Bad luck, beastie," he said, reaching into his pocket to pull out the stone he had previously tucked in there. Drawing it back to ready a throw, he whispered *Fila glaciem* and then cast it hard at his injured foe.

At the truck, the blocky man swung and missed, tumbling forward and rolling with his weight and the energy of his swing as the bunyip raced by. It had singled out the young blonde man standing in front of it, pacing back and forth a couple times as if to antagonize him before lunging forward with its jaws fully bared.

The man turned his lithe body and the enemy brushed against his stomach, biting into thin air. The force of the bite was palpable. Had it been closer, it might have shaved off hairs along with his shirt with its abrasive skin. Instead, a solid line of thick saliva was painted in a swath across his middle.

Not wasting a second, he used both hands to pull a couple long screwdrivers out from his tool belt. Twirling them amongst his fingers, they glinted in the morning light as he grabbed the handles tightly and drove the shafts into the creature's passing neck. As they sunk in with a gratifying squelch, he rotated them like joysticks to enlarge the wounds. Brown fluid globbed out of the gaping punctures, accosting him with the smell of rancid chicken. Catching him off guard he gagged, loosening his grip right as the beast jolted, knocking him into the side of the vehicle. Now winded, he grabbed at his aching back while writhing on the pavement, the sharp soreness spreading down to his legs and up into his shoulders.

Stepping forward and latching on with a large claw on the roof of the truck, the creature's heavy drool pooled in chunky splats around the young man as it hovered over its next meal. A large blob accumulated on its chin before weighing enough to come splashing down on his face, smothering his view.

Back at the motel, the rune stone danced its way through the air, leaving behind faint trails of white dust. It landed at the beast's feet, spinning before exploding into a dazzling burst of blue. Swirls of frost quickly settled around its body like thickening ropes, encasing its legs, torso and snout in icy bondage before yanking it hard to the ground. Water was forced out of the frigid air into a roiling fog that engulfed the creature.

Adrienne fired her pistol from a distance, her aim true despite the thick vapor. With each shot the beast moaned sorely. Before long she had expended her ammo, holstering the pistol and grabbing the long sword.

Confidently, Gage strode past her and up to the impounded beast, placing a boot on its long muzzle. The frosty coating crackled and popped under his weight.

"Enough death today," he said coolly and fired, aiming for the space between its eyes.

The bullet went in but the creature did not die. Instead, its eyes locked in his direction and grew devilishly narrow, a low growl rising to rattle the strands that were restraining it.

"Ah shit," Gage groaned, quickly reaching for serrated steel but not before the filaments shattered and sent him zooming through the air. A short distance later he whacked the inflexible ground along with a hailstorm of numbing shards.

On the ground by the construction vehicle, the blinded young man worked feverishly to wipe away the slimy goo that had coated his face. It was difficult to remove since it was incredibly sticky. After a few seconds, he was able to clear his vision enough to see through a murky sheen. Slopping the smelly gunk off his hands, he saw nothing but a forest of imposing fangs in front of him.

"Mother fucker," he said, realizing there was nothing he could do. The sharp teeth came down and he dodged it once, then twice. He looked out under the truck and a murky outline of a green dress caught his eye. He opened his mouth as if to call for help but as he did so, teeth came in over his head like a clamp and in one powerful bite it was gone, swallowed whole.

Shouts of rage came from behind and the stocky man struck the distracted beast hard on the side of its face with his wrecking bar while the other man popped it with a solid hit from his sledgehammer. The devastating barrage continued with swipe after brutal strike.

Adrienne turned and slid as the bunyip shook loose its tattered constraints and leapt over her on a frenzied charge toward Gage. She raised the long sword up above her as her soft knees skidded bleeding across the pavement. The sword tip sunk into the creature's hardened flesh, squelching as it tore through its dank and pungent innards.

With a final cry it collapsed to the ground, skidding to a stop just before those infamous scuffed boots.

Dizzy from the salvo hefty strikes, the last bunyip stumbled into the construction truck then hunched over into the large dent it made in the side. The men walked over to it as it struggled to gain composure, reaching into their reflective vests and pulling out hidden knives. With arms raised in unison, they struck at it with their short stubs of metal and a loud *boom* ushered out of the wounds, storming through the crowds as if a bomb had gone off.

Gage looked across toward the source of the noise and saw the creature keeling over just after the men stabbed it. He could swear he saw a faint red glow, visible just for a few seconds, but it was hard to make out and could have just been a trick of the the morning light. Had he blinked, he would have missed it.

"Ady," he said softly, "come this way." He started to walk off briskly, without waiting for a reply.

"Gage?" she asked, concerned at the tone he was using. Realizing that he was not going to answer, she caught her breath and got up off her knees, falling in a few steps behind him. "Gage, what is it? Gage?"

He was making his way directly for the GMC, sure to ignore the men as he walked by. However, Adrienne didn't get the memo and made eye contact with the ghoulish one, noticing the fallen bunyip had large gashes in its side.

The men lowered their blades in disturbing synchrony as they continued to look at the two of them, still slobbering tobacco from chapped lips and churning wads of gum.

"Well, well," said the large one, the freakish cracking of his voice hinting at something devious. "Lookie who we have here."

Gage panned across them each in turn and they stared emptily back, not saying a word. Their beady eyes, however, held back secrets which spoke directly to his gut.

"Ady, do you mind going to collect our stuff please?" he asked and the tone of his voice indicated he wasn't going to accept no as a response.

A little confused, but sensing the tension in the air as tight and uneasy as a plucked guitar string, she walked over to the front of the shop to pick up their bags.

"It's time to go," stated Gage. He climbed in and cranked the engine.

She hopped in after him and grabbed her trusty cap from the glove box while Gage pulled out of the gas station onto the service road. She tipped her hat and waved briefly as they drove away.

"Well, not to stereotype," she said to Gage as she rolled down her window, resting an arm on the edge, "but they fought pretty good for creepy hayseeds."

He stayed focused on the road ahead. "Yeah," he replied faintly, "too good."

As the GMC returned to the highway and shrank away on the distant horizon, Amarillo police and emergency services began to flood the scene.

The two workers watched Gage and Adrienne's vehicle disappear and turned their attention back to the beast they had slain. They were joined by a middle aged woman, her vibrant green dress made dingy with stains of blood and chunks of gore.

All of their eyes were now black as night and rimmed with crimson.

CHAPTER
Thirteen

HELL KNIGHTS DIVIDED

THE SANITARIUM'S COMMAND CENTER was jammed in an old cafeteria on the ground floor of the building, gutted of all traces of its previous life except for the aroma of French fries and peanut oil that forever drenched the walls. It normally bustled with activity, but this afternoon was different. The buzz had increased ten fold after six fateful words came across channels from Amarillo: *Gage Crosse was on the move.*

In the three years since he had blazed onto the scene and into the chronicles as one of the most successful slayers in history, many a demon both lesser and great had come to respect and fear his name. How ironic it was that they no longer feared the cross, long the bane of their existence, but would now cower at the mere mention of Crosse.

Fueled by the electricity that permeated the air, they all moved to and fro with purpose, like a well oiled machine. Their hosts and associated attire looked to have been plucked right out of a high level corporate office in London and plopped right in against the decrepit innards of the long abandoned institution.

A few sat at neat little ergonomic desks lining the walls to both the left and right of the entrance arch, typing away on their glossy keyboards in front of state of the art computers. Others stood at tall wood tables distributed between the rows of desks, their gnarled tops spilling over with a wide variety of exotic ingredients. Some were pleasing to the eye, others delicious, as evidenced by a demon stealing strawberries off the table next to his station when nobody was looking. A few were downright disgusting and appropriately demonic, like the murky jar containing the brains of feral mice floating in a vinegary stock made from the full skeletons of fairies.

Yet more demons milled busily like bees in between the desks and tables, heading in and out of the run down chamber. However, all the hustle slowed to a crawl when three large shapes appeared at the entryway, following close behind Keli and Agares. Their mere presence sapped the room of its energy and the rabble made sure to clear out of the central pathway as they walked in.

Keli had donned another outfit, smoothing out the lines in her one piece of tight, form fitting leather. A deep cut plunged down the front, over her breasts and past her belly button. Its outer edges were trimmed with small black feathers, ruffling ever so slightly with each deliberate and slow step. Hardly an outfit that screamed leadership, many whispers began to fly like notes passed around a classroom when she sashayed by. It was the general consensus that one in her position should be wearing attire that garnered respect, instilled fear, or some combination thereof, instead of percolating mere lust like a majority of hers did. That said, it was pretty apparent that she gave no fucks about it. To her any sin, especially one of the seven, was something to be celebrated.

The same could not be said for Baal, one of the greatest of the seven Hell Knights who were once proud kings under Lucifer's grand rule. Time and again, he made sure plenty knew of his grievances, but those concerns and complaints were often overruled by the voices of Knights Paimon and Astaroth, who found themselves siding with her many times more than him these days.

Baal had fallen back, passively defiant, positioning himself the furthest away from Keli at the rear of the small entourage. He looked up at both Paimon and Astaroth while shaking his head subtly.

They were bookending her like some whoreific grimoire, likely mumbling ass-kissing rhetoric in each ear to see who could receive the most brown nosing credit. It was a term he coined and was particularly proud of, one most fitting for his views on their relationship.

Baal continued unabashedly behind them and was not dressed, unlike the other two, in suits, business casual, or pathetic human attire. He was traditional, his large body clad with elaborate plate armor that was forged in the deepest pits of Hell and used during the great war in Heaven ages ago.

The armor was obsidian, its close fitting helmet filigreed with traces of cold silver. His fiery eyes peered out from the slits, made more menacing by two spires that rose up on either side like horns. His large torso was covered by a full cuirass and etched in the center of it was his ornate sigil, glowing bright and orange like molten rock. The remainder of the armor was equally as robust, traces of magma lining the dark suit's menacing spikes and sweeping curves.

His presence managed to do what Keli's could not: exude fear-inducing intimidation upon those around him. Demons nearby shaded their eyes and turned away as he thundered by. When he opened his mouth to speak, his hoarse voice came forth from beneath the helm and caused those around him to tremble. What he said, he did so openly and without care.

"Onoskelis…" he began, hating the humanization of her name, "I have been asking you since being called forth to this dump: what is the purpose of this meeting? We have too many important things going on right now and your trivial distractions are only serving to cause major delays."

She continued to walk as if she hadn't heard a thing. The riff between the two of them was had been building for some time, but was about to reach a head, threatening to burst like some great throbbing boil.

Her blatant disregard of him caused anger to flare in his gut. "Listen here, I-"

"We are almost to the circle," cut in the tall man to her left, his tailored blue suit clinging well to his body as he stretched and ran a hand through his crest of red hair. He turned slightly so he could see Baal out of the corner of his dark eye and then continued. "Respectfully, Baal, silence yourself until then."

"I was not talking to you, Astaroth," Baal stated, waving a gauntlet dismissively his way. "I know traditions, something this bitch could use a major lesson in, and I do not need anyone's permission to speak. I can see now that the Prince of Inquisitions has been reduced to a mere lap dog, as if parading around wearing a soulless ginger weren't enough."

"Stop it, the both of you! No wonder a congregation hasn't been called in years. You should know better than to bicker in front of the lessers!" the other man snapped, his blood red suit and jet black hair standing out from the drab blacks and grays of the other demons about which he spoke. "Be silent until we-"

"Reach the damn circle, yes Paimon," Baal interrupted while shaking his head, pinching his fingers together mockingly as if they were speaking his words. He then pointed it ahead. "Ah, it seems at last we have arrived, so I bid the two of you to shut the fuck up."

"Always the instigator!" Astaroth popped off, turning to face him with fists balled up and sparking. He was not intimidated in the slightest by the dark armor in front of him, so similar to what he had also worn during the war. "For one that touts the old ways so frequently, how quick you are to forego the very foundations of our beliefs. The hierarchy is everything!"

Agares crossed the threshold first into the celebrated circle, actually a line of dried blood that outlined a semi-circular area where the cafeteria's kitchens once were. It was about twenty feet in diameter, its primary purpose to serve as a place of council and debate amongst the great demons. The size and shape of this one paled vastly in comparison to the ones of old that surrounded entire temples. Keli and her two yes-men took up in the rough center as Baal followed, last to enter.

He thrust a metal arm out to his side expectantly and suddenly, a large sword appeared in his hand out of thin air; its blade like ruby and its skull-adorned hilt of black diamond. Twisting in his hand like a key, smoke rose up from the line, wrapping around the five of them like an opaque shield. From the inside, they could see out at the inquisitive faces in the room, but to an outside observer all sights and sounds could not escape past the swirling barrier.

"Now may I speak?" Baal asked sarcastically, shoving the blade into the cracked floor. It singed back at its master as if to grant him permission.

"Baal, you must learn to control yourself! We are already having enough trouble keeping the lessers in line," said Paimon, "and certainly do not need to stoke the fires of their protests. We would be much further along in our plans if we had a more… obedient workforce. Operations around the Great Lakes alone could be doubled if we didn't have constant bickering amongst the staff."

"Workforce?" Baal scoffed at the notion. "That Paimon, is one of our greatest problems right there: they are not workers; they are slaves meant to serve us. Back to the hierarchy you all are so quick to tout, there shouldn't even be a need to reference performance or output or the numbers that you cling so desperately to like haggard maids."

Astaroth shifted his weight from leg to leg, back and forth to stem his temptation to silence Baal. He knew damn well he could not do a thing about it; at least not yet. Even a pop to the chin would be difficult with that helmet on.

"You speak to me as if this budding insurrection is my fault," Baal continued as Astaroth dipped his head and turned away, "yet I am not the one bringing in new age ideas and corrupting the older, purer ways." He directed his gaze over to Keli, who had remained silent while her dogs attacked. "Need I remind all of you that I am the only one appropriately dressed for this occasion?"

The two Knights couldn't dodge that fact but Astaroth had reached his fill of Baal's arrogance and started to retort, "To deny change is to invite one's own-"

Keli spoke at last, "No need to bother, Astaroth. Baal is closed minded. Ancient."

"Is that supposed to be an insult?" Baal asked, clearly not offended. "I'm not surprised to hear such things from a lesser that is wearing shoes that are far too big for her own hooves".

Back and forth more insults were exchanged; heavy, powerful and hurtful.

"In Lucifer's name enough!" shouted Agares over the noise, having had enough. His outburst managed to silence them all but quickly he shrank back to normal, realizing all eyes were now on him. "My... apologies," he muttered, bowing his head low.

"No need to apologize, Duke Agares. You're right of course," Paimon said reassuringly, noting that Baal and Astaroth were continuing to eye each other up. "You two, save the cat fighting for later and if you must, you can whip out our vessel's dicks then to measure who is bigger. Keli, Your Grace, please... why have you called us here?"

Moving to the side so she could address everyone in front of her, she began. "As we've wasted precious time, I'll cut straight to the point. I think it is time we began implementing Infernal Tide."

All three knights were wide eyed. That was certainly an end goal of theirs, but to suggest starting its operation now while a majority of preparations hadn't even begun was a bit surprising.

"What brings you to this decision?" Paimon asked apprehensively.

"This would be quite the large undertaking," Astaroth followed, taking Paimon's tone of voice as his own.

"No, Astaroth, this would be quite the *stupid* undertaking at this stage," Baal said with absolutely no filter.

"I didn't say we would be finishing it by tomorrow," said an embittered Keli. "I merely stated that I think it's time to begin implementing it. Why, you ask? Gage Crosse appears to be heading west..."

Those words were enough to renew Paimon's interest and Astaroth nodded as well, but Baal was still being his stubborn self.

"You do realize where he is likely heading, don't you?" Paimon said. "One of the Solo-"

"Of course I do," he interjected. "I'm not ignorant of the facts, but my point is, we shouldn't be leaping right into the final plan. These things take time, patience and skill. There are several hurdles to overcome first in order to ensure such a colossal plan flows without issue. With the rabble now protesting the way they are, do you really think things will go smoothly for us and that we can afford such things? We must bring order to that mess first. My stance is to focus on freeing the other four Knights from their prisons and using them to oversee operations before we tread too far down this path."

Keli exhaled. "There just isn't time for all of that."

Baal ended up laughing at her. "We're immortal, girl! There is all the time in the world."

"If we are right, Gage will arrive at his home later today," she said, "and should he get his hands on it, our problems will multiply. What would you have us do then?"

"Why are we bowing to the whims of this mortal?" questioned Baal, who could not fathom the power this one stupid mortal had over all of demonkind. "Are we so crippled now that a bag of watery meat holds that much sway over us? He should be killed. Now."

Paimon rubbed his forehead. One of the problems with human hosts was that the demons were subject to their ailments and a massive migraine had started to build in his head. "What do you think we have been trying to do for the past three years, invite him over for brunch?"

The mood was fast becoming rocky and Agares wouldn't be interjecting this time. He slinked behind Keli as Baal continued to assert himself over the others, who continued to side with her in turn.

"We would be far better off if Dajjal were here," Baal finally proclaimed.

Keli's eyes burst into flames at the mere mention of that demon. "Absolutely not!"

Paimon stepped between the two of them and his expression was gravely serious. He addressed Baal directly. "You cannot think the Deceiver would care about any of us if he were above ground?"

"Yes, I do think that," Baal affirmed. "He would be doing a damn sight better than this debacle we called an operation. 'The Night' we call ourselves, yet we act as though we are blinded by the dark, instead of using it to our advantage. Dajjal would keep Hell first and foremost."

"I have had enough!" Keli shouted, overwhelmed by her hatred of Dajjal and Baal's support of him. "What is your problem with me, Baal?"

"Have you not been listening, *lesser?* Oh, where shall I begin?" he mocked. "You are playing a very dangerous game, miss, and you best realize this before you end up… getting hurt."

"Your Graces," Agares finally cut in with a hushed breath, "the masses can be updated later on our plans. You both should go and calm yourselves so we can discuss matters with level heads." His eyes raised slyly and they met with Baal's, ending their journey with a wink.

"I've grown tired of this," the armored demon expressed. "We are obviously done here. Call me when there is need for a real Hell Knight."

Grasping the handle of the embedded sword, he yanked it out of the floor and turned it again in hand. In an instant he vanished, the smoke around them burning itself away to leave the four of them exposed to the gawking control room.

"Don't you all have work to do?" Keli asked as she stormed out of the room, all eyes on her for all the wrong reasons.

THE MUSIC WAS NARCOTIC, its deep base spilling out well above the evening streets. Inside Club AfterNight, sat atop one of the tallest buildings in Shoreditch, the wild beats coursed through the veins of everyone on the dance floor and lining the bar.

In one of the private suites attached to the club, available for high paying clientele to use for whatever purposes they saw fit, two bodies writhed under silken sheets in the cool blue hues cast by the dim floral lamps overhead.

Their moans were muffled by the ongoing dance music, bodies rising and falling with the beat until one of them sat upright. The shimmering covers fell away from her nude body and there she continued to grind on him, taking pleasure from the thickness filling her and ensuring he felt the same way.

He was gorgeous, as if a fashion billboard had mated with a fitness magazine. Piercing blue eyes looked back up at her own and his short cropped hair was so neat and trim, with nary a stray hair in sight despite the rough action.

Feelings upon ecstatic feelings were mounting; his abs began to tense, veins spidering their way across them as his back arched. As he grabbed her hips, his arms were swollen with veins and he guided her where and at the pace he wanted with those massive biceps.

Faster he went and faster she took it, taking his bare skin all the way to the base.

"I... I'm about to..." he said, deep voice still a tremendous turn on despite the stutters.

And then he did, filling her with himself as it spilled out onto his balls with satisfaction.

Satiated, she rose, his still huge dick flopping over to one side, glistening with their emissions.

"Thank you," she said walking over to the nightstand and opening the topmost drawer. A flicker of light danced across her eyes.

"That felt amazing," he said, sitting up on the edge of the bed. His member dangled invitingly between his legs, twitching and growing as the blood started to flow back into it for another round. "Want to go again? I'm sorry I didn't catch your name earlier."

"Oh that's fine, it's Keli," she said meekly, straddling him once again and giving his large pecs a rub with her left hand.

"That's a pretty name, Keli," he said with such boyish charm. Pity.

"I'm so sorry, Chris," she said with a hint of remorse, "but round two will have to wait; I have a call to make."

"Right now?" he asked, slightly puzzled.

She nodded and with a quick strike, she cut his throat.

Desperately he grabbed at it while falling forward to the decorative carpet, a massive red stain growing out from his lifeless body.

She looked down to the damp floor, letting out a sigh as she stepped into the warm liquid. The wet fibers squished between her bare toes and as many times as she'd done it before, she couldn't get over how medieval this method of communication was. She would often joke with herself that she could rest assured knowing it would always be cheaper than cell phone bills.

"*Spiritum meum, victor erit, in malign positus, loquar!*" The words she spoke knocked loose the abstract art from the walls. Her eyes grew darker and her voice deepened as if calling from the very pits of hell as she cast it out to the demonic legions that were spread across the planet and beyond.

Raising her arms out to the side as if standing on a high precipice in front of thousands, she looked out the expanse of windows over the twinkling lights of London and spoke, "This is… Onoskelis and I address you all now with a message and a mission. You have done your part to get us to where we stand today – from a loose and ragged rabble into a primed and well oiled machine. As components needed to be replaced, we eliminated the old and brought in the new. Now look at us: nearly unstoppable by our sheer will alone.

"The Journeymen are now fearful, frightened that they may have overlooked this pathetic little assembly of demons and what we are capable of; that they no longer have the power they held in the days of old."

She spat on the floor. "The arrogance and pride of these humans, newest to the worlds but the most wanton."

Raising her voice, the speech continued, "They may be onto our plans, but that will not stop us. What they know is limited and fragmented and it must remain that way at any cost. In response to the Order's increased interest in our affairs, I shall be sending a small contingent to Bennett Peak for closer… involvement in things there. Perhaps we can show the Journeymen how demons take to being underestimated.

"All of you take heed of my words, now: they cannot stop the oncoming tide poised to rush over this earth, suffocating all who oppose us. This world is ours for the taking; time of demon kind has come!"

With that her speech concluded, the last words echoing across the globe, soaring on the wings of cacophonous cheers. The world was about to change.

CHAPTER
fourteen

HOME SWEET HOME

THE SUN HAD CRESTED ITS highest point of the day and was well on its return journey back to the horizon. Flocks of starlings whirled overhead, twisting and turning like living clouds playfully riding currents in the sky. It was all a gorgeous spectacle: the orange sunlight, the dance-like movements, the flow of air past the open window. All worked in beautiful consensus, holding Adrienne's attention as they entered the the outskirts of Denver.

Not long after they left the highway in lieu of more sweeping country roads, the sight of whooshing gray that had become all too familiar was slowly replaced with nature's own greens and browns. Stubby hills of grass rolled gently out to the north toward the city's skyscrapers and also to the west before rising sharply into the mountains. Green shrubbery and equally tall boulders mingled with the sprinkles of far off lights that began popping in against the darkening landscape. To the south, a thick row of bushes streamed by and blocked the view, but through fleeting gaps in the branches a similar sight extended out into the vast open country.

However, the scenery wasn't the only thing changing with the diminishing roads. There was a notable shift in Gage's demeanor, his expression now a disproportionate mix of happiness and consternation.

The truck swerved along the now dirt paths as he looked ahead, keenly scouting the right hand side for familiar sights. After a good stretch of nothing, they rounded a corner and a rusty mailbox with the number sixty-four perched on top came into view. Barely clinging onto its oxidized sides were a line of stickers spelling out the faded name 'Crosse' in block letters and adjacent to the mailbox stood five jagged poles moving up the property's gravel driveway, each affixed with diamond shaped reflectors.

"We're here," he told Adrienne as he steered the truck over to the right.

Ahead, the path disappeared into a thick line of pines and the loose stones beneath them sputtered and clinked on the chassis. The trees bobbed in step with their heads as they went by, the bumpy ride made more so by the not-so-high quality shocks of the GMC.

All this churning reminded Gage of the day he had driven off in the opposite direction, much faster and full of rage like a bat out of hell. Heading back this way, along this very road, was something he had not expected to do for a long time, if ever again.

The two of them sat silently, nothing to say or do at the moment except take in the surroundings as the drive dove, snaked, and dipped through the rest of the encircling trees until finally it emptied them out into a wide open field.

Out in the rough middle of the grassy tract sat a large, two story plantation house, its symmetrical and weather-beaten facade adorned with light brick and cream clapboard siding. Porches ran along the entire front of both floors, their simple off-white railings spaced evenly between six substantial, square columns that supported the entire thing. Between each set of pillars, tall floor to ceiling windows were evenly distributed to let in the most of the south-facing light and on the lower floor, a simple staircase drew up in the middle allowing access to the front door.

The house was surrounded by oak trees, peppered with the colors of autumn, larger than any Adrienne had ever seen. A traditional white picket fence wrapped neatly around the property, enclosing the main house and two smaller buildings, one on each side, in a quaint box of rustic bliss.

As they neared, Adrienne spotted a rose garden within the fence line which brought a much needed smile to her face. It started neatly along the front beds and extended casually in sweeping red and pink curves off into the backyard. Surprisingly, the untended flowers were still majestically in bloom.

Beyond the petals, a couple of metal gates were closed and locked amongst a broad area of wire fencing that had once contained livestock. A dilapidated barn, smaller than a matchbox from where they were, peeked out in the distance.

Gage looked over into the fields, immediately recalling the squishiness of cold mud percolating up between his mischievous six-year-old toes, his rubber boots lost on purpose somewhere between there and his bedroom. A concealed chuckle escaped as he remembered one particular day when his mother was chasing after him through the pasture, gardens, and even around the entire first floor of the house, those tiny boots flapping in her hand hand while his equally tiny feet left footprints everywhere behind them. His mom was quite bothered by the end of that day; she discovered the mud he had be playing with was not so much muddy as it was fertile.

So indeed, the place where Gage had grown up could have been on the cover of any country living magazine, radiating feelings of coziness and well-being out of every wooden board and stone brick, despite the years devoid of any personal care and attention.

The truck slowed and came to rest in a circle of gravel a couple hundred feet from the porch and wearily, both passengers popped their doors open at the same time.

As Gage stepped out and took everything in without the barrier of metal and glass in between, it was quite emotionally overwhelming. Unsure if it was the freshness of the breeze at this altitude, the smells it had blown his way from the garden, or some combination thereof, his eyes had gotten misty.

"Welcome home," he said openly in low tones before drifting back into the comfort of quiet; it was going to take him a few minutes to compose.

Adrienne had been propped up on her door when she heard him speak. Concerned by his odd behavior, she left it open and worked her way around to his side, finding a space between his arm and locking her own into it once she got there. Nestling her head against his mammoth shoulder, always so soft yet inherently strong, she looked around while he continued to stare out across the garden.

For all intents and purposes everything was picture perfect, until a dark red symbol on the front door caught her eye. Unnoticed until now, its color nearly matched the door's, making it practically invisible from afar unless viewed at a the right angle where it reflected a dim sheen. The design was odd as well, one she was unfamiliar with: a large circle enclosed three interlocking triangles and in the middle of the arrangement was the outline of a hand, an open eye resting on the tips of its closed fingers.

"Gage?" she asked timidly, careful not to startle him out of his thoughts. "What is that?"

"Huh?" he replied lazily as she guided him across with her finger, pointing it toward the door. He winced. "Hell," he answered, "I can't remember."

Being here was definitely having an effect on him. Normally witty if not the slightest bit facetious, Adrienne could actually sense his internal struggle like heat off a stovetop; he just seemed lost.

"Think we should take a closer look?" she asked as a nicety, planning to investigate it herself should he drift off again.

He didn't answer right away, instead continuing to stare at the symbol questioningly, as if it were alive and knew damn well what it was, but wasn't telling.

"Sure thing," he replied, gradually settling back into his normal skin, "but before we do that why don't you leave that cap in the truck and get a little more comfortable?" He popped his finger playfully on the brim. "I'd love to see that gorgeous hair of yours."

She grinned, immediately obliging by tossing the cap through his open door. It spun and landed right in the center of her seat. "Is that better?"

Gage nodded as he ran his fingers through her flowing locks. "Oh yes."

Shutting the doors, together they walked up the path and through the gate, thirsty for oil. Adrienne took that as a signal to slow down before falling back to arm's length as they neared the porch. She watched him take a slow, hypnotic step up, his right cheek popping her way. Another teasing step followed and the left one flexed gracefully over to the other side.

Mercy.

She decided then and there that this was far too unhealthy a thing to be doing, light headedness seriously setting in, but she managed to convince herself that a couple more seconds, or possibly minutes, of watching beauty pitching itself from side to side wouldn't hurt.

Damn the only thing that would make this moment even better is a roll of quarters.

Gage, unaware his tight end was the topic of so much dedicated thought, reached the decking and stepped off delicately, as if a gentler tread would help avoid a rush of memory. To either side of him sat decorative wicker furniture he had once played on and daydreamed the days away, their once ornate weaves now caked with mildew and the low cushions slowly rotted by the elements. He walked up to the front door and saw withered topiaries on either side planted in those long lost childhood boots.

Cautiously, his hand reached out and fingers wrapped themselves around the handle. Half expecting it to spontaneously combust or set off some kind of deadly spike trap, relief won him over when nothing happened.

He then attempted to physically open the door to no avail, as it was sealed up tight by a magical force that resisted all attempts at turning the handle or pushing and pulling at the stubborn lumber. Even a couple of robust kicks in the middle didn't budge it nor smudge the paint.

The earlier relief changed into frustration and he stomped over to the windows on the left, banging them like a madman trying to get inside. A similar force continued to keep him shut out; the glass could not be opened or broken.

Grumbling, he cupped his hands to the glass and pressed his face firmly against them to look inside for any clues. As luck would have it, the heavy curtains had been shut so he couldn't make out much detail. However, he confirmed that the power was still out through the narrow gaps in the panels, the generators having been switched off when he left.

Pretty defeated, he trundled with hunched shoulders back over to the ward and stared at it while it stared back at him. Making a fist, he wanted to pop that smug, unblinking eye so hard. His blood pressure rose and he began to tremble.

Ok Gage, calm down big guy. There's absolutely no rush to get inside, so breathe.

Following his own advice, he inhaled sharply and took in a lung full of air, holding it in for a moment with his chest heaved before releasing it slowly through his pursed lips.

Now, let's approach this logically.

Obviously this was an entry ward of some kind, similar in construction to the Hamsa but slightly rearranged. Gage postulated that it would be keyed to his handprint or fingerprints so with that in mind, he aligned his hand precisely with the symbol and pressed hard against it.

Nothing happened.

He tried a couple more times for good measure and…

Nothing happened still.

The eye must then play an integral role in the spell. So bending over, he held one of his green eyes open just inches away from the mark as if it were a high tech retinal scanner. He then tried the other one before repeating each open eye in turn with his hand again pressed on the door.

It was quite the spectacle and crowning all these amazing efforts: a big, whopping nothing.

This was getting old. He had to have been in quite a state of mind, or completely out of it, when he placed this thing. The latter mood was speedily resurfacing with each passing failure.

Adrienne appeared behind him before he managed to start any more obnoxious contortions and her touch calmed him right down like a sedative.

"Any luck?" she asked with a slight laugh.

"Sorry, this noggin' is drawing a total blank at the moment," he admitted.

"It's all good, Gage," she reassured him, "it can wait. At least we're here now and it's starting to get a little dark."

He pulled away and turned, waltzing over to the railings where he placed both arms and looked out to the right as the sun dipped below the far off tree line. She was right, night was fast approaching and they needed somewhere to rest up. His eyes drifted over to the small building attached to the house by a narrow, covered walkway and he got an idea.

"Looks like we may be sleeping out here for the night," he revealed.

Her face was full of excitement at the prospect, but that quickly fell to apprehension as the quality of the available porch accommodations sank in. They were less than one star, possibly even zero: equivalent to the amount of fucks the elements had given while laying assault to the furniture on a daily basis.

"Um, hopefully we won't be chatting with the sandman on these things," she said, poking the wicker sporadically; it caved in at the slightest amount of pressure.

"Nah, darlin'," he replied with a devilish smirk, "I have somethin' far better in mind for us."

He turned back and looked to the truck. In the golden hues of the hour, she looked almost as inviting as a warm, cozy bed. Almost.

CHAPTER
fifteen
A NIGHT FULL OF STARS

Gage wasn't sure that Adrienne was fully sold on the whole truck camping idea, but it was one of their only options other than sleeping on rotten cushions set atop moldy chairs. She'd soon change her mind after she saw what a Gage-styled camping session was all about. He thought on that for a moment, the first thing popping into his head being one of those infamous eye rolls of hers and he convinced himself that the gesture must be avoided at all costs.

Now a man on a mission, he walked confidently over toward the building he spotted earlier. It was a utility area his mother had built primarily for crafts, but his folks had also converted part of it into a large laundry room. He continued to walk along the the covered path, looking to his right. There, three long clotheslines extended out from the side of the building and off into the back yard, each dancing its own carefree shuffle in the wind.

When he reached the door, he heavily scrutinized every square inch of it. Nary a ward or fleck of misplaced paint was in sight, so he attempted to open it, secretly praying his efforts wouldn't be stopped before they even started. To his delight, the handle moved and the door was open.

The first thing to hit him when he entered was the fragrance of crisp sheets, baby powder, and lavender mixed with bergamot. Dulled by the years, the freshness of it all was still surprisingly potent.

The smells triggered more memories and he could almost feel his mother in the room: crocheting elaborate table coverings and doilies, making multi-tiered macramé plant hangers, customizing Christmas stockings with chunky characters and sequins, and simply repairing the brand new clothes Gage had managed to rip up within a few minutes of putting on. Some of these projects were finished long ago and some, sadly, never would be.

Gage proceeded to open the closest set of cabinets on the left as he went in, but found them empty. The ones situated beneath those were full, but with sewing tools and a surplus of different colored yarns. Helpful at one time, they weren't useful at all now, so he moved his way along the line of cabinets and drawers, finding more fabrics and threads tucked away inside. A huge plastic bin squatted at the end, overflowing with various toys from a childhood long past.

He stopped, grabbing two of the topmost stuffed animals – which happened to be his favorites – and held them up to the inviting light streaming in from a nearby window. The first one was a dog that resembled Snoopy, but he was taller and wearing a tiny bomber jacket. Looking around, he couldn't find his matching leather helmet and goggles, so assumed they had fallen to the bottom of the pile if they hadn't been lost to time.

The other one was a palm-sized parrot with a large beak, bright green and yellow, mere threads where the orange zig zags for feet used to be. Gage supposed that Duffy, their family Shih-Tzu and his best friend growing up, must've got a hankering for them back in the day and tore them off while playing.

As much as he liked going down memory lane, there were still plenty of things to do and there would be more time for this later on. Propping both toys up on a nearby shelf next to a cowbell, he continued on his trek for bedding. Part of him began to hope this wouldn't turn out to be a bust, because had already vowed that no eye rolls were allowed in this man's future.

He didn't have to fear too much longer, as he finally found himself in the right area. Opening a couple of matching mahogany armoires that had been shoved in the corner, stacks of downy comforters, wooly blankets and soft sheets gleamed inside like some long lost treasure. Using his arms like great big hooks, he fished out what he could and placed them all on top of the washing machine to sort through.

The sounds of *Don't Fear the Reaper* cut through the peace.

Normally he wouldn't think twice about it, but that was before all the weirdness of the past few days. Glancing down suspiciously at his phone, his look of trepidation soon melted away into a smile.

It was Joey.

Pressing the answer button, he answered promptly, "What up my man? I think I have enough charge for quick chat. This damn thing keeps dying no matter how much I keep it charged."

Joey responded heartily. "Yeah well, when you get back here we are definitely heading straight to the store and buying you a new one. First damn thing we do."

"Haha, sure thing boss. So what's going on?" Gage asked over the considerable rustling of paper, followed by the sound of many things crashing onto the hardwood floor. "Um, you okay?"

"Yeah, yeah," Joey snipped. "Damn desk organizer fell and made a mess. Trust me, it sucks to always be so full of irony, I'll get it up later. Nah, I called to give you a bit of an update on the situ now that you made it home…" his voice trailed off momentarily, "I assume you've made home, right?"

"Yeah, yeah we are here and surprisingly we made it in one piece."

Gage made himself comfortable on the edge of the large laundry sink, propping himself up with his sleeved arm. Light from the window opposite streamed in and he took a moment to admire the ropey veins that had formed along his arm. Glancing up from his moment of self-admiration, he noticed that his mother really did keep an overabundance of washing powders on hand; the numerous boxes neatly lining the sill looked like some motherly cleaning army.

"Ah good to hear," Joey continued with a lot more than relief in his voice. "So, the Noctis. They have definitely been moving a lot out west and up in the north. Seems they've been forming alliances with all sorts of beasts. Werewolves we knew about from the demon child's little pep talk back at the factory, but get this: they're even finding a way to get some wendigos to join their ranks."

Oh shit.

"Damn, really?" Gage replied with genuine shock and concern. "Wendigos aren't the kind of creatures that tend to shack up well with others. The Noctis must be slinging some heavy demon dick around to lure them over."

Trust Gage to find a means of taking the edge out of any situation. "Haha, yeah the Order has been chatting nonstop about it. The hotbeds they mentioned were in Portland, around the Great Lakes, plus upstate New York. I can't imagine they would be in the city proper but who knows. At least, that's what I could gleam out of the latest batch of transmissions."

"Sounds like that's enough action going on, J."

"If only that were it. Seems there is also some kind of pattern to where the heaviest demon activity is located worldwide, but they're keeping tight lipped about it; something's got them all worked up into a frenzy. The powers that be even broke out some form of code and those of us in the field aren't even aware of what it is, never mind the cypher. So we are in the dark relative to that."

"Huh, that's weird," Gage replied, shifting his weight to his lower back and crossing an arm over to rub an itch out of his left pec, "why would they want us to be unaware and unprepared for where we may encounter heavier smoking?"

"My thoughts exactly, but I am sure they have their reasons. I'm thinking they may have caught onto some of the Noctis' fabled 'master plan' and therefore don't want to tip their hand just yet, in case anyone is listening. I know it's not the only explanation, but it's the only one I have at this point. Plus, they already know we know they're up to something since, well, 2010 and run in with your folks."

"Agree. Ya think there are any near here? The Noctis I mean," Gage asked, concerned about the possibility of their being demons so close to home.

"There's no way to know for sure man," Joey said just as Gage expected him to, "but since you are further out west than here, I would definitely stay on guard."

"Roger that."

"So, that's all I have for now."

"Thanks, man."

"Of course. On another note, how are things going otherwise? You two getting to know each other better?" Joey asked, shifting the conversation to a more personal level. He waited with bated breath for the answer and when it came, it came all too quickly.

"Oh yeah, definitely so," replied Gage. There was a distinct tone in his voice that indicated he was happy. "She's great! More than I imagined."

"Good stuff," he said back with a bit of dissatisfaction that his idea actually worked, but he was content for him. "I knew it would be a good idea for you two."

He definitely didn't want or need to hear further details on that so changed the subject yet again. "So, did you two see any interesting things on your way there?"

"Well you aren't gonna believe this, but we had a fight with a couple of bunyip," Gage mentioned nonchalantly.

The other end went quiet for a few seconds and Gage began to think the the call might have dropped out. He checked his battery levels and though it was low, it was still adequate.

"Are you serious?" Joey's voice blasted over the speaker with the elation of a puppy getting his first toy. "Where?"

"Outside of Amarillo," Gage said bringing the phone back up to his ear. If it were possible, he thought he could feel Joey's pulse through the airwaves.

"No… fucking… way! Ha! Those things were a little far from home, eh?"

Gage laughed. "Oh, just a wee bit."

"How'd you take them down?" came the next rapid fire question.

Gage took a few minutes and recounted the entire battle in intricate and greatly exaggerated detail. Joey stayed silent the entire time and absorbed every word.

"So… you shot it in the head?" he replied with a pitch that screamed he was unimpressed. "Their brains are in their chest cavity ya know."

"I knew that," Gage rebutted.

"So… in that case why didn't you just use a fire rune to dry out their feathers? Oh, or a few incendiary rounds! That would have seriously weakened them. Hell now that I think about it, a fire rune might actually kill one outright it were big enough."

It was now Gage's turn to remain offensively silent; that is if the grumbling he was doing under his breath counted as quiet.

"Um… yeah… well, where would the fun in that be?" he replied in unflappable Gage style.

Joey snickered, fully expecting that. "Damn man, it sounds like you need me more than you let on."

"Oh more than ya know, my man."

With that one sentence Gage couldn't see that on the other end of the line, Joey's eyes had opened to their widest and most delighted point in ages.

"It's definitely… weird not having you around," Joey sputtered back.

"Same here, I ain't gonna lie," Gage replied with ease while lowering his head.

They fell quiet together, only the faint crackle of the line keeping the conversation going.

"Well, I best let you get back to it," said Joey, a bit in awe at where the conversation had shifted. "Oh! Before I go, do you need me to research anything else for you? Other than bunyip lore of course, since you have that adequately covered."

The sarcasm was dripping through the tinny speaker.

"Haha," Gage chuckled. "Actually, I may have one thing. I'm gonna let this phone charge up a bit and send you a photo of a ward that's on the door to the house. Now don't laugh, but I put the fucker there three years ago and can't for the life of me remember how to open it."

"So, you're saying I'm your saving grace yet again?" Joey inquired in jest.

"In so many words."

"Haha, I'll take that as a compliment then, sir."

"You're so good to me," Gage acknowledged. "Wouldn't be where we are today without ya, brother."

Brother. Ugh, so it's a bromance with the B. Not that it matters Joey, for goodness sake!

"Of course my man!" he replied, snapping out of his short-lived funk. "Ok, I'll keep an eye out for that photo and let you know what I find. Depending on what it is, it may take me a bit."

"No worries and thanks J. Will talk soon; Much love."

With that, Gage pressed the end call button and let out a deep breath before looking back to his collection of bedding.

He walked over and grabbed as much of it up as possible, exiting the building with the patchwork of blankets and sheets. This was going to take a couple of trips.

ADRIENNE RETURNED FROM HER walk around the property wondering what Gage had been up to. She rounded the corner back onto the porch and looked out to see the GMC transformed into quite an amazing sight. Her breath was sucked away and she was speechless as the old truck now looked like an actual canopy bed.

The big brute had moved the truck closer to one of the oaks, a low slung branch acting as a tie off point for two sheets that were wrapped snugly around, each pulled loosely to a side and secured with clamps. He had loaded the hard metal with comforters, tucking them up along the edges of the truck boxes for added cushioning. Atop that sat all the blankets and sheets, and upon those more rolled blankets for use as makeshift pillows.

Damn.

She was impressed, even more so when she felt those strong hands ride along her hips.

Adrienne turned around, smiling; she'd been doing a lot of that today.

"It's..." she began.

"Gorgeous," he finished, bringing her in for a kiss. "Now I don't know about you, but I'm beat. Wanna hop in?"

All she could manage was a half assed nod as they walked over together. Score one for the big guy.

The sunlight had all but gone by the time they slung themselves onto the covers, the orange and cranberry sky replaced with the gentle twinkle of a starscape so vast above them.

They both laid there in the stillness of the moonlight, gazing up while their thoughts wandered from pinpoint to distant pinpoint, a light breeze sweeping through the tree limbs like distant ocean waves.

"Ady," Gage whispered in her ear, "I've been meaning to ask ya what your tattoo meant."

"Oh pillow talk, eh? I was beginning to wonder if it wasn't up to par," she joked, her voice going into movie-narrator mode. "After all, it is simple in comparison to the elaborate etchings found upon THE mighty Gage Crosse."

He moved in to punch her arm in slow motion, making a soft exploding sound. "Damn right I'm mighty," he agreed proudly, "but in all seriousness, I've been meaning to ask since seeing it up close, and with all that's happened, it slipped my mind. Call it the bunyip effect."

"Well, there's not a huge or profound meaning behind it," she admitted. "I got it as a symbol of the infinite love I have for things like family, especially my mom."

"Ink that represents love is the best kind in my opinion," he replied, "and the most profound."

"I suppose so," she hesitantly agreed. "Even though she didn't like me 'marking myself up', it was the least I could do to show how much I cared." Her eyes dropped forward toward the house before she continued. "My family didn't have the easiest life, even before we were targeted by a coven, nor the biggest house. All I remember was Mom busting her ass each and every day after Dad was... gone... to keep us fed: me and my brother."

Gage moved a hand under her neck and patted her head, again feeling her soft hair through his fingers. He didn't think he could ever get tired of doing that.

"Moms tend to go out of their way and leave that effect on us," he told her softly. "I miss mine."

"And I miss mine too," she said, returning her gaze skyward; the stars looked incredible and so clear.

"So while we are on this subject," she interjected, "spill it on the rest of your ink. I'm curious."

"Who me?" he asked facetiously in a high pitched voice. "The mighty…"

"Don't do it," she warned, knowing what was coming next.

"Gage," he continued. Oh yeah, he was going to do it.

"I mean it," she reiterated.

"Crosse," he hissed, extending the last part out as if he were a snake.

She reached over to his nipple and pinched it with a hearty twist.

"Ow! Fine," he groaned, crossing his arms while using the inside of his forearm to rub the soreness out of his nipple. "Geez, ya little minx, I guess we'll start right there then. I got the arm sleeved up first as you know, but the chest piece was done around the same time I had those angel wings inked down my back in the fall of 2013."

"These two pistols represent both of my parents," he continued, pointing at the right one. "That one's for Mom and this other one's for Dad. They represent their fighting spirit as they struggled for their lives against Noctis… and lost. I had the artist put them on a bed of thorns since the pain always eats at me, but they also sit surrounded by three roses, representing the three of us, plus they were Mom's favorite as you're intimately aware of." He looked her way and threw out a wink before drawing his arms back behind his head.

"And the script?" she asked, scrolling across the words 'Death Fears Me' that were inked in black on his upper chest.

From the outside it may have appeared like her three simple words were asking about another three simple words, but the meaning in these carried great personal significance to him; a great weight.

He quickly grew silent.

"I didn't mean to-"

"Nah, it's okay," he reassured her, taking a deep breath as though he was hesitant to say anything, "just been a fair while since I've had to think about this.

"It was back in early 2014, just before meeting you and Joey. I was on the trail of a mothman that was making Kentucky its bitch. I was just passing through when I heard a story come across local radio that caught my attention: pale skin, red eyes, yada yada. I thought it was very weird that one of them was so far west, so I got really interested really fast. Knowing what we know now about the Noctis, factions, and movements it makes total sense.

"Anyway, long story short it was indeed a mothman and I managed to put it down after quite the fight outside Louisville. When all was done, I tore out of Dodge and was in a pretty bad mental state from the battle- we had locked eyes a couple of times too many. That's when I didn't notice the kid crossing the street in front of me. He was no more than ten years old I would guess, so young and innocent."

There was a long pause.

"I… I hit him going about forty-five… sent him clean out of his shoes and down the road a stretch."

Adrienne felt tears welling up in her eyes as she saw a glistening kaleidoscope forming in his.

"So," he continued cheerlessly, "I stopped the truck right away and ran over to tend to him as he laid there dying. Dying because of me."

"But it wasn't you, Gage, it was-"

"The mothman's fault?" he snipped, a hand pounding back against the makeshift pillows. "No, that fucker was dead and I was the one behind the wheel. I tried to stop the bleeding, poor kid, but it was too late. Or so I thought.

"As we sat there in the middle of the street, a hooded shape formed out of the nearby shadows and approached. It stood, well hovered as there were no feet, and just looked at us in the bright sun. Its silence was the creepiest thing. I thought it was a demon at first, but it didn't want to possess either of us and there wasn't any telltale smoke or sulfur.

"When it finally said something, I gotta say it was like all the warmth around us was sucked up into its faceless hood and I could see my own breath even though it had to be in the upper sixties that day."

"What did it say to you?" she asked, wide eyed.

"I'll never forget it," Gage said before he put on his best scary voice, which was much scarier in his mind, and went on, "I am the living death and the death of the living. I am come for the soul that is owed us this moment."

"Death?!" Adrienne gasped. "What, as in *the* Grim Reaper? Skull face, black robes and all? You're pulling my leg."

"Always the tone of surprise," he replied. "He did vaguely look like that, but was… different. All I know is that Death was there, in the flesh."

"I know, I know. I'm just… Wow, okay."

"That's not the best part," Gage said sheepishly as Adrienne grew afraid to hear what he had to say next. "As the boy was laying there, I offered my own soul up as a substitute. Now don't look at me like that; I was tired, Ady, and at quite a low point.

"Death reached out to me with his bony fingers and I closed my eyes awaiting my fate, but he stopped just short of my face, refusing to take my soul with him. He told me it was not my time and that he would also spare the boy's life for the lack of fear I showed that moment. With a wave of his hand my addled state of mind was gone and then he said that he feared me: a man that did not show fear of death but respected it. He finished by saying neither Heaven nor Hell could console me for the things coming ahead."

"Gage, I… I had no idea."

"We all keep a lil bit of ourselves hid from the world, Ady. I know you have secrets locked up inside, too. For fear of not letting people know them, for weakness, for pride, whatever. All I ask is that ya don't think less of me."

"That's definitely true," she agreed with a sigh, "and I certainly don't think any less of you. Do you know when… your time will be?"

"No, he didn't tell me. Suppose it's because we aren't meant to know ahead of time."

Silence grew between them for a good ten minutes.

"I love how meaningful all your ink is to you," she told him, breaking the silence to continue the conversation they had started. "Are the wings similarly so?"

Gage had somewhat recuperated and his eyes playfully darted from hers to the sky and back again. "Dammit I wish," he admitted softly, "but I just liked the way they looked on my back."

"At least you're honest," she said with a giggle as his hands came down over his eyes like a 'see no evil' monkey.

"The rest of 'em aren't that meaningful either, more for utility really, except maybe the one on my quad." He then pointed over to the pentacle on his left shoulder, flexing with a mind of its own as soon as attention fell on it.

"That's an easy one. It's for protection against evil," she recited as if reading out of a textbook, "and thou shalt be assured that no enchantment or being, magical or otherwise, shall hold sway over the bearer of this mark."

Gage laughed, pointing to the gash on his brow. "Either mine's broken or something must've been lost in translation, but that sucker delivers one hell of a burn to any supernaturals that touch it."

"So do the runes around it do anything or just add to the 'mighty' factor?" she asked, knowing that Futhark runes generally did imbue qualities such as luck, strength, and defense to weaponry and standard seals.

"Honestly, I added those since they looked cool around it," he confessed. "It's the entire set of runes, so I'm sure if something was working, it's probably being cancelled out by something else."

"I knew it!" she exclaimed, clapping her hands together as if she had won a bet. "I'll have to tell Joey when I see him."

Gage raised a brow again. "Say what?"

She stuck her tongue out at him and he responded by kicking the sheets off his left leg. Their fall was delayed briefly by a gust of wind, showing a clear and lingering view of the sleeping giant before settling back over him, leaving his meaty thigh displayed in the cool light.

"Just for that you're going to have to translate this last tattoo all by yourself, darlin.'"

She propped herself up and gave the leg a good once over. Futhark runes ran horizontally in several short lines spelling out some sort of spell or phrase.

The symbols were resting atop scalloped clouds shaded in the background, which flowed along the defined peaks and valleys his muscles formed. She brought a hand down to help study the runes as if they we written on a delicate scroll and the fibers involuntarily flexed under her touch.

"Now let's see," she stated confidently. "It looks like we have a Bruce Lee fan here ladies and gentlemen. Seems to say: 'Do not pray for an easy life, pray for the strength to endure a difficult one.' Am I right?"

Gage kept his mouth shut.

"Haha. Love it," she said, leaving her hand to linger there on his quad while starting to trace its way up along the deep lines.

"Well that's enough looking for you," he said in fun, pulling the covers up high. All of him was encased in a fluffy cocoon except for his beaming face, white teeth shining with a light all themselves.

Adrienne repositioned herself to stare directly into those emerald pools of his, caressing him on the chest and rubbing his tender nipple.

He unfurled an arm out from under the blankets and rested it next to hers.

"I know I can come across as a big badass," he stated, half expecting another love tap from her. "Someone that can handle themselves and loves to be alone. Reality is, that's as far from the truth as you can get. Being alone… it scares me."

In a heartbeat her hand nestled itself into his again and she looked up, unbelieving of how clear the stars managed to get out here.

"Gage," she said back, "we've journeyed together for a while now, mostly working and placing the safety of others ahead of our own feelings. It does makes it worthwhile, doing it for those you care about… those you love. But I'm glad our feelings for each other are finally getting acknowledged and we're acting on them. Life is a lonely road, but only until you find someone to travel with. My road, no our road, is a lot less lonely now."

Gage hadn't ever considered it that way, always shoving his own feelings on the back burner in the hopes of not getting them hurt.

"Well then, I can safely say that I'm not afraid," he declared.

"Goodie for me," she acknowledged, again looking at his irresistible face.

He returned the glance and laughed. "Oh really now? Just for you?"

"Yup. You are very attractive, sir," she mentioned casually.

"Damn right I'm your 'sir.' Ya better get used to calling me that," he commanded. "I think I like it more than Gage now."

She nodded. "Oh you won't have to worry about that, sir. I'll continue to stare; it's kind of involuntary at this point."

He smiled that unbelievably charming smile one more time as he lifted her hand up in front of them. "Well take a sec and look at this," he said, keeping their hands out. "See that right there? Since taking everything from me, and I mean it all, I've become the best at haunting the dreams of monsters. Now I have someone to haunt them with me. Plus, if things went to hell and ended at this moment and I never got to see anything else in this fucked up crazy world, know that I have all I need in this life right here, right now."

Her grip tightened, a single tear escaping her eye. "Yup," she said. "Everything."

As their hands fell back to the truck bed, they both drifted to sleep underneath the canopy of twinkling stars.

Gage coughed. "You forgot to say sir."

CHAPTER sixteen

A SURPRISE FROM THE PAST

ADRIENNE WAS AWAKENED BY the morning sun dancing on her eyelids as it filtered through the canopy overhead.

Apparently, she had kicked off most of the covers during the night. Gage was notorious for being a scorching furnace and as such, holding onto him for any length of time under a massive stack of blankets would have been a death sentence, or at least a good way to lose a good bit of excess weight. Speaking of that grizzly beast, she prodded the man shaped mound of cloth beside her and discovered that he was already gone. Par for the course, she took a final stretch before tossing the sheet aside to start the day.

Leaping to the ground from the tailgate, her bare feet hopped across the craggy gravel before cuddling up to the carpet-like grass. A little too much winter blew by, forcing her to tiptoe back and reach into the truck to snatch up something to cover herself with before making her way toward the house.

When she reached the picket fence, a lone figure standing out by the pasture caught her attention. Coming around the porch line and into the back yard, she could now make out that it was Gage propped up soulfully with his elbows on the metal gate.

He was looking off into the distance, mind wrapped up in a secret thought, so she found the nearest tree and huddled against it to admire the view while making sure not to disturb him. Perhaps the sheet around her had grown a bit too effective, but it was getting ridiculously hot. It had to be the sun, now peeking over the trees to the east; that was as good an excuse as any.

Calmly he shifted in her direction, the dreamy amber glow settling across every detail from his naked, arched back down to his lower, jean enclosed curves. When their eyes finally met, they didn't need to say a single word, yet spoke volumes.

In her heart, Adrienne knew at that moment it was going to be a great day; the most perfect day.

"Good morning dear," he told her, his voice having a sexually charged raspiness to it. Turning fully around, he placed the small of his back against one of the metal bars and a bead of salty sweat left the center of his chest on a journey down beneath the sweet lines of intimate denim.

"Morning to you, too, mister," she replied while gliding up to him, throwing her arms around his neck as her feet kicked back off the ground. The sheet fluttered around her like an elegant white dress as their lips met.

"Don't think I'll ever tire of that," he said when they finally pulled apart.

"Good thing," she replied, tapping a finger across the middle of his lips. "I don't plan on stopping anytime soon."

He wrapped his stalwart arms around her, drawing her to his side as they settled back on the gate together, admiring the house in its provincial glory; so warm in the morning shine.

"I managed to get the utilities back on," he murmured in her ear, slowly raising his voice to match his elevated mood, "but the house is in a kind of 'low power' mode: the lights are on, but aren't going to get very bright and the large appliances won't be working for us at all. I'm sure we can find a way to get the coffee pot working though, if a three-year-old blend tickles your fancy. Let's see, I also got the pumps fully operational and, oh, you're gonna love this: there's even hot water available through the solar heaters. Thank you, Dad!"

"Oh that's fancy," she said earnestly, thankful that there was an opportunity for a relaxing soak in the near future. Nothing beat that feeling of hot water on the skin, especially after a long stint of road travel; it seemed no matter how long a trip lasted, it always brought the same level of muckiness along for the ride.

Yet the harsh reality of all this fanciful daydreaming about steaming baths underneath dim lights hinged on them actually being able to open the door, and when they last attempted it that was still a no go.

"That sounds fantastic, but are we any closer in figuring out how to get in?" she asked pragmatically, the 'we' undoubtedly meaning 'you' in this case.

"That happens to be what I was mulling over when you came by," he answered. "I sent Joey a text last night with a photo of the ward, hoping he could help me figure it out."

"And… he was able to?" she asked with a little apprehension. Even though she said there was no rush last night, the mere mention of hot water earlier made her realize just how dirty she had become.

"Yeah, thank God. Seems I had the right idea, doing all those circus acts on the porch. As entertaining as that was, I was forgetting a key part of the deal: the passphrase. J called it an 'amalgamated ward' or something technical like that, so it needs all the different elements to be in play correctly and at the same time for it to work." He paused to toss a pious look her way, "Trust lil' ol' me to mix shit up from different cultures when I drew that out. At least the phrase isn't a long one: same number of words as triangles within the circle."

"Makes sense to me I guess. So… what is it?" she asked anxiously. "Please for the love of all that's holy tell me you have the phrase figured out."

His hands raised in defense. "No need to fret, I got this," he reassured her while gesturing back to the building. "Wanna see?"

"By all means," she said, not wasting any time stepping away to allow him to pass. Why did she have the sense he was procrastinating for time?

He pushed himself off and swaggered confidently by, promenading along the grassy field up toward the house. Adrienne once again fell in behind him, taking stock of his abundant assets and in no time they were back on the porch staring at the unblinking eye.

"Here goes nothing," he said, dramatically putting his hand on the mark while looking directly at it. Clearing his throat, he spoke three words to command the door to open, "Home sweet home."

The mandate was followed by an uncomfortable silence, punctuated with the quaint chirping of far off birds.

"Gage!" shouted Adrienne in a huff. "Seriously, come on!"

He laughed at her frustration, though the look on her face didn't reflect the same sentiment. "Okay, okay. Sorry."

"Fucker," she said modestly under her breath, arms resting squarely on her hips.

This time, with a look of intensity that could swoon the most prude person on the planet, he focused all attention on the ward. The dawning day shut itself out in a darkening vignette as he pressed his right hand firmly against the wood, its surface slippery with condensation. Closing his left eye he crouched, right eye peering on while his mouth was cracked, the three words of power hanging ready from his lips.

"Non... Omnis... Moriar..." he uttered calmly.

With each spoken word, a low rumble coursed through the doorway, its prickly heat spilling out to bubble the siding and shake the glass in its frames. A surge of air rushed at him and he tore his hand away from the now fierce stinging; the eye that had been still all this time now blinking as if alive. Suddenly it bloomed into flame, looking around wildly while the hand symbol spread its fingers wide, catching fire too like some burning starfish. When the fingers reached their widest, near painful point, the triangles around them spun erratically before shooting off in dazzling jets of orange that outlined every window and door, surging three times before fizzling out with a subtle *crack*.

The door, at last, swung open to beckon them inside.

Gage stared at the open portal, partly ready to storm inside, yet also wishing he was still trying to figure out how to get it open. Yet, as usual they had succeeded and there was no point in delaying the inevitable any longer.

"Time's come to find out if y'all were right about this being a trap," he said to Adrienne while stepping over the threshold. Care seemed to fall away the moment his foot came down on the other side, followed by the other.

Adrienne was soon inside herself, entering the foyer and closing the door behind her. It clicked softly, securely shut again after all the effort put forth to open it.

Gage had stopped a few paces ahead, mulling over a collection of photos that were neatly arranged across two wooden tables, one on each side of the archway leading into the large living room. The drywall behind them shot up a dozen feet, coated with once lively shades of green and tan. Equally vibrant paintings of country landscapes were distributed around the walls, their colors neutralized under a thin layer of dust; the chalky haze covered pretty much everything in sight, leaving a dullness that betrayed the place's former glory.

From what she could make out, Gage was looking at a family photo. She looked at his smiling mom and dad dressed in their Sunday best. Shoved awkwardly between them was a scrawny kid, tall and dressed in an oversized blue dress shirt with black slacks. No more than a buck twenty, his spotty face smiled proudly through a thick set of braces. When compared with the present day version of Gage, the difference was quite staggering.

"No bad omens yet," he said while setting the frame down, tiny motes kicking up after the soft thump of silver on the tabletop, "though I guess my symbol back on the door there didn't conjure up a feather duster for its lil' hand; how the hell did all this dust get in here?"

"Wards only affect living things," Adrienne answered with a smug look as he stepped through the curls of visible air into the living room, "well soul bound things anyway. Duh."

Gage's attention was, noting the fireplace along the back wall still had a chunks of scorched log resting in the hearth and adjacent to it, running along each side, large windows loomed in the shade. On the left hand side, a set of French doors near the end of the breakfast table lead out to another large patio, the once green plants visible through gaps in the curtains having long since withered to brown.

Adrienne continued around the overstuffed sofas into the modern kitchen that was attached to the breakfast area, while Gage took up on one of the largest of the soft seats. His hefty boots made two clunky *thumps* when he slung them up on the coffee table.

"Damn, manners?" Adrienne said to him with disdain, opening up some of the curtains and twisting the blinds to let a little more light in.

"You seen the state of this place?" Gage replied with equivalent scorn.

Good thing she wasn't close to him after that reply, as she might have popped him with a fist, though that might just be the reaction he was looking for. It was hard to gauge if it was all in his master plan or just luck in how the proverbial cards fell, but he had her confused once again, thinking at length about him while he was just sitting there on the sofa, almost innocently, thinking about God knows what.

Attempting to push him out of her mind, she looked around the kitchen; it had a distinctively modern flair with its stainless steel appliances, black granite countertops flecked with gold, and milky glazed cabinetry. However, looking out from various nooks and crannies were motherly trinkets and plaques that tied the space back to its country roots.

A little black sign hung crooked over the backsplash behind the stovetop, decorated with yellow egg shapes and letters that read 'Wicked chickens lay deviled eggs'. With a chuckle and a bit of OCD, Adrienne stepped over to straighten it, passing through an area of intense cold.

With each breath, clouds of vapor formed; it had to be at least twenty degrees colder than the surrounding area and the feeling icicles could form out of the moisture collected in her now sniffling nose was a very real possibility. She leaped back a few feet in surprise and the temperature began to rise again, her hair standing on end.

"Gage..." she called out collectedly. "You might want to come take a look at this, and snatch the EMF reader if you can."

"I was going to ask you the same thing," his voice came from the living room; it was calm and collected as well, though a pronounced vein of nervousness ran through the words.

She took a few steps to her left and craned her neck around the wall, catching a solid glimpse of a rooster shaped cookie jar as it rose off the counter in front of her and floated merrily into the middle of the living room. The lid separated off of the base and both pieces stopped in front of Gage, still resting with his feet up, taunting him for a moment in the air between his legs.

Then, as if someone decided to turn gravity back on, they dropped one at a time to the floor. The base fell with a heavy and expected *thud* while the lid, a few inches further from him, turned on its side and gunned into the floor with a hollow *clank* that echoed through the room.

Gage lifted his feet off the table and took to his knees, puzzled by the different sounds he had just heard, while Adrienne bolted to the truck for some of their gear.

He took a knuckle and rapped it along the hardwoods, searching the space between the sofa and coffee table. The sound went from deep and solid to soft and vacant. Pulling back the edge of the vintage rug, his latest suspicions were confirmed; there beneath the Persian threads was a trap door. A tiny ward had been placed on the edge, damaged by the lid when it dropped.

"Would ya look at that," Gage whispered to himself, running a fingernail along the tiny dent in the broken symbol, "a concealment ward. Powerful one. Where'd you come from, ya little devil?"

Adrienne returned a short time later with a leather satchel, overflowing with ghost hunting paraphernalia. She reached in and brought out an EMF meter, one of their fancier ones that had the Mosely touch for added signal detection. Holding it close to the cookie jar halves, the rows of LEDs flickered green.

"The green confirms it; we have an Earthbound spirit," she said over the meter's faint, Geiger-like clicks.

"That and seein' it happen with our own peepers," Gage responded acrimoniously as he pointed two fingers in the shape of a V at his eyes.

She withdrew the device smugly and returned it to the bag. The lights calmed, unlike her mood, then diminished. "Give me vamps all night long," she stated, "I hate ghosts."

"So whatcha think this door in the floor is?" he asked poetically. "I've no doubt our lil' poltergeist and whatever's down there are related."

"So… let me get this straight: you've no idea what this is or what is down there?"

Gage nodded indifferently and Adrienne looked as though she was seriously contemplating banging her head as hard as she could, right there on the spot he was pointing to.

"If I *did* know, I wouldn't have asked ya," he stated. "Honestly, had no idea a door was sittin' under the living room coffee table this whole time. Heck, I used to lay under there on my stomach and play with Hot Wheels for hours."

"How is that possible?" she wondered out loud.

"All boys played with cars at some point, Ady."

She didn't reply, instead just staring blankly; he didn't like this new look of hers and was missing the eye roll.

"Well… you didn't know my dad," Gage said matter-of-factly. "He was loving and great, but also had a shit ton of secrets. I always thought there was more to him than just a simple nine to five at an accounting firm. Apparently, one of those secrets included the ability to place a concealment charm on a door to hide who knows how many more down there. We only found it thanks to the not-so-random face plant ol' Foghorn Leghorn did; beak broke clean through the ward."

"Oh wow!" she said, her mood improving mood. Wards and weapons were nearly as exciting to her as his own tools- well, one in particular.

"And before you ask me," he said right as her mouth began to spin up for another salvo of questions, "no, I don't know who this ghost could possibly be."

She sunk back onto her knees. "Your dad maybe?"

Gage chuckled a few times before continuing, "Yeah, I thought it might be one of the folks at first, which made me really uncomfortable. Surprisingly uncomfortable, now that I think about it. I don't think I could handle too much of that right now, especially Mom and her finger waving over my tattoos. But seriously, I can't think of anything off the top of my head that would bind either of them here and though Dad might have some kind of unfinished business with his secrets, I don't think any of it would've warranted going all Patrick Swayze, though I could be wrong. Barring them, that leaves us one answer: an unknown spirit tied to an item somewhere in the house, more than likely something that's tucked away down below."

Adrienne dug into the bag and grabbed up the meter again, waving it over the door. With a sudden jolt it sprang back to life, her eyes like saucers taking in the green lights flashing wildly, shifting from the verdant hues of before to deep reds.

"Gage, there's a lot of energy down there," Adrienne reported, "I mean a ton of it. I've never seen the meter go red before; that can't be good."

The clicks, which had been distant pings before, rapidly increased in frequency to become a constant, unnerving buzz. The mere sound of it made Adrienne feel dizzy, her focus wavering as the secondary flag-arms shot up on either side.

"That's a new one, too," she said, both impressed and anxious. She craved the days of having a single comforting emotion at a time, but those were long gone. Looking down to the digital display, she saw that it was maxed out with all numbers at nine; the LCDs fluttering just as nervously as her heart was.

"We have got to open this bad boy up!" Gage exclaimed, his face and body fidgeting with excitement, in direct contrast to her unease. Massive numbers always seemed to get big men excited: weights lifted in the gym, the horsepower of a car engine, or how pegged out a supernatural field meter was. All of that and factors well beyond her female understanding were cause for instant boners.

So it was the two positioned themselves, ready to lift off the coffee table. Without warning, one of the photos in the entryway slung itself from the table with a loud crash.

They both stood straight up in unison, attention drawn toward the front door. Soon the rest of the pictures followed like a herd of lemmings, cascading onto the floor in a raucous metal and glass waterfall.

All around them, the paintings on the walls began to sway in their frames, the crooked pinnacle of an obsessive-compulsive's worst nightmare, while the lights flared up brightly with supernatural energy.

Suddenly, a chilling scream burst its way through the room, cracking the mirror over the fireplace.

"Ah shit whoever this is, they're comin'," Gage said hurriedly, "Is there any salt in that bag of yours?"

Adrienne rifled through the contents, pulling out a long plastic container of iron filings. There was a crinkled sticky note taped onto the side; it was from Joey and read, 'Sorry, Hometown Grocery was closed so borrowed the salt for steaks. Promise to replace in the morning.'

"No, seems not!" Adrienne said crassly, shoving the note up in Gage's face. "But we have iron powder."

"If we didn't need that kid so much, I swear I'd kill him," he replied after reading the note for himself. His eyes rolled, which was definitely a rare sight. Fighting to suppress his annoyance, he turned and made a mad dash for the kitchen.

As he ran, the pots, pans, glasses and silverware seemed to forget the laws of physics, flying randomly around the room in a culinary cyclone. He dodged his way through with barely a bump until a large copper pot struck pay-dirt on his knee. He stumbled to the floor, but thankfully exactly where he needed to be.

In front of him was the cabinet his mom kept all the spices in. Muttering a little prayer, he reached out to open it, a knife nicking across his forearm as he pulled. His prayer was answered; there inside was a plain blue box of pure sea salt.

"That'll do lil' rain girl," he said, tearing it open and dumping the chunky white crystals into the container of iron, shaking vigorously.

Limping, he made his way back to Adrienne while reciting a short Latin spell over the container. Now blessed, he tossed the mix over to her and walked over to the fireplace, picking up an iron poker to defend himself.

Adrienne proceeded to pour out the salt and iron on the floor around them, but the circle she needed to make was too large and the canister was emptied early. There wasn't enough material to close the gap.

"Shit, why can't this ever be easy?" she complained as she bent over and used her hands to spread out the particles dangerously thin. By the end of her efforts, she was successful and the gap was gone.

With the protective circle finished, she leapt back up and stepped cautiously over the line to join Gage in the center.

The wails, tortured and malevolent, continued to rise.

The duo tried to prepare themselves for an imminent attack, looking around to anticipate where their unseen adversary would materialize. They had no idea where the strike would come from. It drove Adrienne crazy.

The screams had grown deafening, stabbing their ears with agonizing precision and bringing them to the brink of bleeding. Gage dropped the rod on the floor and raised his hands to block out what he could of the noise; Adrienne soon followed suit, nearly blacking out from the buildup of pressure.

The strike came sooner than expected and from all around. There was a brilliant flash and everything became white. A loud ringing pounded their temples and continued to echo between their already sore ears for a few more minutes.

Amidst the bleached haze, Gage's sight was slowly returning to normal. He squinted at the random blobs moving in front of him, trying to make out the shifting and undulating patterns. He couldn't, though one area remained steadily bright, possibly growing brighter. He shielded his eyes with an arm while frantically rubbing his eyes with the other.

He looked again.

Oh my God. This has to be a dream.

There, standing before him, clad wholly in billowing robes of rosy light, was a person he had never expected to see again. His mouth agape, the single word he was trying to say took a lifetime to pass over his chapped lips.

"Mom?"

CHAPTER
seventeen

MR. SHERIDAN'S BAD DAY

I T WAS A BUSY AND BRISK morning in New York City as the clock struck nine, traffic reaching its peak while the population took out their aggressions through incessant honking and shouting.

An athletic man, dressed in vintage tweed and a matching hat, rushed along Broadway, dodging oncoming pedestrians. The smells wafting off the food carts teased his senses when he passed by, breakfast having been skipped that morning due to a late alarm.

As luck would have it, he had timed his journey perfectly, catching nearly all of the crossings as they changed to red and being forced to wait. He was left to fidget with his many ear piercings mercilessly to pass the time.

Dashing a few more blocks – traffic laws be damned – he finally made it to 50th. Rounding the corner, he nearly took out an old woman and though he narrowly missed, those colorfully choice words of hers didn't miss his ears.

Letting out a little laugh at the notion that someone's grandma would be swearing that much, he came upon a large roll up door outside one of the theaters. To the left, a simple pedestrian entrance led into a car park, set behind the bars of a heavy but worn security door. It was shut tight and even had a rusty padlock on the hasp, just in case the notion of keeping out evaded anyone passing by.

Speaking of which, he thought to get inside before anyone noticed him loitering. He had no desire to enter the parking lot itself; in fact Marcus Sheridan hadn't owned a car since the middle of 1995. However, he did want to go where the massive gray door would take him.

"This is Marcus Sheridan, Journeyman XI," he spoke commandingly.

As any normal person would expect, no reply came from the inanimate steel, but Marcus was in the Order and the lack of response took him by surprise. He coughed and repeated the statement, after which there was still silence.

Getting frustrated, he kicked at the lowest part of the door and the whole thing shook noisily. Suddenly a response came from the clatter, as if the door itself were speaking.

"Now, Mr. Sheridan," said an altogether hollow voice, "is that any way to treat Order property?"

"Well," he snapped back quickly, "if the guardsman's response was faster, I wouldn't have to resort to damaging doorways to get attention."

The voice fell silent once more.

He furiously knocked against the gray slats, the ink on his hand jostling into a blur. "Um… hello?"

"Password," it responded, falling quiet again as it waited for his answer.

"Wha… What do you mean password? My credentials have always been sufficient!" he said indignantly.

"New requirements have gone into effect as of this very morning, sir, due to current events."

"The Noctis?" he asked.

"I am not at liberty to say," it replied indifferently. "Password, please."

Marcus scratched at thick scruff, light brown and peppered with gray. "So, how am I supposed to know the password if we were never issued one to begin with?"

The Order's methods could at times be incredibly frustrating and that morning was no exception. Marcus began to pace in annoyance and would surely be noticed by people if he didn't get inside soon.

He paused, pretending to rest against the wall while sorting through the vast Rolodex of facts stored up in his head. As Lead Analyst, there weren't many tidbits of information that got by him. Now he knew there wouldn't be many chances at a guess if a password protocol was in effect and likely, there would be only one if the Noctis did indeed have anything to do with this. He definitely wanted to be right, not only because he would be shut out of his place of work, but there was also no telling what the penalty would be for an incorrect answer.

After a few minutes spent mulling it over, he settled on a line from the Order's creed which was recited at induction ceremonies. It was in reference to the golden mean- a position of balance between two extremes like good and evil. It was certainly a risk to choose it, plucked quite at random, but it was not any more a liability than the myriad of other possible choices. He supposed since it was part of a short phrase that all Journeymen would know by heart, it made the most sense.

"*Aurea mediocritas,*" he said with both eyes closed, half expecting to be vaporized right there on the spot. When he didn't feel a thing, he peeked an eye open and found everything still in one piece.

Or perhaps not...

The back of his neck suddenly got very hot, spreading over his entire body like a fever; the effects of an invisibility field were dousing him.

The metal in front of him curled its way forward as the corrugated door split, a gigantic shape stepping out toward him. However, instead of squashing him like a bug, it stepped off to the side to reveal a shimmering portal in the vacant spot where it had stood. Beyond that was a cavernous hall.

"You are correct," said the guardsman, extending its arm invitingly. "Welcome back to the New York offices of the Grand Order of Journeymen, Mr. Sheridan."

"Much obliged," he said politely, swiftly stepping into the portal.

A tightness formed in the lower part of his back, dragging him forward at great speed as if a rope were tied around his waist. He managed to avert the oncoming blackout this time, which is more than could be said for himself ten years ago.

He had been whisked away from 50th to the entrance hall, located about a mile away in the upper levels of a skyscraper on Central Park West. Stumbling slightly when he arrived on the shiny marble floor, its glossy coating reflected back a disheveled version of himself.

Immediately straightening out his hat and other accessories, Marcus looked around the ornate and equally lustrous chamber. It was three stories tall and lined on either side with marble encased balconies capping off long corridors of identical white doors. There were expansive windows ahead of him, offering a grand view of the autumn colors and a massive dome that swept overhead. It was painted with a Renaissance mural of angels and demons locked in an eternal battle in the sky, while the modern symbol of the Order- a hammer, howdah pistol, and sword overlaid to form a triangle- was emblazoned on a large stone tile in the very center.

To his surprise, there were very few Journeymen walking about this morning; it was quite odd considering the area was normally packed with people, all sorts of creatures, and a lot of office gossip.

A sole gargoyle walked in front of the windows ahead of him, his naked and stoney skin catching flecks of the morning light. One level below, a man in similar attire to his own walked across the expansive floor, a beautiful griffin of brown and white with an owl-like face following close beside. Before heading to his own office, Marcus propped himself up on the iron balustrade and continued to watch as the man mounted the creature, flying off from a platform out and across the park, disappearing into the sky. Such beauty and grace; this was why he loved the Order.

A short time later he reached his office and opened the door to his windowless corner of the corporate world. He was greeted by stacks of paperwork sitting in his inbox, strewn across his desk, and even waiting for him in his seat.

Trudging over to the desk, he moved the stack of papers off of the ergonomic chair and placed them onto the already heaping mound on the desktop. He sat down with a look of shock; never had this many reports appeared overnight.

There was no other place to start than the top, so he began to plod through the huge reams. What jumped out almost immediately was the sheer number of reports from outposts reporting increased demon activity and the sightings of all manner of dark creatures, an abundance of them coming from the West Coast and along the northern border. All of this was quite strange, as most activity in the States was relegated to the northeast and south, with the odd occurrence happening in the Midwest or four corner states and of course the proliferation of vampire covens in Texas. Most of those had been taken care of by Gage Crosse.

Ah Gage, now there was a Journeyman living the life, not stuck between four walls analyzing statistics and reports as the highlight of his day. How the Order had changed since the Incursion. Marcus secretly longed for life on the road, despite the hazards and unpredictability of it.

He spotted some messages mixed in among the papers from longtime colleague Om Citta. The topic was all about ancient artifacts and despite his kindled interest, Marcus would have to review those later when there was more time. The priority now was figuring out what the Noctis were up to.

From what he could gather over the next two hours of painstaking review, the demons had suddenly attacked and possibly even infiltrated some of their most distant outposts in Oregon and along the Great Lakes, all of which had ties of some manner to the location and operation of the stateside vaults. Housed within those were some of the most dangerous items in the world. The demons were likely planning to raid them for powerful tools to help them gain strength and for other nefarious purposes, but Marcus couldn't shake the feeling that there was more to this, much more that laid hidden between the lines. Regardless, he didn't like it and it made him incredibly uneasy.

He swiveled in his chair to face an elegant rotary phone tucked away at the corner of his desk, its twisted cord poking out from underneath the piled up paperwork.

"Edith," he said after lifting the golden handset and dialing seven. "I need to schedule a meeting with the Council."

"Yes, Mr. Sheridan, of course. When are you looking to do so? Their current calendar of events takes them to next Thurs-"

"I need to see them today," he interrupted, the seriousness in his voice could not be denied. "I fear we do not have much time."

There was no choice in his mind, a Grand Assembly would need to be called.

CHAPTER eighteen

THE CURSED HIGHWAY

B ENNETT PEAK WAS A monolith that stood alone amongst the rest of the flatlands of New Mexico, along the cursed stretch of road formerly known as the Devil's Highway. Although the humans renamed that stretch to the boring US Route 491, it was still known by its old name to many.

Its isolated location and natural rock formations provided the perfect cover for the Noctis and their operations, although due to the area's public reputation and ties to the supernatural, they kept their numbers small to lessen the risk of detection. Thus far they were able to remain hidden from the Journeymen, while any odd, unsuspecting hikers would become a part of their ranks, or worse.

The sun had moved into position at high noon, uncaring for what went on underneath as it dumped copious amounts of heat onto the landscape. A sudden flash of lightning burst from unseen clouds, heralding the arrival of Keli at the secret base.

Immediately, she set to walking up to the tallest point, looking out at the drab landscape around her as a hot breeze caught her hair. The expanse stretched for miles in all directions and here she was, now able to breathe and to think – her thoughts free like the stirring sands below

She found beauty in the utter desolation and this was why she loved the Noctis.

"Your Grace," came a gritty voice from behind. It was the demon Ronove, primary watcher of the peak. "Welcome. We have just received updates on our alliances per your request; would you care for an update?"

His skin was brown and parched like the grasses below them and he bore a rickety staff in his wizened hands. Pleats of dull fabric wrapped loosely around his frail body, rippling in the ongoing breeze.

She took a moment for a last look to the horizon before turning to him, her blue eyes meeting his sunken, colorless ones. There was an emptiness there that, unlike the desert, made her feel barren and somber.

"Yes, of course," she said, withdrawing her gaze and stepping past him down the steps.

He followed closely behind her, stopping when faint, anguished chirping reached his ears. He paused, looking for the source of it, and soon found an ailing sparrow tucked in amongst the folds of stone. Its wing had been broken and was twisted back on itself. Its feathers ruffled and sickly. Ants were crawling over its body, biting and eating as it squirmed in the dirt.

"Poor, decrepit soul," Ronove said calmly. He placed his weight onto the staff and slowly dropped down to one knee. Extending a hand, it hovered inches away from the suffering creature and then, with a subtle *pop*, it was dead.

A faint whorl of light rose up from its body and into his arthritic fingers, becoming a strand of his robes when he stood back up.

He carried on down the steps to meet up with Keli in the caverns, soon reaching the base of the winding stairs where she stood waiting for him.

"Delayed?" she asked pointedly.

"Only slightly," he replied peacefully. "Helping a suffering soul be free."

She had stopped underneath a single pillar of light that streamed down from the outside. Behind her, a great door hung from a towering frame and across its ebony surface of glass were wicked carvings of heinous things unlike the world had ever seen. From the other side, something knocked, forever waiting to be answered.

They both ignored the base desire to open the door, turning away to walk deeper into the grotto. Soon they reached a branching corridor with paths heading off to the left, right and center. Ronove headed down the central one and into a small chamber. Stone shelves were carved directly into the walls. Upon them were stoppered flasks and bottles of various colored liquid and in the middle, a stony basin rose from the ground. Its inner surface was smooth as glass.

He walked over to a large round flask of black fluid and unstoppered it, pouring half the container into the basin. It was thick like tar and bubbled once it settled.

"Your hand," he said, extending his own above the boiling fluid.

Keli followed suit and his hand doubled backwards to seize it. Producing a dagger from beneath his robes, he swiftly cut a gash across her open palm. The blood pooled as she attempted to withdraw, but he kept her firmly in place. It overflowed into the bowl and when the deep crimson hit black, the liquid went clear, swirling like a drain to show them brief glimpses from far off demonic settlements around the world.

Keli proudly observed the forests of Tillamook as the Bigfoot there walked openly amongst her agents —many had assembled for such a rare creature. Their towering frames and dark hair blended seamlessly amongst the surrounding foliage.

The scene whirled to Kenora, Canada where a grizzly sight met their eyes. Emaciated Wendigo were feasting upon still living flesh and Keli did not turn away. Their long tongues lapped up fresh blood and she couldn't help but applaud herself for bringing at least a few of these terrifying beasts to their aide.

The dank cave then spun away, replaced by rapidly shifting images of megalithic ruins, ancient statues, deep mines, and high volcanoes. All were visually striking yet forsaken, as if they sat poised for greatness.

Suddenly the liquid raged and the destitute lands dissolved into an assembly of non-aligned supernatural creatures, gathering under the dappled light of an old barn. At the front of the group, the head vampires of three covens paced.

"Shifting the purpose of the Sight is a dangerous thing, Your Grace," Ronove chastised. "Do it too often and our eyes will be detected."

"I know," she said, "but we have to know what our adversaries are up to. Where is this place?"

Ronove fell quiet, allowing the magic to work its way into his mind. "Durango," he answered.

"Ah, so they're close then?" she replied.

He nodded.

Rippling once more, she tried to direct the Sight into the Journeymen outposts, but they were blocked from entering by powerful warding. The fluid surged back, spilling over onto the floor; only a thin sliver remained along the bottom of the basin.

She finally thought of Gage and his homestead appeared, quite distant in the shallow pool.

"The Crosse home," Ronove confirmed. "We cannot yet penetrate any closer than this, but my agents have corroborated that he is there."

A devilish smile slithered across her face. This was just the news she was waiting for.

"All we need to do now is wait," she said eagerly.

"Most excellent Your Grace," Ronove concurred as a lesser came into the room. He approached him, whispering into Ronove's ear before stepping back a few paces.

"It seems that your quarters are now ready as well," he informed her. "I can take you there now if-"

A sudden *boom* rattled the chamber, knocking Ronove to the ground. Keli struggled to maintain balance as Agares' voice echoed throughout the room.

"Keli, my apologies for interrupting you but there is a... situation here that requires your immediate attention."

"Agares, we need to limit this form of communication! Especially to here!

Can you not see to these matters yourself?" she asked sharply, questioning if he could do anything but grovel. "I have only just arrived and-"

"It's Dajjal," he cut in, not wanting to waste time mincing words.

Ronove watched Keli vanish in an instant as he rose to his feet, leaving them both alone among the dark rock and stone.

Agares was pacing amongst the dead plants when Keli manifested outside the church.

"Where is he?" she asked hastily.

He stepped out of the blood puddle and quickly led her inside, still barefoot..

They didn't have to wait long. The doors had barely closed when she was addressed.

"Ah you are finally here," a deep voice rumbled, knocking loose rotten scraps from the timbers above.

"I'd keep you waiting for all eternity if I could," she answered. "What do you want, filth?"

A giant firestorm erupted in the middle of the church, setting the dark altar alight. It took the shape of a horned skull as she screened her face from the searing heat of the flames.

"Do not continue to toy with me, little girl," he said with utter malice. "How such a lesser demon, a satyr no less, ever managed to crawl its way out of Hell and even possess a mortal escapes me. Yet, I shall be sure to get those answers. I am the bringer of pain and death, born to make you suffer."

Keli approached the fires, now swirling in a circle above the altar. What little glass remained in the windows began to melt and flow down the walls as if some enormous candle were weeping.

"I happen to be full of surprises, about as much as you are overblown with hot air, Dajjal," she replied spitefully. "I intend to keep those secrets to myself as well. Looking at this situation, I see that you are still down there,

172 | GOLDEN CZERMAK

roasting away in the pits while I'm up here actually getting crap done with our ever growing legions."

"Forever the peddler of great words and little deeds. I agree that shit is all you have managed to accomplish," he said with a coldness that could douse any normal fire, yet the hellfire continued to roar.

"You dare speak to me like that? I will show you what I am capable of..." she began.

"No, you unremarkable ass," he said, cutting her off and making her feel insignificantly small in one fell swoop. "Let me show you."

A flash of hot silver flew out of the breach with a roar, the spinning razor finding its way across Agares' neck before gliding back through the portal like a boomerang.

His eyes flashed, widened by an incredible pain. He then crumpled to the floor without a word. There was no blood from the cauterized wound, only death.

"That is but a small taste of my power and it is growing. I will be there soon, Keli," he warned, "and you are incapable of stopping me. There is nobody there who can."

A loud crack of thunder shook the entire place and a great gust of wind arose, extinguishing the flames. All went dark, along with part of Keli's confidence.

Hesitantly, she departed back to the Devil's Highway, leaving Agares' body alone in the middle of her once sacred sanctuary.

CHAPTER
nineteen

A FATEFUL REUNION

G AGE CONTINUED TO GAWK in disbelief at the ghostly woman who was standing, well in fact floating, in front of him.

"Mom?" he asked, unable to fully comprehend what he was seeing. It definitely looked like her, but she had youth upon her face. He looked over to Adrienne. "I can't…"

"Gage," interrupted Adrienne. "Is that?"

"Yes, it is I," his mother interrupted mockingly, whilst waving her arms about in a ghostly fashion. "You know, either of you could direct your questions this way. It took me years to work up enough energy to manifest."

She floated around the two of them, their mouths still agape. "Gage for goodness sake, you're gonna catch a bunch of flies if you leave it open like that. Now, where was I? Oh yes; manifesting alone takes an incredible amount of power, but then to remotely call a phone by way of the EM spectrum? Outlandish! Yet, I managed to do it and there you stand with your mouths open as if you've never even seen a ghost before. I know better than that, or shall I say 'boo' to make you feel more at ease?" She shook her head and looked directly at her son. "And Gage, honey, upgrade your phone. There's all sorts of wrong going on in there."

Adrienne just stood there, staring straight at and through her. She finally closed her lips after the trio stood awkwardly in the middle of the living room for a few more minutes. It was hardly the picture perfect family reunion, but Adrienne finally moved, stepping out from the salt circle while using her shoe to break the solid line.

"My apologies, Mrs. Crosse," she said. "I… I meant no direct offense when I said I didn't like ghosts earlier. My name is Adrienne Elkins and it's a pleasure to meet you. I'm a Journeyman based out of Houston, Texas. I came here with Gage to… wait," she paused, noticing Gage's mother was taking all this information in without so much as a blink, "do you even know what a Journeyman is?"

She smiled. "Oh I'm *all too familiar* with them, yes, and no offense. I'd hate ghosts too if all I encountered were the tormented spirits that you both do so often."

"How is that possible?" asked Gage as he trudged out of the circle at last, pausing to take in his mother's face up close. He reached out to rub her cheek but his fingers fell straight through as if nothing were there. Her feel was notably warmer than the other ghosts he had encountered, but still wet. It was an odd feeling that was, to date, unique to spirits.

"Oh Gage, what on God's green Earth have you done to yourself?" she asked as her eyes rolled their way up his tattoo sleeve. "You look like a-"

"Thug?" he finished for her, looking over to Adrienne who was already giggling. "I told you she would say that." He glanced back over to his mom mischievously. "You know, I have a *lot* more of them too," he teased, raising his eyebrow.

She raised hers in return, indicating who he learned that expression from. "Is that so? Well, good thing you don't have a brother then, since he would immediately graduate to my favorite right now."

Adrienne couldn't help herself and laughed loudly before throwing a hand up to her mouth. She peeked over Gage's way and found that his still furrowed brow didn't look all too happy now.

His mom drifted over to the fireplace, looking at its cold hearth. It reminded her of how she had felt the past three years. "I am joking of course," she said softly, turning back to look at her son. "It is so good to see you again my boy, I can't even express it. And dear, it is a pleasure to meet you too; Adrienne, was it?"

"Yes ma'am, and the pleasure is all mine," she said as she took to lighting the fireplace with a lighter out of the satchel.

"My name is Madeline Crosse," she said, formally introducing herself. "The big lug you've brought along as your traveling partner is, as you know, my stubborn son… is he stubborn with you too?"

Adrienne was reluctant to nod, but turned away from Gage and did so meekly.

Madeline laughed. "Not surprised. Somehow, despite Charles' best efforts, he still ended up in the employ of the Journeymen." She saw a puzzled look settle on Adrienne's face as Gage slumped himself onto the sofa, returning his feet to the coffee table.

"Manners," she said.

Gage shrugged. "Demons and shit tend to pull out your manners and yank ya into the life whether or not ya want it, Mom. So, Dad was a Journeyman?" Gage prodded. "I gotta say, I had no clue."

"Yes he was," she said timidly, as if admitting a lie.

Gage bowed his head, "So where is he? I gather from your solo appearance that he's not here with you."

"No, he isn't," she replied, looking back to the now sputtering hearth, the fire quite pitiful in size. "Sadly, I have no idea where he is. Part of me hoped that he would be here to help explain things, possibly even aid you in a vastly superior capacity than I could, but when I first managed to appear he was nowhere to be found. I was alone and scared, unsure if he was utterly destroyed, sent to Heaven or Hell, or even in the astral plane. For a long time I was unsure I could even contact you. Thank God I did."

"Well, I'm glad you're here, Mom," Gage said with relief riding heartache.

"I'm so sorry to hear that," Adrienne said, still a bit lost on the conversation.

"So, Charles Crosse was part of the Journeymen? I have to admit I've never heard of that name before."

"Oh, you wouldn't have. Charles didn't use his real name when he was in the Order, as if a simple name change could protect us from all the things that came our way. He went by the name Landon Merryforth. God awful, isn't it?"

Adrienne was certainly aware of that name. "Maniacal Merryforth?" she asked with the enthusiasm of a elementary school child. Realizing what she said, she looked apologetically at Madeline. "No offense."

"None taken my dear, yet we are talking about one and the same," she replied. "Here, take a seat."

The three of them sat in the living room, Gage and Adrienne taking up the sofa while his mother hovered over the armchair.

"Loopy Landon, Maniacal Merryforth- these and many other nicknames were bestowed on your father after his odd and disturbing behavior came to light. He had taken a liking to – no quite an obsession for – collecting rare and powerful artifacts, along with other paranormal things. How he came to collect them is unknown to me, but I would not be surprised if there was criminal activity involved with some, if not most, of the acquisitions. Only a handful were gifts and so as you can expect, this made us a target for many different groups, none more foul and dangerous than the Noctis.

"But, he wasn't always so crazy or so completely driven, at least not with trinkets and treasure. He used to be madly in love… with me. Then when you came into the world, the both of us. Let's see, he joined the Journeyman back in 1979 if I remember correctly. Yes, yes, it was two years after we first met. I had no idea supernatural things even existed before I met him, apart from stories and fairy tales. But he showed me things I could never imagine. Great and terrible things. He and I both believed that it was possible to live a happy, virtually normal life while he was in the Order and for six years we did. Everything was remarkable, almost magical, the best day being July 27, 1985 – the day you were born."

"I do remember having a great childhood here," Gage said, reminiscing.

"Indeed all our time in those days was wonderful," she continued. "This is home and it will always be. However, when you eventually left to live your own life, it was as if your father needed something to pour that extra time and attention into. We had both aged, and I'm not going to say the love I had for him went away. But that said, it was certainly diminished and so it didn't fulfill him as it once had. So, Charles became consumed again by the unknown and the supernatural, and we all began to suffer for it."

A childhood memory ran into Gage's head at that moment – visions of a ruined holiday. "Was this around the same time we all had that huge blow up at Thanksgiving and ended up missing Christmas together for the first time ever?"

She nodded. "Indeed. From then on, we decided it best to try and frame our troubles as 'traditional' marital issues, versus the whole otherworldly thing- it was just far easier to accept all around. He had realized, perhaps too late, that what he had become was a shell of his former self and he didn't want you to have any part of it for fear of the same thing happening to you. But sometimes even the best of intentions are in no way good enough to prepare you for what is to come. Once your father obtained the amulet and chain after his travels to the Middle East, the biggest target imaginable was painted on us."

"Amulet and chain?" asked Adrienne.

"Two artifacts of immense power, relics from a more ancient time. Charles had extensive notes on them. He ended up delving too deep in a world he understood very little of, despite his many years as a Journeyman. It's amazing how much we know pales in comparison to the magnitude of what we don't."

Gage took a moment to stand up and stretch, shifting his neck from one side to another before cracking his knuckles. "So, this lil' trinket and collar?" he asked. "Where are they now? Tucked away in some Order vault I imagine. I hear that's where they put the most dangerous and powerful items." He shot a look over to Adrienne. "See, I do listen sometimes."

Madeline continued, her voice growing antsy. "Well, they are locked away…"

Gage was curious about that response, so pressed her. "Okay, in which vault?"

His mother's eyes drifted down to the rug beneath their feet.

CHAPTER
Twenty
THE AMULET AND CHAIN

"You have got to be joking!" Gage blurted out as he dropped himself back onto the sofa.

"I wish I was," Madeline confirmed. "Ultimately, all of your father's collection was stored in the cellar. It's sealed with all sorts of magical protections. No supernatural creatures are able to get down there through the door or burrow into the cellar from the outside. It is essentially a lock box as powerful and secure as any of the Order's vaults."

Adrienne was amazed at what she was hearing, having no idea such a thing was even possible. She was intrigued by both the level of skill needed to pull something like that off, but also the hubris of a man who could conceive something like it.

"So all of that… is still down there?" she asked.

"Yes," Madeline answered. "As time passed, Charles suspected the Noctis would come looking for blood. Toward the end of our time he removed all the barriers around the property and focused entirely on sealing the cellar, even making sure the only way to open the door again was by one of us after death. I suppose that's why I was still tied here and able to come back as a ghost. Unfinished business and all that."

"Wait, so you're suggesting we actually take out-" Gage started to ask with heaps of trepidation.

"Yes," she said before he finished the sentence.

"But why?" he rebutted. "It's secured down there and the Noctis are unable to get to it."

She sighed. "All I can ask you to do is read your father's notes; they're also down there. Perhaps that will shed some light on the situation."

Gage glanced over to an ornate wooden clock sitting on the mantle, an antique his mom had picked up from an estate auction in Aspen when he was five. It seemed that collecting old and ancient things was an unavoidable family trait and he was steadfastly against doing the same himself.

Its hands indicated that an hour and ten minutes had passed and while the conversation and stories were engrossing, he was getting restless.

"Might as well see what we have down there," he said, eagerly wanting to change pace. He grabbed the coffee table before anyone could say no and effortlessly lifted it out of the way.

"What? Right now?" Adrienne asked.

"Yeah, time's wasting."

Madeline floated into an upright position and held out her hand. "Well alrighty then. I told you Adrienne, he's as stubborn as a mule."

"With the attention span of a fork," she added.

"With the attention span of a fork," Gage mocked in a high pitched voice. "A damn manly fork."

Both women laughed and Madeline pushed the rug away with simple wave, rolling it up neatly at the base of the sofa. She then hovered over the door's recessed handle, reaching out to grab it, but her hand passed straight through the metal ring.

Adrienne recounted what Madeline had said: *the only way to open the door was by one of us after death.* She was curious to see that in action and so repositioned herself for a better look.

Madeline tried again, this time closing her eyes and concentrating fully. Her hand clouded, becoming opaque as she grabbed hold of the now glowing handle. A faint whistle coursed through the wood as she pulled up. The door was now open and stale air rushed out to greet the party.

Adrienne's eyes were again wide as she stuttered, "I can't even... How... How were you able to grab that iron ring?" A thousand more questions popped into her inquisitive mind, balanced with a bit of candor. "It's not possible, or shouldn't be."

"There are certain things in this house, down there, that allow the rules to be bent if you will. Not broken mind you, as they're absolute."

She held up the ghostly hand used to open the door and a solid line of ebony ran clear across it. The darkness began to flake away and her form underneath became ethereal once more, but had grown notably dimmer where the metal touched her.

Adrienne replied with wonder, "I'll never cease to be amazed."

"Don't ever lose that," she replied motherly, flexing her hand a couple of times, "as the world is full of many wonders. Despite the darkness, it is an amazing place."

Gage stepped up to the opening and looked into the dank and musty hole. A ladder plunged down from the side closest to him.

"Anything I should be concerned about down there?" he asked.

"No," Madeline replied. "At least nothing I can remember."

"Great. Wish me luck," he said as he straddled the ladder and slid down into the gray void.

His boots hit the floor with a resounding *thud*, echoing for what seemed like ages. Years of caked dust rose up around him, forcing him to clear a path with a few swings of his arms.

The cellar was a shambles, a disarrayed assortment of aged notes and endless, unmarked boxes. He couldn't make out much more since the light streaming in from the open hatch fell off unnaturally fast.

Searching around the entrance for some kind of switch, he soon found a thin cord dangling just behind the ladder and tugged on it.

A set of fluorescent lighting fixtures lining all four walls sprang to life. Dim at first, they slowly grew brighter and filled the room with a pale radiance.

The cavernous space turned out to be deceptively small, no more than twenty feet in any direction from where he stood. However, the light didn't diminish the number of boxes that had been crammed into the tight space.

Not knowing where to begin the unsurmountable task of sorting through it all, he grabbed a random box that happened to be close by and opened it up.

Inside he found a pair of decrepit leather boots and a bearded hatchet decorated with serrated edging. A hole was in the center of the blade. There was also an ornate helmet crowned with long horns wrapped in cast vines, and a palm sized coin, white with a red cross upon it, which grew into a full size battle shield when held firmly by the handle in one's hand.

Setting that box at the base of the ladder, he reached out for another, finding a hundred or so animal figurines mixed in with stones that had been inscribed with ancient writing. A mummified left hand was buried beneath them all, along with a set of five fatty candles, each with wicks no thicker than a hair.

Gage stared at the wizened appendage for a second. *Surely this isn't…* he thought to himself before shaking his head and returning the artifact to the box and closing the lid.

He picked up another; an assortment of peculiar clothing ranging from shirts, pants, and caps were neatly folded inside.

As exciting as looking through all these boxes was, he had no clue what most of the items he was turning up actually did. In fact, some of them were so strange looking that their intended function was a mystery too.

He decided the best bet would be to take some back to the Lodge so Joey could have a look and possibly unlock their secrets. If anyone had the drive to do it, he did. However, for that to have any hopes of succeeding within their lifetime, he would need some notes to serve as a starting point. So, albeit reluctantly, he set about looking for any paperwork he could find.

The next few boxes left him empty handed with respect to the document hunt, but nonetheless they were chock full of mysteries.

It was then that a dark green container, suspiciously alone in a corner, drew his attention.

He strode over and picked it up, finding it surprisingly light for a box of its size. Shaking gently, there was no sound so he assumed it was empty at first but when he managed to pry the tight lid open, he realized that he had struck the mother load.

Reams of parchment were stuffed inside, handwritten notes messily sprawled across dingy yellow pages. Taking the box with him, he moved over to the opposite corner and sat down on an old stone bench that was there. He removed the topmost pages and settled in for some reading.

He noticed a few demonic symbols emblazoned on the sheets in red ink.

"Hello, what do we have here?" he said aloud, rustling the papers to smooth out some of the wrinkles.

The symbols appeared to be examples of various wards, as the pages went into some detail about demon kind in general, kind of like a CliffsNotes version of a lore book.

Demoniacal Studies by Kultan Sylas
Notes by Landon Merryforth
Journeyman Order I.
January 7, 1979
Demons are evil spirits that some conjecture may be fallen angels who reside in Hell. (I wonder why there are so few mentions of angels in any the lore. It's quite odd, especially if Hell is as populated as we are being told. It's almost as if they aren't as common or prevalent as demons are. I must investigate this further.)

Sylas is referring to Hell as the 'lower plane' of existence, implying that Heaven is the upper one and that Earth (our universe? Are there more?) is in the middle, sandwiched between two distinct astral planes that some of the other recruits are calling ghost realms. Those sound utterly chilling and not the place one would want to reside in for more than a second, never mind eternity.

January 14, 1979
In our next session, we learned that demons and their 'true' forms are varied and wide, seemingly a conglomeration of animal parts mixed with human elements; horrific when you think on it. That said, a common trait amongst them all seems to be that their bodies are composed entirely of black ectoplasm (a "smoke" if you will)

when on Earth, which can sometimes take on the outline of their Hell-bound bodies. When I asked if the smoke was tangible, he stated that it behaved as normal smoke does, although some demons can use telekinesis to interact with Earthly objects when in this form. This smoke, along with a powerful odor of sulphur, are their most recognizable features when here on Earth, almost serving to subvert their disguises in all but the most powerful cases.

On this topic, demonic entities can roam the Earth freely if they escape from Hell (numerous methods exist for such; investigate further) but only if they are contained within a human body. This serves as some kind of anchor to the Earthly realm; they are unable to possess animals, even monkeys, which are not that dissimilar from us genetically. I did not get an answer to my question about monster possession.

January 21, 1979
For some odd reason Sylas hasn't gone into, demons must be allowed or invited into the host, though it is believed that some of the most powerful demons can forcibly enter a body at will. Our instructor believes this act is incredibly painful for the entity and has lasting effects on both the body and mind of the demon and its host, should they both survive a hostile possession.

Though it sounds sick, I wonder what it feels like to be possessed – the lack of control over one's own cognitive functions seems quite frightening. It would be like watching yourself perform actions, whether for good or ill, with no ability to stop it.

January 28, 1979
Today we learned that demons can be exorcised from a host using Latin spells and ejected back to Hell if it departs early and cannot find a new host shortly after retreating, or if a banishment spell or stone is used. I am sure there are other items in the world that can perform an exorcism, but we did not discuss that today.

Demons can be contained in both possessed and demonic forms by iron and with certain symbols. Other symbols can also act as wards to prevent entry into places (interesting topic to investigate further).

Demons can apparently be killed by supernatural weapons or certain beings and should this happen, their death is final; the entity will not return to Hell but instead be consumed by the void.

Crap, there was nothing here that Gage didn't already know about or have plenty of experience doing himself. He set those particular sheets down on the chilled rock, rifling back through countless other sheets on demon lore. He found something new, pulling out a short scrap of torn paper about a third of a full page; the rest was missing.

> Notes by Landon Merryforth
> Journeyman Order XVIII.
> March 8, 1997
> A demonic group calling themselves the Noctis, which is based off the Latin for 'night,' have emerged domestically. From all accounts, they appear to be loosely organized and currently pose no significant threat to the Order.
> However, it is rare and suspicious for demons to form large groups and even more so that they appear to be at odds with vampire covens up in the northeast, driving them south. I am going to investigate along with a few colleagues. We shall determine if they pose a long term threat.

Another page, notably weathered, contained a detailed recipe for creating a Hand of Glory, confirming his earlier suspicion that the severed hand he found was one of these macabre tools. He supposed that his dad used it to obtain the items that were stored alongside it in the box, and perhaps most of the materials in the cellar. Of course the extent of his father's transgressions would never be known, but nevertheless it was upsetting to see.

He put the papers away, discouraged to read his father had resorted to thievery for his collections. Unsure now if he even wanted to continue for fear of finding out more negative things about his dad, he had to force himself to press on. The next document he pulled returned to the subject of demons.

> Notes by Landon Merryforth
> Journeyman Order XXXI.
> October 22, 2010
> The Order is in a massive state of disarray. A disastrous event known by all as The Incursion has affected the world, cutting our ranks by nearly a third.
> As much as I would like to, I cannot speak anymore on this matter, for my heart is too heavy with grief at the sheer loss of life.
>
> October 31, 2010
> I may be crazy but I believe the Noctis may actually be looking to open a portal of some kind, to Hell itself no less. This little necklace I obtained from the Middle East may play a part in the tide that

would rise out of that foul place and wash over the Earth.

February 14, 2011

I bear grave news. After months of probing, inquiries, and research, my suspicions have been confirmed. Indeed, the Noctis are seeking a way to open a doorway to Hell. Where is unknown, but they are planning to usher in a new age of the Earth: the Demon Age, where they will rule. I will be returning home to Denver in order to plan what to do next. I cannot help but think the Council does not want this information out.

On the subject of the necklace, as fate would have it both the pendant and its chain are two necessary elements in this diabolical plan. Sadly, I am unaware if any other pieces are needed for these plans to succeed.

April 13, 2012

Gage, if by some remote chance you are reading this...

The Noctis are coming for us and they are out for blood. I am sealing both amulet and chain here in this cellar. Though they are keys to opening the doorway, as such they are also keys to stopping the Noctis dead in their tracks. I have learned that there are at least three, possibly four other items that are necessary for the Noctis to have in order to complete their goal. I unfortunately do not have a list of them, but a long time colleague of mine, Om Citta, has made a vow that he would continue researching to find out.

Now, I have enchanted the container that the objects are stored in so they remain hidden even if a Hell Knight entered this chamber and its eyes fell upon it, but you should be able to find them easily when your heart and mind are in the right place.

This will be the last entry in my notes.

Your mother and I are left with no choice but to stand and fight against the Noctis here, within the walls of our own home. As safe as they have been for us, there is no security left in them against this fate. I intercepted a communication; they are sending a demon named Camio to deal with us and the Order will not be here in time to counterattack.

Gage, my son, I implore you to remember these things if nothing else:

Their leader and the one who gave the order calls herself Onoskelis. Remember her name. Remember that Keli is the one that sentenced your parents to death.

Also, if you can, seek out Om Citta. He should still be anchored at 252 Front Street in New York City, unless some ill fate befalls him.

Don't fret, we won't go down without a fight. I love you, my dear son. We both do. Always have and always will.

Charles Crosse
Dad.

Gage sat in total silence, dropping the paper from his hands. It fluttered to the floor without a hint of turbulence before coming to rest between his feet. Looking down at the cream parchment, he glared at the last line which was facing back at him. Unable to look away as he kneeled down, he handled the document delicately between his fingers, mulling over what he had just read.

Those final words repeated over and over in his mind.

"I love you too," was all he could muster.

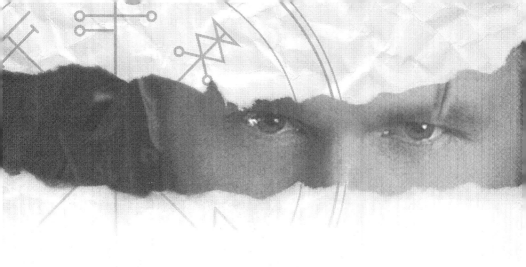

CHAPTER
twenty-one

THE HERALD

A FTER A COUPLE HOURS, he climbed back out of the cellar, hauling with him a large box of select artifacts. Slinging it off to the side he descended again, returning no less than three times with yet more containers of strange looking gear, a hefty collection of books, and reams of unsorted notes.

Pulling himself out of the opening, he sat on the edge wiping away a bit of sweat while his feet rested against the rungs.

"Ady," he said exhaustedly. "Can you help me load these in the truck? Take the light one over there and I'll be sure to snag the heavier ones in a few. I think there's a ton of stuff here that J would downright have an orgasm over."

She nodded, taking a gulp of her water and setting the glass down on the end table. "Ha! I bet so," she replied. "It doesn't take much for that guy to lose himself, does it?"

"Oh, you have no idea," he replied snarkily.

With that, she stood up and grabbed the box closest to her, carrying it out toward the front door. Madeline opened it with a wave, leaving the door cracked for when she returned. Her attention then turned to Gage.

"Any luck finding it down there?" she asked.

"No not yet," he said. "Dad left it a lil' messy down there and I had no idea you could fit that many boxes into that small a room."

"I'm not surprised at all," she agreed, rubbing her hands together. "Organizing was the least of his strong points."

"I did find some unique ammo and artifacts down there; you weren't exaggerating 'bout his obsession. I have zero clue what a lot of that stuff does and Dad's notes on 'em are, at best, sparse."

Madeline paced, worried for a moment that all of this effort were for naught. "What if someone managed to make it in there before I manifested? No, that can't be possible. It has to be down there."

Sensing her concern, Gage reassured her. "I'll take one last look tonight," he said, mounting the ladder again. "If don't find it now, I'll continue the search in the morning after getting some rest. We'll get through all the stuff down there… eventually."

He receded from her nodding head down to the bottom. Placing hands on his hips, he surveyed the area one more time.

"Now if I were an ancient relic of death and destruction, where would I be?" He looked around impatiently, eyes darting from one box to another random container to yet another unmarked box. "Ah fuck!"

Embittered, he punted the tower of boxes just off to his right and a couple of loose coins that were scattered across the top fell, bouncing off the ground with a few light dings.

He was so drained, both physically and mentally, without a clue as to which was winning the battle to wear him down. Propping a hand up on the stack for support, he drooped his weary head.

That's when he noticed an indentation creeping its way out at a ninety-degree angle from the base of the pile, not unlike a grout line. Curious, he kneeled and ran a finger along it. There wasn't any grout there, but instead a fine gap between the surrounding stone.

With renewed vigor he cleared out the stack directly above the line and in record time, squatted back down. The lines formed a corner of a now uncovered square half a meter wide. In the opposite corner was a tiny divot, which upon closer inspection was a stamped rose.

This has to be it, he thought anxiously.

Shifting his fingers fastidiously around the edges, he searched for a means of getting some kind of grip or leverage but it was to no avail. There was no way those meaty stubs of his were going to fit in between there.

Gage then heard what he thought was a faint chirp, but it disappeared before he could really hone in and listen.

Steadfast, he stood and walked with purpose over to a foot locker brimming with swords. Yielding one of the stout ones, he returned to the square, drew back and plunged the blade into the space in the floor. Leaning hard into it with all his might for leverage, the side of the stonework rose a couple inches but no more. He slumped back off the sword, reserves spent, and the stone settled back into its locked position.

"What was it Dad said? 'When your heart and mind are in the right place'?" Gage whispered, tapping his forehead. "Right then…"

He took a deep breath to recharge himself and shifted sides, lowering the blade gently into the crack. "Heart and mind, heart and mind, heart and mind…" he repeated aloud as he closed his eyes and slowly pulled down on the pommel. He cracked an eye to take a peek at the progress and saw that the stone moved drastically…

… less distance than it had before.

What the fuck? he thought, releasing his grip which sent the sword shaking. As it did so, a tiny tag wiggled itself loose from underneath the cross guards.

He sat expressionless, staring as the minuscule piece of paper flaunted itself in mid air. Mid-flutter, he snatched it and took an impertinent look. There, written in his dad's distinct handwriting was the word 'Excalibur'.

It might as well have sprouted arms and four heads with the look he was giving. "Oh that's just fuckin' ironic, isn't it?" he said, crumpling the label and flinging himself down on his knees. Balling up a fist, he smashed it against the debossed rose, a faint light kindling from the impact.

The light grew to cover the entire square and Gage backed away from it, startled. The solid stone became like gravel then dissolved into powder before his eyes. The motes took on the muted shape of Solomon's third seal before getting carried away by a soft, unearthly breeze that wafted from the hole.

The alcove was barren except for a mahogany jewelry box which sat in the exact center. It was adorned with baroque, golden floral patterns on each of its eight corners and sat upon four small clawed feet. The lid rose without prompting and settled wide open.

There was the amulet perched atop a wadded silk cloth that shimmered between ephemeral shades of blue and gray, itself crowning a mound of jewels of various shapes, sizes, and colors.

There it waited as he reached out carefully, unwilling or perhaps unable to touch its plain metal surface. His hand quivered a hair's breath from the shiny disc before an overwhelming urge to set his fingers down drove him to do just that.

As his flesh touched the cool metal it scalded his fingertips, the pain surging straight up his arm and into to his temples. Visions surged into his mind and forcibly commanded all of his senses.

A foul odor of rotten eggs rushed him as he was whooshed away from the cellar. The sting of sparks cascaded over his body, naked under the night sky.

The pendant hung low and heavy upon his neck as he looked to the endless stars above. He took a step on an invisible set of stairs, climbing higher as the chain sweltered and the disc burned brightly. The eighth seal of Solomon flashed brilliantly in front of his eyes. He raised an arm to shield his face from the heat, yet the symbol was gone in an instant, consumed by a swirling vortex of fiery tendrils.

Sparks stung mercilessly again as the cities of humankind burned across the horizon. Packs of hell hounds hunted openly in the streets, flames spitting from underfoot while soot churned like dust devils high into the air. The screams of countless souls rose up in those swirling columns to join monstrous behemoths that loomed overhead, sending great swaths of shadow across the land as the skulls of hundreds poured from the sky.

Gage looked down as the shade swept across him. Two rings appeared out of thin air, landing in his palms. The one on the right was made of platinum entwined gold and on the left, a thin circle of rust was on the verge of falling apart.

The ferrous metal grew thick and weighty, sinking into his skin with an effervescent hiss while his bones were crunched into foul shapes. Black ash leached out of the fissures in his cracked skin, the plumes dancing spherically around his other hand, unaffected as if a barrier protected it.

Unable to hold it in any longer, Gage screamed as the pain and soot overtook him. He felt a pinch at the nape of his neck and was cinched backwards before blacking out.

Awakening on a small island set above a sea of stormy clouds, the roiling vapors stretched out beneath him as far as his eyes could see.

The land abruptly heaved to and fro and Gage became ill from all the rocking. He looked up from the horizon, blazing like a distant sunset, in an attempt to alleviate his motion sickness. It didn't help, as far above another blanket of darkness quaked, sandwiching him in between.

Lightning flung its way from the topmost clouds to the bottom, building in rage until a massive bolt whipped free and tore a path through the ground.

Solid rock was obliterated and fell away into the abyss. Gage soon followed, pummeled by the many fragments of sharp stone. As the distant lightning pulsed, he saw things take shape in the swirling debris.

A golden crown, wreathed in flame, was set upon the silhouette of a man. He turned and …

An army of Journeyman, both supernatural and human, were locked in a great battle against a legion of demons and other foul beasts that defied description as …

Joey turned away, disheartened, while the faint sounds of a woman's scream rose in his ears…

Adrienne?

Gage raised his hands to cover his ears and tumbled end over end before facing into the endless pit of black. Silence arrived as a hint of gray flickered way ahead and he realized at last the bottom could be seen.

However, he was approaching too quickly with no indication of slowing down. As the hard ground raced toward him, he held out his arms in an impotent attempt to brace himself before he struck. The impact was so great his entire body broke.

As blood trickled from his mouth and eyes and his last few breaths escaped in coughs, Gage saw a hooded figure approaching, wielding a sickle in its ancient hand.

It stopped before him and looked down through empty, sunken sockets. Extending a skeletal arm toward Gage's arm, it snapped his hand clean off just below the wrist.

Gage tried to scream, the loudest he ever had, but no sound came.

The figure placed the end of the sickle against the frayed appendage and they shimmered, the sounds of Gage's delayed scream echoing as the objects melded together. As the painful cries subsided, Gage watched motionless as Death raised his newly formed scythe above him and came down in one fell swoop.

The gruesome and prophetic flashes subsided and he was left in the gloom with far too little breath. Lying in a heap on the floor he worked to build his capacity back up, eventually setting up on his knees.

The weight of the world seemed to drag his shoulders down and he was drawn down to the thin, spiky chain and round bit of silver that threatened to turn his life upside down. There was a choice that needed to be made, right now.

A large part of him wanted to ignore the problem at hand and just leave.

You know, you could just forget about this tiny trinket here in this dark and dusty hole. Keli and the Noctis, they would all be none the wiser, still struggling to grasp power.

But he continued to stare. The treasure glimmered even though no light was overhead.

Yet, that's still the problem, isn't it Gage? Murder. Death. Kill. Repeat. You said it yourself, it's what demons do. It goes on and on and on, whether you leave this glorified piece of tin here or carry it out with you.

But if you do take it, there's a chance of fucking over the Noctis and their biggest plans, stopping them dead in their tracks.

That brought a loose smile to his face.

And who better to fuck them over than you?

Now convinced, Gage brought the chain over his neck, the necklace coming to rest on the red rose in the center of his chest.

The items seemed to get heavier, as if they were securing themselves in place. A slight buzz then came from them, penetrating his skin like a massage. It felt comforting yet mildly irritating.

Empowered, he rose to his feet and gave the area a final once-over. What he thought were the most interesting items and notes had already been secured in the truck whilst the big prize sat firmly around his neck. He took a last whiff of the chalky air before turning, heading back to the ladder to climb out.

As he took his first steps, deja vu fell upon him, then again as he took another. He continued on up, passing through the warded threshold.

A low rumble rolled in the ground and shook the very foundations as the talisman floated away from his chest, coming to rest in mid air before his eyes.

There it remained while he paused, spreading his arms for balance. "What the-"

Without warning, vivid red spindles erupted from the center of the pendant, spinning high into the late afternoon sky. They coalesced, the clouds themselves groaning and cracking under the onslaught. Forks of intense lightning careened down and out across countless miles and everything that the violent bolts touched vaporized in bursts of shadow and flame.

Then, in an instant, all was gone.

"What the hell was that?" asked Gage, voice peppered with cumbersome gasps. "Getting a lil' bit weirded out by the deadly laser beams that seems to shoot out of this thing at random!"

"It was a signal," said Madeline.

Adrienne had returned to Gage's side, helping him out of the doorway.

She turned to Madeline. "To whom?" she asked.

She sighed, her ghostly form especially grave. "My dear, to everyone."

CHAPTER
twenty-two

THE SIGN SEEN AROUND THE WORLD

KELI SAT ATOP A PILLAR at the highest point of Bennett Peak, looking out to the west. A hawk flew by, diving down toward the ground in pursuit of its prey. Darkness would arrive within a few hours, although she already felt as if the chill of the night air was on her skin.

Agares was gone, the look on his bare and pained face hung in her waking thoughts. Even closing her eyes could not shield her from that vision. Another of the ancient Greats, a supreme demon of Hell, had been ended in an instant – this time by the hand of Dajjal, who was still trapped in the blistering fires and bound in eternal chains.

How was that even possible? Never before had a demon been able to send an item to Earth from Hell, never mind control it.

Doubt for her fate had entered into her once secure and confident mind. His powers were definitely growing and she began to question herself and her actions. Was she being too lax? Was she too lenient to the throngs? Was she blinded by her own arrogance?

Regardless, she wanted to be like the hawk, now soaring away with a rabbit in its talons. Quick, efficient, and deadly.

As she reflected and the claws of depression threatened to close on her, there was a distant roar like a great beast piercing the stillness. It was accompanied by a scarlet luster, her lengthening shadow indicating that the light was coming from the northeast and it was growing brighter. She turned and what she saw compelled her to rise.

The sky was alight as a barrage of lightning came down to strike the mountaintops, plains, and anything in between. There, at the very center of the monstrous and sudden storm, was a vivid red column that penetrated the heavens. The Herald called out for all to see.

"In Lucifer's name…" she said with her mouth open in awe.

A stray bolt leaped from the distant and dark clouds, striking a forlorn gas station sitting along the desolate highway. The fuel was ignited and the place exploded in a burst of fire, smoke, and dirt. The debris rose high into the air before it rained down around the wreckage.

The pillar stayed for a moment longer, then faded, the broken vestige of clouds the only evidence that something odd was ever there.

That was it: the moment she had been waiting for. Instantly all her doubt was erased, or at least pushed back into the depths of her psyche where it would be harmless, for the time being.

IN A LARGE CONFERENCE room on the uppermost floor of the New York offices, Marcus completed reciting his findings to the Council, tapping the thick stack of papers end first on the glossy tabletop.

The window shades of the corner room had been drawn to keep out the blinding sunlight at this time of day. Around the arched mahogany table sat seven individuals. Five of them were there in person, seated in luxurious leather chairs and the other two were at remote locations, displayed on two-way mirrors that had been set in place of their empty seats.

They all took to murmuring amongst themselves, voices raising high and low, all but relegating Marcus to the the status of a wallflower.

"Excuse me," he interrupted, following a throat clearing cough; protocols be damned during a time like this. "Do we call an Assembly for the matter at hand? What do you say to this?"

The supernatural members of the Council stared back at him, unblinking. Tensions had certainly increased between the supernaturals of the world and humans in recent years, who some viewed as prideful. In a way they were right, such pride from a human archmage leading to the most devastating event in Journeyman history just five years earlier. As such, humans found themselves outnumbered in the current iteration of the Council.

"This shouldn't be up for debate," Marcus continued sternly, placing his own personal feelings aside but unable to shake the notion that he was still talking to the walls. "You've heard and even seen the evidence. We need to act...now."

"We shall be the judge of such things, Mr. Sheridan," said Fenran pointedly, an elf from the rolling greens of Ireland. His high swept ears were tucked up beneath a brown cap and a pair of spindly elbows jutted out from Earthen robes, planted firmly on the table. The tips of his thin fingers rapped together annoyingly.

Another voice came from across the table, somewhat tinny as it passed through the glass. "An Assembly of this magnitude hasn't been called since the days of the Incursion," stated a haughty, beast-like creature with coarse burgundy hair. Behind his goat-like horns, snow fell over evergreen trees growing amongst high mountain peaks.

"Yes, Tyrol" confirmed Drogir as he sat upright with membranous wings folded behind himself like a cape. "We mustn't be hasty and cause a panic where none is warranted."

Marcus let go of his paperwork, simply stunned. Trying to calm himself by twisting the ear bar piercing in his left ear, he remained astonished by the hurdles being faced. "Panic? How about being well prepared; what more do you want?" he asked with desperation, pointing toward the conference room door behind him. "Would you have the Noctis march right up and knock on that very door, asking to come in?"

"Don't be silly, Marcus," urged the calming human voice of Jane Carter. Though stern in character and carrying a corresponding amount in appearance, she garnered a great deal of respect from her fellow Councilors and the Journeymen alike. She did not have time today for such an obvious pissing match, turning her attention to the naysayers. "He is right you know, despite your reluctance to believe it."

Fenran shot her a slow and deliberate stare down the bridge of his nose. If had been wearing glasses, he would've been peering pompously over the rims.

"Agreed," Councilor Timothy Randall chimed in, adding his support. Like Jane, he was one of the three humans on the Council, the last being Allete Popov, who was away for personal reasons in her native Bulgaria. In his late forties, Timothy was quite the gentlemen who respected the seat he held. The thought of using it for ill purposes or to let the power go to his head never crossed his mind. The very notion of it was offensive to him and he found himself disappointed by the others.

"Of course you humans would be agreeable with each other's views," Fenran finally said.

"You humans?" Jane repeated, taking offense. "Lest you forget Fenran that we are all on this Earth together and face the same enemy."

Fenran waved his hand dismissively in reply. "Humans," he said conceitedly, "again pretending they know all in the matters of the worlds."

"If you both are finished, I was not. We have also received a communique from England," Timothy resumed, "from one of our own no less: a Mr. Henry Abington."

"He was found wandering the streets of Grimsargh, alone," cut in Quileth, a human-like creature with the features of a tiger. His saucer shaped eyes looked directly over to his gargoyle colleague before continuing. "You of all here should know that feeling, Drogir. From what we hear, he sustained grave injuries from his encounter with this self-proclaimed Noctis 'leader' as she calls herself. We should definitely bring him here after he has recuperated enough for travel and find out what he knows. In the meantime, we-"

Quileth was interrupted by the deafening scream of klaxons and the strobing of alternating white and orange lights. Those seated in the room stood immediately, ready to listen to the upcoming announcement while the two that were offsite departed.

They were not left waiting for long.

"Alert!" came a voice over the intercoms. "Alert! Level Four anomaly detected."

Marcus smirked, making sure that Fenran saw him do so. "Well, there's your knock."

KELI HAD MADE HER way back into the caverns and was speaking to Ronove.

"I think it's about we time paid Gage a visit," Keli said confidently, suddenly pausing as if a great idea entered her thoughts. "But, I think we should stop by Durango on the way, for a little bit of housekeeping. This seems like the perfect opportunity for a certain Hell Knight to put his money where his ever-complaining mouth is."

Ronove raised his lips into an accursed smile before bowing his head in agreement, vanishing in a snap of air.

CHAPTER
twenty-three
THE BATTLE OF DURANGO

B AILEY, EVANS, AND MILLER stood in front of the congregation of monsters, the last light of dusk creeping in through the gaps of the rough hewn walls. There were of course vampires present, hidden in the growing shadows, along with beast shifters, kappas, and even a rogue mountain troll.

The floor was covered in dirt and a smattering of hay; the earthiness of the smell underscoring the importance of this world to those in attendance. Dim lanterns hung randomly around the different levels and from the loft, casting an inviting warmth around the interior.

These vampires, proud and tall, were the leaders of an esteemed triad of Houses, rebels against demonkind and their rise to power.

"Thank you all for coming," the tallest of the three said. It was Bailey, dressed in casual clothes like the others, dirtied from lack of washing. "We know that times are not how they used to be."

"Yes," added Miller. "Where things were once balanced, the scales have now tipped. Sadly, they've not done so in our favor. It has become far more dangerous for those of us who choose not to align with the demons. Far more… deadly."

The crowd rumbled in agreement; their ears and horns and hair all nodding.

"So why run?" asked a kappa, water sloshing around awkwardly in the divot on its head. "Why not just join them?"

Everyone got quiet and looked forward.

The last of the three leaders stepped up as the other two parted to each side. Evans was the oldest of them all, having turned Miller and Bailey himself and as their original coven grew, he gave them an opportunity to lead their own. They had done so quite successfully.

"Nothing is forcing you not to join them, river child. Any species or member thereof is free to do what they will in the times ahead – at their own risk or peril. However, it has been decided that all vampires will not bow or take direction from the demons. They are not even of this world and cannot, in our eyes, be trusted with the fate of it."

Many in the crowd agreed but some less so. Vampires would not bow or take orders yet seemed to give them quite well.

Miller paced in front of the others, noting the mood. He wore a hopeful look on his face while he gestured with his fist. "There are more of us; groups just like this one forming and growing to combat this darkness."

It was an astounding sight made more so by the words being spoken. Foul creatures from every corner of the world referring to a threat that was darker than themselves. In this, they weren't that different from the Journeymen with their very way of life and existence in jeopardy.

Miller continued, "They are the very concept of darkness incarnate. Do not be fooled by their words or ploys or promises. They will use you until your need is spent, then dispose of you like the trash they really think you are."

"We can all agree that the demons are untrustworthy, but what makes us trust you any more?" asked a voice from the crowd. He was a shifter, able to transform at will into the shape of any creature he had consumed.

Bailey stepped up to answer. "You don't have any guarantees, other than our word. Plus, think of it this way: the demons use humans as hosts, parading around in them like some kind of suit."

The crowd chattered at the unsavoriness of the idea.

"We feed on humans," he continued, looking to the shifters. "Well, for the most part. I know some of you have an affinity for wild bears. But in any case, not only do demons want to exterminate us monsters, those of us that do fight them, or do nothing, or even join their ranks are going to be hit with the harsh reality of dwindling food supplies. To me that's hardly an ideal world to live in."

A passing glance scanned over the crowd and he could tell by their expressions they were swayed by his words.

"I am not going to lie to you: this will not be an easy fight," Bailey admitted. "The demons have vast numbers on their side and each victory for us is just a single step on a very long road to victory."

The crowd was hushed except for the sounds of deep breathing.

Then came the match…

"Death!"

"Yes!" Evans encouraged.

That ignited the inferno…

"DEATH TO THE DEMONS!"

"That's it!" Evans shouted, raising his arms triumphantly amongst the chanting. "We will continue to fight… with every claw, every bite, every single damn breath! For as long as we do, they have not won and we will still be free!" Bailey and Miller joined him amongst the sounds of intense applause. Finally their efforts were paying off.

A faint burst of noise like far of firecrackers barely rose over the chorus of cheers.

Evans was concerned, thinking he had heard something out of the ordinary. He stepped forward. The barn doors flickered with a distant light.

Another *boom* came up and over the boisterous crowd, much louder than the last one. The trio looked to each other, wondering if the sounds of screams were mixed in amongst the noise.

The applause died down as the structure began to tremble, followed by yet another earsplitting roar.

By now Evans and Bailey had reached the doors, peering through the warped gaps before flinging them open. Miller walked up behind them both and his mouth fell open as the other's had already done, his fangs extending as he curled his lips into a snarl.

There on the hill fronting the farmhouse stood an imposing figure, dressed in obsidian. The dark and menacing flames rose from the burning home and spread out like wings of shadow on each side of him.

Baal had come.

Damn you, demon, Miller thought, distressed. *How did you even manage to breach the-*

Like a flash he looked to the sides of the barn, behind the tall copses of bushes and grass. His suspicions were immediately confirmed: the wards had been smashed in with a hatchet; their power negated. The guilty, rusted blade was still embedded in one of the protection sigils as if to mock their efforts.

"Traitors!" Miller spat.

"Well," replied Evans as his fangs and claws grew out to their full length, "time to put our money where our mouths are."

The tone of his voice was confident, yet worry clung to his words. It was as if they needed more time to prepare, yet no more would be given.

Baal was not there to play games or parlay. He held his great sword aloft as a glowing beacon, pointing it at the barn and the monsters that were gathered inside.

"Annihilate them," he commanded, saying nothing more. By his order, a dark tide swelled over and rushed down the hill. Within it, demons charged forward and were joined by werewolves and possibly a wendigo; it was moving so fast that it was barely a streak against the dark surroundings.

The demons had brought with them destruction runes of fire and ice, brandishing the magical stones before launching them at their enemies. The front of the barn, with its protections defaced, erupted into a dazzling and deadly display of blistering and frost-bound bombs.

Luckily for the monsters, some of the sigils on the roof were still intact and their defensive charms were activated. A large part of the blitz ricocheted back on the demons, killing a swath of them. Their mangled bodies tumbled down the hill, coming to rest at the bottom where they were trampled into the damp soil by those still drawing breath.

Ten men came screaming out of the barn, kicking off high into the air. Half of them extended their teeth and claws, now equipped to lacerate demonic flesh. Bones snapped in the others, contorting into the monstrous shapes of boars and bears, now poised to mutilate their canine brethren.

The shifters and vampires raced uphill side by side, clashing with the oncoming pack of werewolves and demons; the sounds that filled the dark skies when they met were brutal, laced with suffering and lament.

Meanwhile inside the barn, a bale of kappa wove water spells on the fire and the flames started to shrink.

The mountain troll took the distracted opportunity and moved in from behind, snatching up two of them in its gigantic hands, revealing himself as the treacherous snake. He wasted no time in dispensing with them, cruelly pouring the water from their heads down his gullet before biting clean through their reptilian necks. His thick and crushing teeth made sure their deaths were not painless.

The rest of the group spun around to assail the troll. Surrounding it and extending their scaly arms in a rough circle, they chanted in Japanese while avoiding the powerful swings that were striking the ground around them. Hay flew around like a blizzard and seconds later, a faint blue circle pushed out from the kappa to enclose the troll's feet.

Almost immediately the beast gagged, reaching for his neck that swiftly filled with arid breath. The chanting was able to continue uninterrupted and water began to gush out from every pore, floating as if weightless and drawing out into long strands. The lances of water grew with each passing second. He must've been nearly drained when nothing but a flaking husk was left standing.

His dry and wrinkled eyes struggled to see the watery filaments as they turned in toward his torso. The glowing circle rose up from his feet to instantly freeze them into icy lances.

That's when the kappa's chanting ended and the troll was impaled where he stood. His shrunken body collapsed with a soft *whoosh*. Their nemesis out of the way, they returned to battling the flames consuming the barn.

Bailey and Miller watched as the skirmish continued in front of them. Countless were dead on both sides, the ground made darker than the night around it.

"This is unbeliev-" said Bailey, his words cut off by a rush of air that raced between them.

"What was that, Bailey?" Miller asked, his attention still on the battle ahead.

"Hayden..." Bailey whispered, looking down at his waist; it was stained red from a huge gash across the belly button. He tried to stop the flow of blood, but it was too much.

Miller twisted around at the odd mention of his first name, catching his kin falling to his knees. Blood soaked the entirety of his lower body and he was fast fading. By the time Miller reached him, he was dead.

"What...?" he asked hysterically." What on earth is this?" A wound, even one this extensive, shouldn't have killed Bailey. His vampiric healing would have kicked into high gear but something stopped that from happening. Instinctively, Miller reached out to the gash to investigate, but stopped just short of it. A faint yellow glow twinkled along the outer edges. This was no normal cut at all.

There was a growl from something that had approached behind him, breathing fast and heavy. Its hot breath caressed the hairs on the back of his neck.

Ah fuck, it's you, Miller thought, closing his eyes briefly.

He opened them as he turned, catching a glimpse of a long, serpentine tongue between razor sharp teeth, just before the wendigo closed them down over his face. All went painfully dark.

Further up toward the hill, Evans stood proudly in front of the armored fiend approaching him, his claws scraping against each other like nails on a chalkboard.

"What's the occasion, demon?" he asked mockingly, unimpressed by the garish outfit that was being paraded in front of him. "All Hallows Eve isn't for a month yet."

"My, such audacity in the face of your betters," Baal said, unfazed by the vampire's nattering. He continued his gradual and deliberate advance as they began to circle each other cautiously.

"Betters?" Evans repeated with distaste. "In whose book?"

"The only one that matters…" Baal was suddenly close to him; way too close. "… MINE!"

His sword came down with a sharp whistle and would have sliced Evans in two, but the vampire happened to be faster, nimbly dashing out of the way just in the nick of time. The blade struck the dirt with a mighty *clang*, lodging itself into the ground.

Evans took a chance to strike. He looped around and swiped across the back of Baal's armor, his claws digging into that dark shell. It was nowhere near deep enough.

This fight was not going to be easy.

Baal yanked his sword out of the ground and lunged toward Evans, flames blazing from beneath his helm.

Four werewolves raced across the clearing and through the fighting crowds, bearing a large golden vase between them. It was adorned with a fiery leaf motif and strange, curled symbols, sitting within a middle of rickety wooden frame.

They made haste for the barn, tearing through what little resistance remained inside and placed the container on the ground. One of the wolves stepped up to the vase, its golden surface gleaming in the firelight. The rest backed away as he pulled off the lid.

"*Aistadeaa*," said the wolf. It was the last thing he or any of the others would do.

Back outside, Baal kicked Evans to the ground and looked down his nose at the pathetic vamp, soiled with muck and a battered in face. He shifted in his busted armor, placing the full weight of his boot on Evans' chest.

As fun as all this was, the time for play had passed. He raised his sword for the kill, ready to cut that ugly head off that marred body, but before he could bring it down, a massive explosion ripped through the barn. The shockwave wasn't far behind and it flung him away like a rag doll.

Evans looked over to the barn, or what was left of it, his head stuffed full of intense pressure and ringing.

A great shadow emerged from the tempest of fire. It was difficult to make out in the swirling torrent, but its massive wings and thick, swept back horns were unmistakable. The sight of that alone was enough to widen his eyes in fear. This was not a fight Evans could win even at full strength. So bruised and battered, he limped off into the woods alone – away from the fight, the noises of death, and the light.

Baal got to his feet a few minutes later and noticed he was by himself. Swearing under his breath, a distinct cry pierced the silence; everything else had fallen still and afraid.

He looked to the decimated structure, a mere scattering of planks amongst a curtain of flame. Though his sword was in hand, a chill moved down his own spine when he saw it: the infernal jinn, Ifrit, was loose upon the Earth.

"Foolish mutts!" he yelled. "Do you know what you've done?" The question went unanswered as all things in the barn had perished.

This was of no surprise, for this wasn't a moderate weapon, nor someone's tamed pet. It was a force of nature far worse than any wendigo or group thereof. Everyone and everything within a mile had been placed under a death sentence.

Baal cursed the ineptitude of Keli and those following that lesser she-beast for allowing such a stupendous misstep to happen.

He had little choice but to face it; running was a coward's move. Approaching the wicked creature and pointing his sword at it, he spoke sternly. "I am Baal, Lord unto Hell and Knight in service to Lucifer the Great. Foul creature, I command you to retreat back to your confines. Now."

There was a long period of silence.

"What is your answer?" he demanded.

A great fireball made its way toward him. Baal extended his free hand and a shield appeared in it, deflecting the energy on its skull façade. The land around him burned to cinder.

He lowered the shield. "So be it!"

Baal held his sword aloft and it became a frosty blue. He charged and the sharp tongue of ice was quick to chew its way into the beast's belly. The jinn halted, burning from the freezing cold spreading out from the wound.

The exchanges continued, back and forth, potholing the earth and their bodies alike. Before long the entire area was smote to ruin.

The Ifrit threw Baal to the ground and held him down as it laid upon him, the heat conducting through the dark armor with ease. As his body burned, it belched molten salvia into his face, bubbling the host's skin into a disgusting, peeling mess.

With what strength that remained, Baal released his sword and shut his eyes, commanding the blade to fly through the beast's skull. It was an order it gladly followed.

As the sword pierced the Ifrit, the end had come. Without releasing its grasp, the Ifrit slumped forward, shaking violently as energy built. Finally, its body could not contain anymore and it exploded violently, the both of them engulfed in a massive surge. Fire fell from the sky like rain, relegating themselves and a significant portion of Durango to memory.

THE MOON BLANKETED ITSELF in the warmth of the black smoke as Keli walked amidst the smoldering devastation that was once Durango. Motes of char entwined with floating embers moved without a care over the what remained of the dead.

She stopped just ahead of two black spires sticking precariously out of the gray powder and bent over to pick them up. Out of the ash she pulled Baal's lofty helm. It was empty. The host's body had been obliterated, mixed in amongst the dusty remnants and his demonic form fared no better, since carried away by the wind.

Baal was no more. It seems her idea of stopping by Durango for a bit of housekeeping took care of two birds with one massive, molten stone.

CHAPTER
twenty-four
AT LAST

"**Y**OU'LL HAVE TO LEAVE very soon," Madeline said sternly to Gage. "There is no telling who, or what, saw that beacon but they will be on their way here."

"Did you know that the signal would be sent?" asked Gage amidst heavy breaths.

"No," she replied. "I had assumed they would remain dormant until actually used. Obviously that didn't happen."

"Used?" Adrienne asked, her curiosity piqued. "How so?"

"There's not a lot of time to go into that right now," she answered. "It's... complicated. You have Charles' notes on it and from what you've told me about your friend Joey, he does a great job at figuring things out." Her eyes locked back onto her son's. "I implore you to leave... soon. You have no idea what is coming for you, baby."

"Okay, okay," he said, trying to place his hands on her shoulders. They passed straight through. Oh how he wished he could actually touch her right now. Hug her dearly. "We'll get the truck packed up now with the rest of our stuff and leave at first light."

Madeline nodded. "Alright," she said, voice breaking.

"I love you Mom," he said. "Seeing you again was much needed."

"You too, Gage. I cannot tell you how proud I am of you. I know that your father would be too if he were here."

She raised a hand, the fainter one that she had used to open the cellar door, and closed her eyes. A balmy draft wrapped itself around Gage, its tender heat rising from his feet up his entire body. He felt motivated to return the gesture and to his surprise was able to push against her soft skin with his own fingers for a brief moment before his hand fell through the mist.

A tear pooled at the corner of Adrienne's eye and she wiped it away before it had a chance to trickle down her cheek.

"Well," said Madeline. "I'll let you two get to it. Let me know if you need anything, I'll be floating around. Otherwise, I will see you both off first thing in the morning." She stepped back a few paces before fading away, leaving Adrienne and Gage alone in the room.

Each of their hands found its way into the other's and they brought their foreheads together.

"I'll take the rest of these boxes and see if there's anything else we can go ahead and pack up in the ol' girl," said Gage as he rubbed his nose on Adrienne's. "It shouldn't take me too long. I'll see you upstairs afterwards?"

She moved her hands up around his neck and gave him a kiss, savoring in the prickly goodness of his beard. "Okay then," she whispered. "I'll see you up there soon. I'm going to see about grabbing us something to munch on."

Gage smiled profusely as he pulled himself away, moving toward the stairs. "I have something that can take care of that, too. Just in case you turn up empty handed."

AS HE THOUGHT, THERE wasn't much left to pack up other than a few clothes and toiletries. Gage strode back into the bedroom and noticed that Adrienne wasn't there yet. She was probably still on the hunt for something to eat.

He took the opportunity to plop himself down on the edge of the bed, wondering if he had made the right decision to come here. Not one to doubt himself, a shade of skepticism had entered his mind now that an extremely powerful relic dangled around his neck. Letting out a lengthy sigh he bent over, the amulet tucked tightly between his clasped hands. It gave off an enticing warmth and for the first time in his life, he contemplated praying.

"Well," he said aloud into the empty room. "I'm not even sure I believe you exist, but I'll give this a go. Ironic isn't it? Here in a world of demons and monsters, the guy that slays them has doubts about your existence.

"But I'm wondering, yet again, if it was the right choice coming here. Especially with her. I need answers, else I don't think I will ever be able to get rid of this shred of doubt that keeps lingering. I mean don't get me wrong, things seem to be going great, but now the weight of the world is on my shoulders, quite literally strung around my neck, and I don't know if I am remotely up to the task."

He opened his hands and the silver disc stared blankly at him from his calloused palms.

"How is it such a small thing can be the key to something so overwhelmingly large as the end of the world?" he pondered.

As he sat there contemplating the words he spoken to himself, an inner voice resounded in his skull. It was distant at first, like a shade of a whisper, but before long was booming, filling his body with both vigor and contentment. Oddly, it was the same voice that always spoke to him since the day he first could, yet it felt different… more paternal.

"Gage, you must always take positive inventory on what you have and what've done in your life. No matter what, don't get bogged down in the overwhelming and nagging little details as that can drive even the sanest man to throw himself over a cliff." There was a brief pause. "And let's face it, you're far from the sanest man on the planet. After all, you fight demons and things-that-go-bump-in-the-night as your career. Hardly the stuff of sanity… it's the stuff of legend."

Gage chuckled a bit. "There's no denying that fact. But, I still don't know."

The voice continued, "Far too often there are times we find ourselves down and out, lonely whilst circling a pit of despair, thinking about nothing but all of the insurmountable things have gone wrong or questioning every decision we made to evaluate if it was the right one: Should I have slayed that creature? What about the repercussions of leaving that one alive? Should I have come back home...

"Don't do it. Focus instead on the positive, going with what your gut or your heart tells you, and most importantly believe in yourself. There is certainly no shortage of good across your thirty short years; the lives you've saved alone are worthy of record."

It dawned on him then that he had frankly lost count of the sheer number of lives he'd saved over the last three years. Each and every one of those souls would have been lost had it not been for him or his teammates.

"Life's direction and the direction of the things churning within it can change in an instant. We win things, we lose things, we learn from those things. Use that gained knowledge and the impact of the lives you have kept safe on this Earth and use it to carry yourself through the day, months, and years ahead."

Gage was still dubious. "But how do I know if I'm good eno-"

"Gage, just stop thinking about it. Simply immerse yourself in the depth of the world. You ask yourself now if you have made the right choice. You have, if only because it was a choice you made for yourself. You also wonder if you are good enough for the task at hand. Only in situations where we place ourselves outside our comfort levels can we discover who we truly are. Only when we challenge ourselves can we grow into who we are meant to be..."

Gage felt compelled to nod his head in agreement as the words rang resoundingly true to him. The voice diminished, its departure leaving his body colder as the muted ticking of the wall clock became louder.

"Immerse yourself in the depth of the world, huh?" he repeated softly.

In his head, thoughts swirled like ink in water and Adrienne's supple form solidified, walking slowly down a long highway. She was alone, the sun setting in a dazzling display of churning light and cloud before her. In the distance, the smoky figure of a man loomed against the brightness and as she continued toward him, he began to stride toward her. Step by slow step he advanced and soon Gage's distinct features crystallized from the roiling dark.

Soundless, he stood in front of her before taking her close for an embrace. They held each other for a moment, locking hands together before continuing into the setting sun. As they grew distant on the horizon, their forms merged and became one with the sunset and the land.

"Yes indeed," he said. "I made the right decision. Well, we did. Love may certainly bring with it pain but together we can, and shall, endure the challenges ahead."

He sat for a moment longer before a modest whiff of a bad odor caught in his nose. Lifting an arm, he took a breath and discovered his deodorant was on the verge of giving out. It was likely the pendant's doing, as he'd felt strangely feverish ever since putting it on.

After the day's crazy events and the fact Adrienne wasn't back yet, he decided that a shower was certainly in order. Pushing himself up off the bed, he walked over to the linen closet, collected a towel from middle shelf and made his way into the bathroom.

ADRIENNE WENT BACK UPSTAIRS empty handed. It seemed that during the excitement of the day they had forgotten to get any fresh food supplies. She supposed that finding ghosts of dead relatives did tend to shift one's priorities. Eating the MREs Charlie had stockpiled in the cellar wasn't an option, even though they had over twenty delicious years of shelf life left. Her stomach however didn't care and still grumbled in admonishment.

As she entered the bedroom, the dim light from the bathroom fan caught her attention as it fell out into the surrounding darkness. She walked toward it and the sound of running water could be heard whilst steam wafted out of the slightly open door.

Pushing it open, she peeked inside, watching keenly as the warm drops rained on Gage's ever impressive shoulders, rolling along every line to begin their long journey down to the drain. She focused on the divot formed between his thick traps, teeth curling her lower lip while those drenched wing tattoos funneled the water to the center. The stream flowed all the way down the muscular path until it had no choice but to spill over that glorious behind. Jesus, she had never in her life been envious of water but there's a first time for everything. Tonight she wanted to be it in such a bad, bad way.

Slowly, Gage turned and ran his fingers through that untamed mop of hair. He opened his eyes and spotted Adrienne in the hallway. He locked in and without missing a beat reached for a sliver of years-old soap, still fragrant, and rubbed his chest. The pomegranate suds traced their way over his front, rising and falling on each one of his abs and down to his hand, resting around his full, aching self.

"Well," he said deeply. "You want in?"

He did not need to repeat himself.

In an instant she was in the shower, being caressed by the same water she was jealous of not ten seconds before. She found herself kneeling in front of him again, the view just as marvelous as the day she first saw it. The v-lines of his abs pointed her in the right direction as she grabbed hold with both hands.

He stepped forward and brought himself to her lips, teasing her with a little taste before she wrapped her lips around his meaty head and went to work. Gage was noticeably aroused, flowing onto her lips with each suck. On she went, drawing more out of him than ever before and his legs started to buckle. After a few more long licks and a kiss on the palmful of man she held, she rose, holding firm while she leaned forward to nibble his ear. "Now it's my turn," she whispered. A hot breath went into his ear, nearly toppling that sturdy frame to the floor. "Does the beast want in, sir?"

A deep growl sent a tremor down her spine.

She reached over to the faucet and cranked it hotter. Steam began to fill the shower, rising along with her body as he lifted her in his arms and nudged her against the tile. His broad back expanded like a cobra to shield her from the falling water, allowing the monster to generously tease between her legs.

Eagerly she locked her legs around his narrow waist while he effortlessly rolled on a sleeve. She looked ahead into focused green, his head crowned with mist.

Unwavering in his return stare, an eyebrow arched its way up as he spoke. "Time to feed the beast."

That's all she needed to hear; those words, that voice, this man. Her arms cradled his thick neck while her uncontrollable wetness mingled with his shaft. She caught scent of his musk as they became one again and she had no choice but to scream.

He groaned, his tone falling with each inch that passed through her door. Heaven was again on Earth and it was the age of Gage and Adrienne.

Grabbing her with one arm he brought her in closer, moving away from the wall to hold her in mid air as she rode. She repeatedly took it all, head to base while her thighs tightened around him.

They went harder.

She began to churn along with his thrusts and like a series of waves, each movement built upon the last.

Harder.

The thrill was amazingly high. As her eyes rolled back she spilled herself around him, but did not stop.

Harder.

She could not stop.

Harder.

The luxurious sensations multiplied. The pleasure was contagious and Gage reached the point of no return, rushing right over the line.

Unable to hold back, he pulled himself out and set her down gently. It was taking every fiber of his being not to explode as she stood in front of him. They fervidly began to kiss as he propped up on her torso, reaching down to yank off the sheath. The feeling of freeing all twelve abundant inches from that latex prison was oh so much to handle.

As they continued to taste each other and rub himself between their slippery bodies, he lost control. Arching his back and grabbing hold with both hands, he unleashed a loud groan while he indiscriminately glazed the two of them, the surrounding tiles and everything in between.

Quivering under the pressures of intense joy, his legs cramped and he lost balance for a second, sending him and Adrienne back against the shower wall.

She bumped her head and let out a soft laugh, looking over the fashionable 'gel' that glowed against his dark hair. Rubbing her head, she noted that she was wearing it as well. A lot of it.

"Well, I guess that means mission accomplished?" she asked, holding a hand out under the water stream.

Gage let out a couple slow breaths, looking down at his satisfied self before nodding. "Oh yeah," he barely got out.

"I guess we should actually take a proper shower now," she said, turning the temperature down a touch. As she drew her hand back, Gage grabbed hold. She was always so silky.

"I love you, gorgeous. Like, I really do." His green eyes shone like emeralds. "I have for quite some time… so much that you don't even know."

She took a step toward him and nuzzled his nose. "I bet I *do* know."

"Nope, you can't. Because I don't even know the limits of how much I have in my heart for you. Now let's clean up, this hair gel smells like jizz."

It was quiet in the bedroom as they laid naked under the covers, the warmth of their bodies and the shower made for a soothing cocoon to entangle oneself in.

"I can't believe you're mine," Gage whispered while shifting to give her a bit more room to come closer.

"Believe it mister," she said, burrowing her head into her favorite spot. The space between his chest and neck welcomed her with that rousing bouquet. She reached down and traced a finger from the bottom of his balls all the way along his soft member before she closed her eyes and drifted off to sleep.

As she did, Gage turned and kissed her on her head. He had an arm wrapped firmly around her, never planning to let go from this day forward. At last, something in this crazy ass world they lived in went right. Neither were now alone, their separate journeys becoming one and the same. Soon he found himself strolling into slumber land a happy man, the most content he had been in ages.

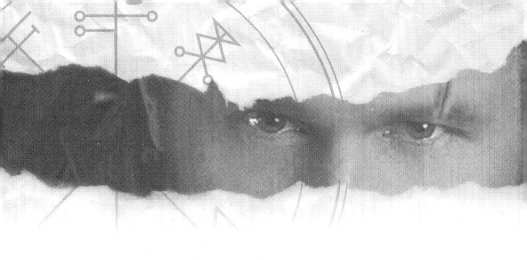

CHAPTER
twenty-five
THE COMING OF THE TIDE

The homestead sat quietly amidst the picturesque scene of country heaven. The moon loomed large overhead, marking midnight across the sparse clouds and bathing the landscape in a cool blue hue.

Bang!

The sudden sound pierced the tranquil night and rumbled over the country hills, echoing far into the distance as the bleating of spooked livestock rose to join it in chorus.

Gage was jolted out of his restful sleep and rose with a start. By instinct he reached over to the nightstand to grab his gun, racking the slide without the slightest trace of hesitation.

Bang! Bang!

The sound of heavy metal beating hard against wood continued to fill the house with each strike. Whatever it was, wanted inside, badly.

"Adrienne," he said, prodding her with an elbow to her still sleeping shoulder. "Get up. Now."

She opened her groggy eyes, struggling to hold onto the luscious dream she was having.

"What is it, baby?" she whispered, still partially under the sandman's spell.

The loud strikes continued, joined now by the distinct chittering and cracking of wood.

"We have company."

With those three words, underscored with another loud boom, she snapped out of her lethargic trance and within a few seconds they were both up on their feet.

"Already?" she asked as she pulled on some underwear and an oversized nightshirt. "I expected us to be on the road before any trouble showed up."

"Seems so," he replied, donning a pair of sweatpants. "They must've had assets pretty close by. Dammit." He took in a long breath to calm his nerves. "So, you ready to check this out?

She bent down and snagged her silver dagger off of her belt, giving him a nod.

"Let's go."

Gage carefully led the way out of the bedroom and down the upstairs hall. Immediately, they were assaulted by the oppressive smell of sulfur which unrelentingly bore down upon their senses. Undeterred, they continued toward the top of the stairwell with arms folded across their noses. There Madeline joined them, shimmering into view.

"Demons I gather?" Gage asked her, knowing full well what the foul odor meant.

"Yes," she replied. "They've taken male hosts; probably possessed some of the neighbors from up the street. By the looks of them, it's the Donnellys. I never much cared for them, always so weird and untoward. So, it's no surprise seeing they've willingly let demons inside."

"How many are there. A lot?" he asked, hoping the answer was small.

"No, not yet anyway. I saw three- the two Donnelly boys are the ones banging away at the front door and Lawrence, their father, is sneaking around the back."

Gage shot Adrienne a confident look as he rubbed the back of his neck with his spare hand. "Sounds like nothing we haven't been able to handle before." As he rubbed, he noted that he was still abnormally hot, the brief time spent rubbing causing his palms to sweat.

She brandished her blade, its embossed sigils catching the dim light as she passed him a wink. "Yup."

Madeline was so pleased by what she saw. She longed for the day that Gage, ever the loner, broke down the walls he had built up around himself. It seemed that day had finally arrived. It was enough to warm this mother's heart, if it were still beating of course. How times had certainly changed for the Crosse family.

"You two take care," she said lovingly, "and I'll see you downstairs shortly."

She vanished in an instant while the two of them pressed on and crept downstairs together.

The crashing grew more frequent with each step they descended, reaching near deafening levels by the time they reached the living room. The front door bowed and cracked each time, threatening to yield to the forces assailing it.

Gage and Adrienne readied themselves as the entryway finally gave way.

The door flew open and two young men rushed inside, their eyes rimmed with a fire that shined in the darkened room. Blake, older of the two brothers, was the first one through the door. He was moving his hefty, corn-fed body surprisingly fast.

Gage wasted no time firing several rounds his way, landing a strike into his broad chest and another straight to his head, knocking him to the ground in an incapacitated heap as the wounds flickered with a faint purple light.

"Shit!" he exclaimed, realizing the UV rounds were still chambered.

Before Gage could change the magazine or take two steps to finish off Blake, his younger brother Preston was upon him. Just as large as the two of them, he landed a solid blow to Gage's chin, knocking him back.

He could taste the metallic hotness of a bloodied lip, wiping the bulk of it away with his wrist. Flinging the sticky liquid to the ground, he swirled the rest around in his mouth and spit at Preston's feet.

"Mother fucker," Gage said before rushing in to knock the shit out of Preston's smirking face. His temperature was feverish, but he channeled that energy into his attacks. He got in double the amount of pain and punishment on that demon's ass before signaling to Adrienne. He moved himself behind the demon and locked his large arms like a vice.

Adrienne came around in no time, positioning herself in front of Preston. Blade ready in hand, she dove in while he struggled to free himself of Gage's powerful hold. The silver shard sunk in deep and a golden hue erupted from the lacerated flesh.

Preston wailed as the shadow within the host, his true self, was vaporized into the nothingness that awaited it.

"Good job," Gage said as he dropped the lifeless body.

"You know it," she replied, wiping the dagger on her shirt.

While they were fighting, Blake had awakened from his short radioactive coma and broke away from the scuffle. He charged toward the back door, planning to let his father in for reinforcement.

He was halted by Madeline, who materialized in the kitchen and blocked the way. She waved a hand as if to toss him aside like a piece of trash, but before she was able to finish the motion, he pulled out a dark powder from his front pockets and blew it all around her. They were iron filings and they were as razors to her. They sparked and hissed vigorously as they punctured her, causing her to glitch as if she were being short circuited.

The attack also left Blake injured and he pulled back his own burning hands and grimaced. With his ghostly foe momentarily distracted, he continued to the doorway. Grasping the handle with a blistering palm, he gritted his teeth and turned.

The door creaked open and Lawrence stepped through, one squalid shoe at a time. He didn't hang back however, charging straight away on the offense and swiping at Madeline with an oversized wrench. The weight of the weapon was unwieldy and caused him to swing slowly. He missed while she weaved herself out of the way.

Lawrence had always been a small man and because of that he was agile. Being possessed by a demon amplified those characteristics and made him that much more dangerous as he continued to bring his weapon to bear. Mercilessly he swung at her multiple times in succession yet Madeline, who was equally agile, was able to tactfully keep him at bay.

Riled by his lack of success, he grasped the handle with both hands and flung it at her with all his strength like a hammer throw; the momentum he had built causing him to tumble forward.

Madeline ducked as the wrench whooshed by her head and impaled itself in the wall. Quickly she held out a hand as he started to regain balance and with a flick of her wrist, he was launched hard into the breakfast area where the furniture broke beneath him as he landed.

Blake then came at her swinging with his own iron bar, which she managed to dodge just as easily as before. Like his father though, he did not give up and did it again and again until he finally lucked up and made contact with her. The bar slid through like butter, the path it traced vaporizing in a cloud of coral smoke.

She gasped in pain as she floated in tatters, grasping at the long shear in her body while waiting another inevitable strike.

"Bye, you spectral bitch!" Blake said with unabashed hatred, but the next move did not come from him.

Madeline heard Lawrence shuffling around behind her, the sounds of damaged furniture snapping beneath his feet. She spun around to face him and what she saw worried her.

He stood there in the ruins holding a small stone between two fingers and thumb. It was emblazoned with interconnecting white runes across its dull surface.

"*Spiritum Ejicio!*" he shouted joyously. The symbols flared up with an intense light that spiraled out toward her, striking her abdomen before binding her body as if with chains.

Incapable of escaping the magical prison, she was ejected from the house as the spell flung itself through the roof, knocking a gaping hole clear through to the outside.

"Mom, no!" Gage bit at his sore lip as his new magazine slid into place.

Both demons snarled back at him, baring their heavily plaque-ridden

228 | GOLDEN CZERMAK

teeth. Scraps of tinder gently rained down.

"You…" said Gage, taunting with a finger pointed sternly at Lawrence, "are gonna suffer for that."

Blake crowed as Lawrence took a step forward.

"Oh really, Mister Crosse?" he said without fear of the reputed demon-slayer's response. "You have no idea the fate that awaits slayer scum like you. In fact, I think tonight I'll have the pleasure of finally seeing you suffer the same fate as your cunt mother and bastard father."

Adrienne felt vastly uneasy.

"Easy now," Gage replied, heat building in the very pit of his stomach. "Those are my parents you're talking about."

"Duh," he replied. "I know them well. In fact, I might have gotten to know them *really* well back in the day before they were… extinguished like a weak candle flame." He made a puffing noise and stretched his fingers out wide like an explosion.

Gage felt his blood pressure rising, hand tightening around the grip of the MK23. *This fucker was there!?*

"So were you the one that did it?" he asked in a low, near indecipherable tone.

"Did what?" Lawrence asked sneeringly, shrugging his shoulders and raising his palms upward in a mocking fashion.

Blake erupted in a fit of derisive laughter.

Gage raised his weapon, pointed it at Blake, and pulled the trigger. A shining bullet emerged from the barrel and struck him directly in the previous head wound. He spasmed for a moment as if being electrocuted before slumping on the floor, lifeless.

Adrienne looked to Gage and his expression was alarming, as if he himself were possessed by something dreadful. "Did what?!" he yelled. "Take my parents' lives just like I took your fucking demon brother's."

Lawrence cackled garishly and clapped his grubby hands.

"So, I ask you again, did you do it?" asked Gage, his stare barren.

Lawrence's lips spread garishly wide, curving upward into a sick smile. "Yes."

With that Gage leapt at him, grabbing him by the collar. He lifted him clear off the floor and bashed him into the window frame a couple of times. He then lowered his feet back to the ground in order to batter him relentlessly with more powerful blows across his face and stomach.

Lawrence wasn't putting up much of a fight. In fact, he wasn't fighting at all, instead standing there like a mannequin. Had Gage released his grip, he would likely collapse.

"Gage," Adrienne interrupted, looking past the two of them out the window. She sensed something off in the distance beyond the tree line. "He's baiting you. I think something else is on its way."

Gage paid her no mind and continued his assault, nearly in tears. "I'm gonna beat the fucking smoke out of you!"

His foe stayed eerily quiet, those roughened teeth smiling at him through a thick coat of fresh blood.

"Gage!" shouted Adrienne. "Enough! Just finish him!"

Without a word back to her, Gage held out a hand, the other firmly around Lawrence's throat as he secured him against the wall.

Adrienne looked anxiously at his quivering palm and then up to his still barren stare, fixed on the demon's face. She slowly placed her blade in his hand and his fingers closed around the handle.

Gage leaned in extremely close to his foe's face, so close that their noses nearly touched. A bead of sweat was able to exchange between the two of them before dripping to the floor.

Lawrence's demonic eyes had shifted back to a more human looking shade of blue.

"I know you're in there smoky," Gage said as he teased the knife edge on Lawrence's neck. He pricked it and blood flowed out along the blade. "Let's talk… eye to eye."

"It's too late, you arrogant prick. They are coming for you and those two magnificent treasures around your filthy neck."

"I'll deal with 'them' when they get here," said Gage confidently. "Right now it's our party. Just you…" he flicked the knife again, "and me."

Lawrence cackled and Gage swiped the blade hard across his chest to shut him up. Those soothing blue eyes bolted, replaced by the foul colors of a crimson midnight.

"Ah now that you're back! Your name," commanded Gage.

There was no reply.

"Your name," he repeated, slicing the blade across the demon's chest again, forming a cross-like shape.

Still no words came. The smell of burning flesh pervaded the room and the demon's feet began to smolder as if he were standing on a pile of searing ashes.

"Your... fucking... name!" shouted Gage as he stabbed the knife into his shoulder.

Adrienne shut her eyes, taking a step back. Never before had she seen Gage like this. As she opened them again, she could have sworn the things around his neck gleamed briefly. As much as she wanted to, she didn't have time to think on it as she caught distant shapes in the window, emerging from the tree line.

"Camio," the demon said, its smoking flesh damn near overbearing. "My name is Camio."

Gage tilted his head slightly and leaned in toward his ear and whispered, "Well, Camio, please accept this parting gift with kindest regards from the Crosse family." He raised the dagger and slowly drug it across his neck from end to end.

The yellow glow from the fatal wound soaked into his vacant eyes and Camio drew his final, garbled breath. Having lived for several millennia, he was no more.

CHAPTER
twenty-six
LOVE IS PAIN

Gage handed the blade back to Adrienne, his hands no longer shaking from whatever rage had overtaken him.

"Gage, are you okay?" she asked as she took it from him. "You weren't yourself just now."

"Yeah, I'm fine," he replied, unsure if he believed that himself. "Just repaying someone that took my old life away. Gimme a few, darlin' and I'll be good."

"Sadly babe, we don't have a minute," she replied, pointing out the back window to the shapes by the distant trees.

There were now thirteen dark forms standing in the pale moonlight, lining up against the forest wall.

"Oh my God," he said, unable to make out what they were at this distance.

Without warning, they all screeched in unison, the sound both ghastly and new. Neither Gage nor Adrienne had encountered these terrors, whatever they were, before.

They then broke away from the trees in turn and sprinted toward the house on all fours, scattering like flies waved away at a picnic. As they came closer, their abominable nature became apparent.

They were bipedal, no larger than an average human, though they could run on all their limbs at great speed. Their ebony skin was tight and smooth but non-reflective, capable of absorbing the moonlight to hide their athletic bodies. From the tips of their whip-like tails to the crown of their tentacled heads ran a ridge of sharp, spiny bone.

They were at the house in no time, rising on their hind legs and using their tails for balance. Lifting their heads high they sniffed, faces otherwise encased in bands of chunky leather sewn directly to their flesh. Their eyes, if they had any, were covered but massive jaws were able to move unhindered. Several large and serrated teeth jutted out from their lipless mouths while sharp claws rasped the air.

"What are they?" whispered Adrienne, forcing her hand into Gage's.

"I have no idea what those... abominations are," he answered. "I don't even recall seeing anything remotely like them in lore." Definitely worried by the unknown, he swallowed hard before continuing. "We have to try and get out of here... head for the truck."

The two of them made their way toward the front door, but were stopped dead in their tracks when one of the creatures stepped inside. It hadn't detected them, stooping down and smelling Preston's body. A long tongue writhed its way out of its mouth and no sooner than the slimy appendage touched human skin, the creature lurched forward. It took Preston's head into its mouth, pulverizing the bone in its jaws while grating on the residual meat.

Adrienne gasped, hand lifting to her mouth to suppress the urge to vomit. Gage guided her into position behind him for added protection and checked his pistol; there was a single demon killing round left. He had absolutely no idea if it would even be effective against these things, but it was all they had and judging by the diabolical appearance of their enemies it could work, in theory.

The only other thing at their immediate disposal was Adrienne's dagger.

It was a sure bet thanks to the sigils engraved upon it, but being a knife it would require him to get way too close for comfort. That luxury he would save as their last resort.

The creature continued mindlessly consuming Preston, as a dog would a bowl of food, while Gage and Adrienne repositioned themselves. They were looking for the prime position to make a run for it.

Matters soon went from bad to worse: two more beasts noisily stumbled their way over the debris accumulated at the back door. There they found the bodies of Lawrence and Blake, wasting no time in devouring them along with Gage's hopes for escape.

The odds were just not in their favor. Three creatures had made their way into the house and blocked the exits, the truck was parked at least a hundred fifty feet away from the closest door, while ten other abominations had dispersed and could be anywhere in between.

He pivoted Adrienne toward him, coming to grips with the reality they faced. Brushing a hand through that luxurious hair of hers, he came to rest it on her cheek, cupping it affectionately.

"Darlin', I can clear you a path out the front door and hold those two at the back. I don't know where the rest of 'em are but at least it'll give you a chance to get yourself to the truck and your ass out of here."

"No!" she said, fighting the very notion of it. "I can't leave you here."

"Yes you can!" he said sharply under his breath. "You have to go. I… I care about you too much."

A tear streamed down her face and was caught by his thumb. He gingerly wiped it away.

"Gage, no," she insisted, making no moves except to get closer to him. "Absolutely no. We're a team… a family, all the way to the end."

He smiled and for once didn't know what to say.

"Now," she said. "Let's get out of here, together."

With a new found resolve, Gage aimed at the creature blocking the front door. "Hey ugly!" he shouted at the top of his lungs, drawing the ire of all three beasts. "Get the hell out of our way!"

It reared up tall and shrieked, gore flecking off of its teeth.

"I sure hope this does something," he whispered, pulling the trigger with a silent prayer. The last of his slayer ammo soared from the barrel and gracefully through the air, straight into the fiend's mouth and out the other side. It stood in front of them frozen in place as if it were stunned.

"Fuck!" said Gage, realizing the bullet didn't kill it. "We gotta head upstairs and-"

A delayed whimper leached out from the abomination as it fell over in answer to their prayers. The bullet succeeded in slaying the foul beast.

Together they dashed toward the front door, the freedom of wider spaces just a few more precious steps away.

However, the universe decided now was not the time for such niceties and threw another curve ball their way. Their feeling of elation was short lived as two more of the things crossed the threshold into the house.

Gage and Adrienne had no choice but to fall back into the center of the living room. He pushed her behind him yet again, but soon the two monsters that had been behind them encroached and were within a couple feet.

They were surrounded.

One of the beasts approaching from the back leapt at them and Gage pushed Adrienne out of the way just as it swiped upwards across his chest with its long talons. They scratched a series of deep, parallel cuts into his right pec. As the nails cut Gage, they struck the chain and its sheer power shattered the petrified keratin like glass.

The beast cringed in misery, retreating to the kitchen as the other one took its turn and lunged. It got a solid kick in the stomach as a reward, sending it crashing to the floor.

Gage strode over to the dazed monster, Adrienne in tow, and placed a foot on its head before pressing down. He could hear the bone start to crunch under foot and feel it buckle, fueling him to press down even harder with his full weight.

"Ady, I want you-"

His words were cut forcibly short when she was wrenched from his grip by the two other monstrosities.

He felt her fingers slipping through his own and he turned, realizing then that the situation had grown dire.

She tried to stab at her attackers, but they were able to keep the dagger from making any sort of contact. Incensed, one slapped at her hand and with an indignant growl sent the silver blade pirouetting through the room. It landed tip first into the hardwood some distance away from either of them. There it wavered for a moment before becoming still.

Time slipped into unwelcome slow motion as the brute viciously pulled back Adrienne's neck and bit into her shoulder, taking a good chunk out of it. Her face contorted from the horrendous pain that blazed its way through her entire body. While still latched on, it walked her around the room as one would a trophy, looping around to the other side as she seared in pain.

There, the previously injured beast stepped out from the dark corner where it was recuperating and made its way over to them. It inhaled the air just above the wound, tasting her warm blood with its probing tongue. It made sure to turn its face toward Gage, who was still standing over the fallen beast. Without warning it thrust the claws of its unbroken hand into her side before slowly twisting it back out.

She screamed as the remaining creatures poured in at the sound of her cries, screeching themselves in approval.

Gage watched in horror as she bled out over her once soft and beautiful skin, her legs marred by the blood and viscera flowing down to the floor. A massive deluge of emotions overtook him and his anger grew to a level so intense that it literally sparked a fire within him. Light and flame blazed from his eyes as if he were Hell Incarnate. The metal trembled as the chain scorched his skin, sending plumes of deathly smoke around him like a twisted hood and cape.

He utterly crushed the beast's head that was beneath his heel, kicking its body away with a thunderous *crack*. He then focused all of his attention on the group of foul creatures that still stood ahead of him.

Adrienne was dropped without compassion there in the kitchen as the remaining creatures encircled Gage. She convulsed, her body in shock as it still clung onto what little life she had left.

Without an ounce of fear Gage stepped forward, the talisman now floating in front of him, vibrating so rapidly that it was nearly invisible. Smoke continued to cascade around him and his eyes shone brightly from behind the veil.

The monsters roared, deafening in their sick melody. They all leapt toward him in the center of their circle of death, baring all manner of sharpness to tear him to shreds.

His eyes became slices of razor thin hatred and there was another sound like thunder that exploded through the room, knocking pictures off the walls and shattering keepsakes. The amulet immediately stopped and waves of hellfire coursed out of it, wrecking the ceiling entirely and most of the back wall. Great chunks of rubble crashed atop the creatures, impaling some while crushing others without pity.

As the ones that survived climbed out from beneath the wreckage, death was set upon them. There was absolutely no hope, for Gage would not let them have an ounce of it. With lash upon fiery lash they were blown back and away, each violent tendril chasing them as if alive and hungry for destruction and torment. The burning whips endlessly beat charred chunks out of their bodies, which disappeared in satisfying whorls of char.

As the last body was obliterated in the raging inferno, its tortured cries were swiftly muted and carried off by the wind. The fires then faded away, receding back into the silver disc from where they came.

Nothing now remained of Gage's enemies, except for the peaceful flutter of ash.

CHAPTER
twenty-seven
NON OMNIS MORIAR

WHEN HE OPENED HIS eyes, he was lost, unable to comprehend what had just happened or how much time had gone by. The ringing in his ears was still deafening and his vision muddy. Instinctively, he felt his neck expecting to have massive injuries everywhere yet there were no signs of any. Amidst the cacophony a figure lay still, focused, and broken on a kitchen floor which had seen much better days.

Adrienne! I'm so sorry, he thought to himself as he rushed to her side. He checked her for signs of life.

Oh thank God.

They were there, but were mere embers. Her eyes slowly opened upon feeling his touch.

"You look like shit," he managed to say, barely even a whisper across his lips. Pulling a hand through her ever-soft hair, he closed his eyes and tried forcing himself to believe the wetness he felt was from the shower they shared earlier.

He couldn't do it.

"Yup," she whispered through a labored breath and a weak, blood stained smile.

"Oh my dear Adrienne," Gage began. "We'll be sure to get you fixed up. Yeah. Fixed up right away. Joey probably has something- "

She winced, taking all her strength to lift a shaky finger up to his lips. "Shhh. Liar."

Gage knew what was coming, fast, and was ill prepared for it. "I love you, darlin.'"

"I... know... always," she replied, her voice feeble and still failing. She stared up and out through the hole in the roof. "The stars... look prettier than... last night."

Gage looked up too and saw the vast expanse of starlight twinkling in the heavens. His eyes welled with regret as he looked back down to find those same stars reflected in her eyes, now full of tears.

"When I... saw you this morning. I knew... that today... would be... a perfect day."

An anemic smile formed. "Was it?" he asked.

"Yes. You're here... with me... at the end . I lo- "

A hard cough came and her hand fell back, eyes widening in an aimless search. "Gage!" she whimpered before the deafening sound of silence took over.

She lay still.

"Ady?"

There was no reply.

"Ady?" he repeated.

There was no way to describe what Gage felt as she still didn't respond; desolate and barren was a vast understatement. His heart might as well have been torn out by one of those monstrous things as it would have been far less excruciating.

His lips turned down and became a thin line as the realization finally settled in. Gently, he pressed his fingers on his lips, then brought them to hers before using them to slide her eyelids closed.

"Sleep well, gorgeous. You'll forever be the brightest star in my sky."

A FEW QUIET MOMENTS passed as Gage sat with eyes closed in the midst of the ruined kitchen, holding firmly onto Adrienne's body.

Then, a familiar voice came from behind.

"Sweetie," said his mother as she crouched beside him. Her hand rested on his lower back as she gave it a loving rub.

"Mom, you're ok?"

"Bastards can't keep me banished for long, especially from here," she replied.

"I've lost everything, again." He kneeled, sinking back onto his heels as his hands fell down to his sides. "You, Dad, now… her."

"It's ok, baby," she said reassuringly. "You're strong."

"Not strong enough apparently. I've failed all of you! This damn thing should have stayed buried in the cellar and I never should have let my emotions bring her into this."

"Hush, none of that," she insisted. "She was a Journeyman. You're a Journeyman. Despite the walls you put up, you're both in the business. Whether or not you both got together, or stayed friends or just fell into being acquaintances, the life follows you. Momma knows best about that. And enough about that other nonsense; you *are* strong. Do you remember what I used to tell you?"

He picked up a small board that was lying nearby and snapped it between his hands. "Strength isn't just physical. It's also in the heart and the mind. Dad reminded me of that in order to get this thing." His fingers grazed the disc before dropping back to his sides.

"Yes!" she said, pointing to his head then chest. "In there it's much more potent and thankfully there is an abundance of both beneath that thick skull and gruff exterior your mother can so easily see through. Your love is powerful my son. It's why I'm here now and it will certainly get you through the toughest times ahead. Love is hope and hope.. well it's all we have in the darkest of times.

"But, I'm not going to lie to you. More of this will be coming for you and times are about to get much darker. Especially with that thing around your neck."

He looked down at Adrienne and nodded. She looked as if she could be sleeping.

"She was a good soul, baby," she said. "Now she's in a better place. We can look at clearing some room in the rose garden to…"

Her voice trailed off as yet another deep rumble came from far off the property. If it was loud enough to be heard in the house and shake what little remained intact in the room, something big was coming.

"Wait here," she said, phasing out.

Gage grabbed at the talisman. *Why me?*

She returned a few seconds later, a terrified look upon her face. "Baby. You have to go!"

Gage shot to his feet and stared out the rear doors. In the distance, he saw a shit storm of what-the-fuck rushing their way. A massive horde of demons and dark creatures was coming fast.

Madeline quickly solidified to embrace him. "Goodbye, my dear son." She spun him around and pushed him toward the front door. "I'll buy you some time; your father had a couple backup plans just in case one of us managed to make it back. You must keep it safe!" she exclaimed. "Now go!"

With a raise of her hand another massive hole tore across the wall, sending debris, the porch rails, and even the troublesome front door flying into the demons that surrounded his truck, impaling their bodies to the ground.

Seeing his opportunity to escape, Gage went for it, looking one last time at Adrienne and remembering her face as if it were the first glorious time he saw it. He took off with the treasures and her enchanted dagger firmly in hand.

Madeline watched as her son safely exited, then turned back toward the oncoming horde. Her demeanor shifted. No longer warm and motherly, she became deep and cold like the ocean during a hurricane. Her wraithlike form held firm while what was left of the back of the house shattered before her. Swarms of foul creatures spilled into her home.

"You are not welcome here!" she commanded. Eyes like lances pierced her enemies and they were frozen in place by the dread that swam in the deep pools of her soul.

Some were not afraid and rocketed forward with all the deadliness they could muster. With a mere flick of her wrist, they were mangled into appalling shapes and sent flying from the property.

The rest dared not touch her, nor could.

Except for one.

Ancient he was, with a name long lost to prehistory. Without fear or remorse for those in his way, the massive serpent barreled into the house and set himself before Madeline, coiled to strike. The moon cascaded upon the leviathan's thick black hide but did not reflect away, the matted darkness crushing the light. His putrid and stinking body rolled and made quick work of all it touched, while his massive jaw unhinged, salivating at the mere notion of feasting.

He lunged with quickness and a pure light enveloped her like a shield, shattering his monstrous fangs. He hissed and flared immense armored flaps from his neck like a cobra, blocking out the stars behind.

He struck again mercilessly and with each strike thereafter her light grew dimmer, but not without penalty to himself.

Madeline had enough and extended a hand through the rippling glow that stood between her and the darkness. A beam of powerful light lashed out, striking the serpent in the face and burning out its eyes.

The ferocious assault between them continued until the shield was but a thin line of silver against the storm. She had grown weak and with one more blow, her only protection would be gone. She would be finished. Falling to her knees, she was ready to accept her fate.

His colossal maw came at her a final time, but was stopped when the living room sofa careened into it. He was knocked back.

Furniture of all sizes followed, shredding in mid air into thousands of sharp splinters that pummeled and punctured the beast outside and in.

Madeline breathed a sigh of welcome relief, but drew back ready for an attack when something touched her on the shoulder. She spun around, ready to throw this latest abomination back, but her fury quickly subsided. She smiled with relief.

Outside, Gage had made it to the truck and slammed the door closed. He looked over his shoulder and was taken aback. The loves of his life stood there, hand in hand in the massive breach, gleaming like gems amidst the waves of darkness crashing around them.

Ady!?

Behind their shining forms the serpent writhed, positioning its crippled body for another indomitable strike.

Frozen by despair, Gage couldn't focus on anything but their aura; he should be leaving but couldn't. They were both so close, oh so close to him, yet infinitely out of reach.

There sat the unstoppable Gage Crosse, powerless in his old truck just watching as the two of them shone brightly amidst the churning destruction. All he could manage to do while they coalesced into orbs was extend a hand in their direction – a sole, empty hand.

Adrienne saw him and returned the gesture, hers full of love and light. She raised her hand up to her fading lips, turning it out to blow him a kiss.

"*Non omnis moriar,*" she mouthed afterward and was consumed by utter black.

His eyes welled yet did not spill a drop and with anguish, his fingers creaked closed around the last memory of her. He pulled in that fist tightly, letting out the deepest breath of his life while thumping it hard against his chest.

The terrible viper roared once more, its victory cries echoing across the fields just before the unmistakable throws of gagging took over.

Gage opened his eyes and watched as a burst of dazzling light slid along the serpent, the shockwave knocking down the demonic legion as two orbs tore their way out and rocketed skyward into the night.

Quickly they faded and were gone.

She was gone.

From the belly of the beast a shadow ripped out like a tempest, whipping through the remnants of the house and horde alike.

His home and life were decimated and his precious memories, those he still had left, were sent straight into the abyss.

There was no going back this time.

The tears, long overdue, finally crested as he stomped hard on the gas, the exhaust belching oil and fire. As he looked over to where Adrienne would be sitting, the very pit of his stomach dropped seeing what was in the empty shotgun seat. Her hat was still sitting there neatly in the middle, unaware of the loss of its owner.

As the GMC raced down the drive and peeled onto the country road, he found himself alone again. Houston never felt so far away.

epilogue

I T WAS NEARLY PITCH black in the room, the sound of heavy rain beating
against the window panes filled the darkness with a threatening roar.

A slender figure awoke and stumbled lazily out of bed. The pale comforter
fell to the floor as it walked toward the windows that groaned ominously
under the intense wind. The room itself seemed to breathe, swaying as if set
on a stormy sea.

Grabbing the curtains forcefully, the figure flung them open just as a
thunderous *boom* shook the glass and rebounded against the walls.

Outside, the horizon shone bright like the setting sun, sandwiched
between two quaking layers of intense, boiling clouds.

"Oh my God," said Adrienne, her face catching the lightning as it began
screaming between the clouds both above and below. Far off in the distance,
a pinprick of light shone out brighter than anything around it. "What have
you gotten yourself into?"

In grim reply, an army of gray hands, lifeless and countless, slammed against the windows, shattering the glass as they tore their way toward her.

THE END

THE JOURNEY CONTINUES IN

JOURNEYMAN SERIES TWO

Main Cast of Characters

Humans:
Gage Crosse
Adrienne Elkins
Joey Mosely
Henry Abington
Marcus Sheridan
Councilor Jane Carter
Councilor Timothy Randall
Councilor Allete Popov

Paranormals:
Onoskelis (Keli)
Hell Knight Baal
Hell Knight Astaroth
Hell Knight Paimon
Dajjal
Councilor Fenran
Councilor Drogir
Councilor Tyrol
Councilor Qulieth
Head Vampire Bailey
Head Vampire Evans
Head Vampire Miller
Geirolf, The Wolf Spear

Made in the USA
San Bernardino, CA
08 May 2017